TABLE OF CONTENTS

K.R.E.W.

STEPHEN P. BENNETT

SECRETS OF AREA 71

THE SEED IS PLANTED

As told by Zechariah D. Mulholland

I had been spending the holidays at home with Mom and Dad. All is the same in my hometown of Bonaparte, Iowa. So far, the winter hasn't been bad, there was still snow and it was cold. After my visit at the cemetery, I drove through town. The stores, Murrey's general store, the grocery and Pat's Bar and Grill and Package, were busy all the way to Christmas.

Christmas Day 1983, yeah Mom got a microwave and Dad got a rocker recliner. Me, well, a very nice card with a gift certificate for a a full set of five brand new tires. A person could have knocked me over with a noodle. Tires the old truck is gonna get its final parts. The old Chevy is my pride and joy. I've spent over two years rebuilding it from front to back. I looked at the gift certificate. There wasn't a cash value, no limits, no nothing. A blank check. I looked at Mom. A little smile slipped over her face with the microwave cookbook still in her hands.

"Dad!"

I was shocked as well as puzzled, as he was doing some kind of nesting ceremony, with a few pillows in his recliner.

He settled into the chair, then a long stare happened as a minute passed.

"Zack," he said in a voice so even and unmistakable.

"Your mother and I have loved you since the day Doctor Walker said that the rabbit had died. You came into this world with barely a squeak. The doctor hit your butt and you sucked a baby size deep breath, but never cried. We brought you home and the first time I picked you up, you peed, crapped, and barfed all at once. Your mother looked at me standing there with all ten pounds of you on my forearm. Barf was running over my pack of smokes, pee was running to my belt and crap was dripping off my arm. She said, You can love him dear but don't hug him so tight. Well, its thirty years later we've seen a lot. We watched you work on your truck and kept track of all your setbacks. We both knew it was time for the tires. So, you go to the tire store and get what you know will work for you and get a warranty."

A few days after Christmas I made my way to the tire shop. The road conditions that day were not all that good. It was messy. Once I got there, it went really well. All five tires were in stock, exactly what I wanted for my truck. About all there was checking the signature on the gift certificate then a two hour wait as the tires were mounted and balanced. The trip home was great; the new tires really held the road. The bill came to $1,150.00 plus tax and Dad didn't say a word about it.

∞

New Year's came and went in the usual way. Mom, Dad, and I went to Murrey's Bar with almost the rest of the town for a social drink or drunk. A few weeks slipped by; the work was starting to really slow down not just in town, but all over. Pat Murrey, the owner of the bar, was my last bit of income. It was only twelve to sixteen hours a week. On January 19, 1984, I handed Pat my two-week notice. Pat asked if he could help or if I needed more money? Me and

Pat got along great, so I felt it was only right to tell him. It was time for me to go, to make my way in the world.

Pat asked if I had any recommendations for a replacement. I told him of a guy on Cherry Street who was retired and not bad on a grill. And to my understanding he was a good people person. Pat only said,

"Cherry Street retired."

As he was heading out the door. No one was in the bar when Pat and my dad came in laughing and carrying on. My dad asked what he needed to know about the job. I stated.

"Long hours, low pay, mean boss, apply today."

At that point, the two of them were sitting in a booth laughing like kids.

"And don't forget to clean both restrooms."

I had three hours that day and was filling in my timecard to leave when Pat said.

"Thank you, Zack, I believe this guy can do the job."

I started home when I ask to use the garage to finish the truck. He informed me Pat had already told him about my travel plans.

I made the turn at Cherry Street like millions of times before, I realized I would be leaving. I thought to myself, well, man, it was going to happen someday so why not do it? I could see Mom in the window she had something in her hands. She opened the door as I stepped in to pull my boots off. She was holding her book of my baby pictures.

"You find anything new in there?" I asked her jokingly.

"Nope"

As we sat down at the kitchen table, Mom looked at me with that look only Moms, Grandmas and some aunts can do then sighed.

"You're going to try your wings."

"Yeah, you lived on your own before you and Dad got married. What was it like for you in the beginning?"

"At first I was scared to death when I moved from home and got an apartment. But after a few weeks, I settled into my life working, playing and became the kind of person. I wanted to be happy. You look like you're ready."

"You know, Mom, you and Dad spent a lot of time and effort on teaching me all kinds of things or ways to take care of myself. Look, I can cook, clean, sew, do laundry, handle money, and fix about anything. So, I think it's time to give it my best shot."

Mom smiled. "If I can help you just say it and I'll be there for you," She said.

"Mom, I need your keys I'm gonna start getting the truck ready," I added.

Mom turned away and went to the sink.

"Go take a bath. I'll put my car in the drive." Her voice was starting to break up.

I made for the shower. I cleaned up and put on my best work rags. The clothes Mom wanted to burn or throw away. In the kitchen she had a sandwich with a soda on the table for me. She wasn't in the house and her car was gone. I finished lunch and cleaned up my mess.

I heard that Mr. Murrey that is Pat's uncle that ran the package side of the business. He had steam heat and had a hook up with a hose and nozzle for doing steam cleaning. I didn't know if he rented to folks or not. I took off in the truck for the store. Mom and Dad's cars were parked in front of Pat's side of the business. I parked the truck and went in. Mr. Murrey was getting ready to close. I asked.

"Mr. Murrey, I've heard you have a steam cleaning device; I would like to rent sometime for using it."

"Zack, you showed up at an ideal time. The system needs to be purged so you give me a bit to close up."

I sat by the door as he got the bank deposit in the bag. Then the front door locked the lights turned off then we exited out the back into a heated garage. The garage was well lit; in the corner was this manifold arrangement of pipes, valves with hoses and nozzles on both sides. Mr. Murrey got in his car then told me to get my truck and park it in the center of the garage. I did exactly as he said. The garage was closed as he was now looking over my truck.

"Zack, the rumor is you're going to hit the open road. Well, here's the deal. The steam cleaner is no charge; however I have a few questions. First is, are you going to paint it and are you going to be working in a heated garage at home?"

"I would say yes to both, but I haven't turned up the heat at home just yet."

"OK here's what we'll do. You be here at 7:00 AM to start cleaning, Next, turn the heat up at home tonight. The paint job will go on much better at seventy-five degrees. I know I've been doing this for years."

"I'll be here first thing in the morning."

∞

The truck was left there for the night. Next door, my folks were about to order supper from the grill at the bar. I told Dad I needed to get home to warm up the workshop side of the garage. Mom handed me her keys as Dad said they would bring supper home for me. The next morning, I was at Murrey's on time and ready to go. If you could see it or near see it, it was steamed off. Ten hours later, not a trace of dirt or oil, just clean. I took extra care in cleaning up when I finished. Mr. Murrey explained it would be best to let it set till morning so it would be completely dry. I agreed and said I would be here bright and early to get it.

The next day I was waiting out front as he parked out front. I had walked over to his business, it was cold out, not a lot of wind. He unlocked the place. Inside, it was warm as he readied the store for the day.

"Are you ready to go?"

"Yes sir. I must owe you something for all the time it took?"

"Nope a deal is a deal."

I got in my truck pulled out of his garage. I put it in low gear so not to throw anything on the clean surfaces on the drive home.

Backing in the garage I parked the truck as near center as I could now begin the vigil. I started working my way down the list to end all lists of all that had to be done. About 6:00 PM January 27, 1984, I called Mr. Murrey to make an appointment for the steam cleaner. He said 2:30 in the afternoon tomorrow park in the same place. I thanked him. I was dog tired from the sixteen-hour days putting it together. I told Mom I was going to bed; it was early I needed sleep. It was a solid fourteen hours of uninterrupted shut eye.

When the camper had been steamed out the work got a little more intense. Everything inside needed to be worked on, serviced or replaced. Dad had called some of his friends from work and things started coming together fast. This guy showed up, to do the inside walls in fiberglass. I ask Dad if I could afford custom walls. He just said he got a deal. It took nearly four days to do but did it look great when it was done smooth as glass itself. The next item on the list was paint, it went fairly fast in a day's time the prep work had already been done. The entire outside was sprayed with three coats. According to the can, the paint would be ninety-seven percent dry in twenty-four hours which meant some serious assembly could start.

I spent a day inventorying all the stuff going back into the truck, as well as the camper. I lined up the pieces and parts in the order of reassembly. The next morning, I was up with the sun. The shop needed to be warmed up a little. Dad came out with a pot of coffee and cups. We talked about the game plan for the day's work. Mom came out in jeans, she never wore jeans, but she was ready to work. The two of them worked on the cab of the truck as I was in the camper. I could see Mom had put a lot of thought into her sewing seat covers and side panels. The interior as it had all kinds of pockets and hiding places. The lines of stuff to go into the truck had been whittled down a fair amount so that only a half dozen things were left to be put in. Mom and Dad were horsing around. All of us were pretty tired so we called it a day and closed up the shop.

By 5:00 PM the very next day, only a few trim pieces were left to be put inside, as Mom was making them. Dad and I ran through all the systems-lights, brakes, belts, hoses, and levels. The camper, my home away from home was completed by noon the next day. All that was left was the LP tank, and water tank to fill and fuel. The slow process of loading my stuff into the camper started; it took a lot of time, as well as a lot of thought.

∞

I had been thinking of the baggage I would be leaving behind-like my cars. Both convertibles the 1963 OLDS 98 and the 1964 Mustang. It was beginning to concern me. I could use the money, but I wasn't going to give them away. Maybe Dad might have an idea that made sense. Dad and I had a talk on the subject. He said he may have an answer, but he needed to make some phone calls. It turned out Dad knew people who were interested in my cars. So, by 12:30 PM Al Johnson, Mr. Murrey, Pat, and Dad were in the back of the garage checking the cars over. Dad did all the talking and in a matter of minutes I had $17,000 cash in hand. I now had some travel money with some to spare. The titles were signed over and business ended.

Mom was clearly unhappy. I caught her in the kitchen crying. She told me how her life had been the three of us for so long and all I had been through. It took a little while, but she calmed down. I asked if she would help me pack the rest of my room. She agreed so we worked on packing all my stuff away. It reminded me of when I went into the Service. When we had finished in my room she joined me in the garage. I continued putting things here and there, then moving them to a better place for storage. It looked strange, but it's all I could do. The things I was most cautious with storing was my notebooks and small bags of change.

∞

Pat had a farewell party for me. It was a blast. The food was great and everyone had a good time. On February 20, 1984, the camper was ready for the highway. I was feeling that it was time to go. In the morning I went in the house with a change of clothes. I took a shower and then had a little breakfast with Mom and Dad. This may be the last one for some time. Dad said he was going into Pat's to help.

"Zack, call us when you get a chance just let us know you're OK."

We shook hands and he gave me a hug. Mom on the other hand looked like she was about to come unglued.

"Mom, I'll be just fine. Please don't worry." It was all that I could say.

She went to her dresser and came back with something in her hand. She opened her hand. It was a handkerchief, no a table napkin. She turned it over.

"Here's a name for your home away from home."

"RITZ, I like it."

Mom put it in a sewing hoop so I could hang it somewhere. Then she handed it to me. I could see the tears filling her eyes as I started for the door.

"It's time isn't it?" She asked.

We walked out to the RITZ. I reached in to set the cloth and hoop on the seat. I slipped in behind the wheel. Mom pushed the button to open the garage door. She leaned in the window and kissed me.

"Well, I'm off, love you Mom bye-bye."

The truck was in gear, and I rolled out the drive.

I had a plan or a place in mind, but for now it was just me and the open road. My first day got me to just outside Miami, Oklahoma. I spent a few days there and then headed south. The next stop was in Vega, Texas for food, fuel, and campground information. I spent the night in a rest area off the Interstate. The next day I was just a tourist with no worries and no hurry. That night I pulled into a rest area west of Clines Corners, New Mexico. I enjoyed the sunset, made a light supper had a shot of Schnapps then cleaned up and closed-up for the night.

∞

I awoke to the nasty taste of hot antifreeze coming in the window at 2:40 AM. I was instantly out of bed, and into some clothes. I stepped into the cab then out into the night air. Outside was a 1963 OLDS 98 convertible. There's no doubt about it, it had blown a hose. This guy was under the hood looking over the damage. He was about to pull the radiator cap.

"Say, friend, you pull that cap the way you're standing, you're looking at second or third degree burns to the face. Very painful, most generally scarring and sometimes disfiguring scarring." I warned.

His hand moved away from that cap like it was poison ivy. He looked my way.

"Mister, do you know auto repair? Are you a licensed mechanic? I had my mechanic go over the whole car before I left on vacation. The son of a bitch had it a whole damn week."

"Well, old boy, here's how I see it. You're pretty upset presently, but the fact is, the car is way too hot for anyone to work on it. It's late and you won't be able to call anyone to look at it. The phone's been

vandalized. I had two years of auto repair schooling. Plus, I rebuilt a
`63 OLDS from the ground up. I got a warm camper, a pad to rest
on, a blanket, food, drink, and tools for repair. The name is Zack
Mulholland. You're welcome to spend the night, or what's left of it."

He closed the hood, turned.

"Robert McCabe. I appreciate and would like to take your offer.
I hope you'll excuse my poor manners."

"Robert it ain't good to dwell on things. Right now, we're just
travelers, good time to get a little rest."

He locked up his car as I opened the back door of the camper. I
had Robert sleep in the upper bed and I took the lower, as I knew I
would be up first. The guy looked beat.

I was up and moving at 6:00 AM February 29, 1984. the odd day
of the year. I made a pot of coffee, grabbed a cup, and started checking
the OLDS. In short it was a mess. It took all of ten minutes to figure
out what needed to be done and where to start. The list of things
needing attention was long. I got to work, as I already knew what was
to be where it went fast so. By 8:30 A.M. I was done. I cleaned up
everything myself as well as the tools, before starting breakfast.

Robert was still out like a light. I decided to use the best wakeup
call ever. In minutes, Robert was up and moving to the smell of bacon.
It works every time. We had bacon, eggs, and coffee. It was nothing
fancy, just food. The morning meal done and Robert was ready to
start on the car.

I brought the coffee out for another cup and some conversation.

Robert: How can I help? You think the OLDS can be saved?

Zack: There's a good chance we can put it back to right.

Robert: Have you looked over the damage yet this morning?

Zack: Yep, just kind of 1, 2, 3, look see. Where you from in Ohio?

Robert: McConnelsville. A nice town born and raised there. And you?

Zack: Bonaparte. It's a small town and fits every small-town joke ever made. I'd guess you to be a salesman. Maybe real estate?

Robert: Nope, but not a bad guess. I'm an attorney.

Zack: Criminal or corporate?

Robert: Criminal, but I'm heading to L.A. to see an old friend. He said there may be a corporate opening.

Zack: Sounds like you'll be in the big house on the hill before long. You'll be driving some jazzy sports car and bitching about not getting the tee off time at the country club.

Robert: Yep, no doubt about it. You appear to be a jack of all trades, but I can't put my finger on what you'd specialize in?

Zack: Well, I've changed careers a few times, but the one thing I can say I specialize in is welding and design.

Robert: What kind of things do you design and build?

Zack: For the past year, I've been working on a design for an egg-shaped, giant size-for lack of a better word-garbage can. It would be as big as a battleship or bigger in heavy plate steel. Its use would be to contain toxic waste, as well as nuclear waste. The hard part is how exactly to bury it to a depth safe from attack. I need to be a physicist. Then I could sell my idea. Probably sounds crazy.

Robert: You sound like you've give this a great deal of thought and put some work into it. Well, I think you'll sell it.

Zack: Say, could I give you a retainer, so if the subject ever comes around you could make a presentation or something like that? Being an attorney, you would be a lot closer to people that might be in the market for my idea.

Robert: OK I can do that for you. Now, when are we going to start on the car?

Zack: In just about one minute.

I took off for the RITZ and in seconds returned with pen, paper, a piece of carbon paper and an envelope of money.

Zack: Robert, would you write me up an official type of receipt please.

He folded the paper over and put the carbon in.

Robert: How much should I write this for Zack? Let me see your license so there are no misspellings.

I set my license on the table.

Zack: All I can afford right now is five dollars American money.

Robert smiled then began writing out the receipt.

"On February 29, 1984, at 9:20 A.M. I, Robert McCabe, Attorney of Law received from Zechariah D. Mulholland the sum of Five Dollars American Money as retainer for my assistance in promoting his new idea of waste disposal, created by Mr. Mulholland." He read it when he had finished writing. Robert handed the top copy and carbon to me,

He put his copy in the envelope.

Zack: Well, I got an attorney pulling for me. I'm going to be a success. OK, now you need a little news. I was up at 6:00 AM and fixed the hose and a few other little things that didn't look right. Just don't run the A.C. and it will work like a Swiss watch. Another cup of coffee?

Robert: Sure, if you say it's ready to go, I guess I can relax a while longer before getting back on the highway. Say, if I can sell your idea how much do you want to get for it?

I had a big smile on my face.

Zack: I want enough so I'll never have the need to wear a watch.

Robert: You've got some good goals Zack.

We talked and joked around till about 10:30 AM or so. With safe travels along with goodbyes said, Robert started the OLDS and was on his way. I busied myself with getting the RITZ ready to go. About 11:00 AM I was on the move and listening to the radio for road reports. The roads were clear through the Sierras, so I decided to drive on into Las Vegas to see my old friend from our school and service days, Jake Pauly. It was going to be a scream to see the look on his face when he found me at his door.

THE FIRST MEETINGS

As told by Jake Pauly and Arthur Fellows

Zack had arrived at my house in the night to find no one at home. He knew it was my house as my beat-up old Ford truck was in the drive. He had stopped at the store for snacks and a newspaper. He'd backed into the drive for the night, at some point he found it in the paper. The reason I was not home.

March 1, 1984, 5:30 AM. I pulled in my drive to find a yellow pick up with a camper parked in my driveway. I was mad and beat on the door.

"Get up you sons of bitches and get the hell out of here, this ain't no RV park damn it."

I screamed.

The camper door swung open it was Zack.

"Jake Pauly, you're going to lose friends with talk like that."

"Zack is that you man? I'm sorry, but the past two days have been the worst in my life. "

I was in shock as my good friend looked at me as he climbed down from the camper.

In that weird calm voice of his he said.

"Jake, old boy, I got here hours ago. I saw it in the paper. I'm sorry for your loss. You and Janet were together for quite some time. Look man if you're needing some help I'm here or would it be better if I took off?"

"Zack, you stay. I'm not in the right frame of mind. Here's a key to the house. Give me a call in the morning. I need to do some heavy thinking on my own. OK?"

"You go in and do what you need to do. I'll see you later."

Zack climbed into his camper for the day.

I went in the house and laid down on the sofa. My kids were at my folk's house in Kelso. My wife is gone. There were no signs of her being sick in any way. Her heart just quit. It does not make sense. The last cake she made was sitting in the cake safe. I had been staring at it for some time. At 3:00 AM I buried it in the backyard and then fell asleep. Zack let me be until 9:30. I made it to my feet and headed to the kitchen. I followed the smell of coffee. Zack was listening to the radio. He turned and said.

"Morning old man, there's coffee. And call your kids. They're not sounding happy at all."

"Oh no, it's almost ten. Look Zack, I'm a little short on cash, so could we take your truck into Kelso. I told the kids I would pick them up at noon."

"Take it easy. Your mom remembered me on the phone. I said you were still sleeping, and she was pretty cool about it. Just give her a call."

My friend was offering to help. If it were anyone else, I would have to think about it, but not Zack. The half-crazy guy has been the closest thing to a brother in my life.

I was choosing my words carefully.

"Zack, I'm putting you in for a big promotion."

"Oh, yeah?"

"How does Uncle Zack sound to you?"

"Sure, why not? I've never been an uncle, but I'll give it my best shot."

I went to get cleaned up for the trip to Kelso to get my kids. Zack had found the vacuum and was working his way through the house. When it sounded like he was in my den and he was freaking out.

"Jake is this really yours? It's great."

"I'm getting dressed we need to get going. We can talk about that later. Let's get the kids. They're going to flip when they meet you."

I grabbed my keys and glasses. Zack had his vest and shades. We were about to step out the door when there was a knock on the door.

In a flash Zack had his illegal shot filled gloves on! I remember the night he got those gloves. A lumber jack was using my face as a parking place for his fist. Zack hit him two or three times and he hit the floor like he'd been shot.

"Zack, open the door please."

It was Mr. Allen, my boss. Zack was like a spring about to uncoil.

"Jake, can I have a minute? I need to talk to you."

I stepped between Zack and Mr. Allen.

"Mr. Allen, I'm sorry it's been rough; I'm going to get my kids now. I've had a lot going on the last two days."

"You're needed at the shop Jake. I need you at the shop. Please put your life and household in order. If your friend needs some work, I'll help Jake."

Zack was patting me on the shoulder.

"Mr. Allen, just a day or two and I'll be back. I still have to talk with my kids and Zack has offered to help."

He said goodbye and left.

In a minute we were in his truck and on our way to Kelso. Turning on to the ramp at Tropicana and I-15, it was an hour and a half on the Interstate. When we hit the Interstate the conversation began.

Jake: What's the little gear shift? Is this a four-wheel drive?

Zack: Nope, she's no four-wheel drive. It's a ten speed-a highway type five speed trans and a two-speed rear end.

Jake: You put this whole thing together yourself?

Zack: Yep!

Jake: How long did it take to build? There's something else that's strange about it.

Zack: Well, I'll tell you, old boy, it took a little better than two years to build. Getting one thing at a time, then working on it part time. The camper only took two weeks to rebuild and restore. Mom and Dad helped so it went pretty quick. The strange thing you probably noticed is that there is little to no road noise.

Jake: How'd you do that?

Zack: Simple! I just put spray type insulation between all the body panels in the cab and doors. There's one inch polyurethane foam under the carpet and seats.

Jake: She's a nice piece. You did a great job putting it all together. So, what in the world made you head out this way anyhow?

Zack: Well, it was time I got out on my own. I was back living at home. The work slowed down real bad, so I packed up and decided to give it a shot out here.

Jake: Look, you're welcome to stay and live with us. I'm going to need help with the kids, house, and all. Mr. Allen is a jerk. I know he's going to have me on twelve hour shifts till doomsday.

Zack: OK, I just hope the little Pauly people are up for all these changes in their young lives. I mean one if they take to liking me right off the bat and two how much of a ghost thing will they have about their mom. I can be an uncle, but will Janet and Jake Jr. let me be an uncle?

Jake: You forget, I'm the dad. When I say to like somethings they will. Hey what's this about an attorney anyway?

Zack: I paid Robert a retainer. He's my attorney.

Jake: What do you need an attorney for? Are you having some kind of problem?

Zack: No problems. Look, you know money hangs around money, so I paid him to present an idea of mine to the right person at the right time.

Jake: Sounds pretty crazy to me, but I guess that's one way of getting an idea to someone with money. You use someone with money. Pretty clever man how much you figure on making when it sells?

Zack: Let me put it like this. Sending Janet and Jake Jr. off to school for their doctorates will be no different than going for an ice cream cone-what ice cream you want, what school you want.

Jake about your den that's nice. Was that a computer you got in there?

Jake: Yeah, and two-word processers and the engineering calculators. Why?

Zack: Those things could really help with a project I'm working on.

We talked all the way to Kelso.

At my folk's house he was looking a little nervous. We went inside, where Mom was waiting for us.

"Where are the kids, Mom?"

"At the cemetery with grandpa. He said that he was going to explain some about life to them."

It wasn't all that long the three of them came through the door.

"Hi Dad, you and the kids have a good outing."

"I believe we did."

"Well, what did you two learn today?"

Jake Jr. spoke up.

"Dad, some people get old and die. And some people just die like Mom. It's not a good thing to think about it all the time."

"Dad, we'll be OK. Just don't die right away, I don't think I could take it." Janet whispered.

"The both of you sound like you got some very good advice today. Now I have a surprise. You've never had an uncle."

The two of them looked at me with confused faces.

"Uncle Zack you can come in now."

Zack walked into the living room.

"Hello Janet, Jake. You ready to go home?"

Both of them were staring at me in disbelief. It took almost a half hour before we were in the truck to start back to Vegas.

Janet was in the front seat looking like she was on a date, while Jr. and I rode in the camper. We made it home in two hours which is not bad. Zack said he would stay in his camper for the time being. He did remind me he had an interest in my den and library. My folks remember him from years ago, and my kids like him a lot. I think this is going to work out just fine.

At home, my son asked the question I was waiting for.

"Dad who is Uncle Zack really?"

I felt it best to only tell the short version.

"Son, Zack and I were in the service together and he was my best friend. We were in town one night and this guy started beating me up pretty bad. Zack got him off me then took me to the hospital. Zack saved my life that night."

My son looked at Zack for a while.

"Dad he doesn't look like a hero."

Janet brought up the subject of dating, so I let Zack set up the rules. He gave a beautiful dissertation on the rules of dating. The part that hit home was when he said she could start dating tomorrow at 4:00 PM. That's when she broke down.

"He'll never ask me for a date. I'll be an old maid."

I was fighting to keep a straight face. My little lady was in love with her new uncle.

The hardest thing was getting the school to understand that Zack was their uncle without doing a ton of paperwork. I went back to work. Zack took over the house and housework like a pro. Janet started teaching Zack how to use the computer. Zack found a stable not far from here, as Jake Jr. was into horses. We were becoming a family.

∞

March 1, 1984, 2:00 P.M. Los Angeles, California

I just received a call from my college roommate Robert McCabe. My old friend apologized for his delay in arriving here. He'd had car problems; however he was enroute and would be here as soon as possible. My guess for his arrival would be in seventeen minutes. My thoughts were focused on our days at college-the countless hours face down in a textbook. Then all the fun we had at break. I didn't miss by much. Robert is here and he's driving the same car from our college days.

It's been many years since college. We have become professionals. I only wonder what Robert's climb was like.

I made it a point to answer the door myself. The doorbell rang as I opened the door.

Art: Robert, come in my friend and welcome to my home.

Robert: Art, it's good to see you after all these years.

Art: My manners must be on break. John!

John: You called sir.

Art: Yes, this is Robert McCabe. He's a very good friend of mine from our days in college. He will be staying here; do you have a room ready for him?

John: Sir, I have made up two rooms. Mr. McCabe may choose which he prefers. Your luggage, sir?

Robert: Oh, yes, here are my keys. It's in the trunk, John, and thank you.

John: You're most welcome, sir.

Art: Let's go to my den and have a few cocktails. Then you tell me about your trip here. How's business back east? Wait tell me about the trip is first.

Robert: I'll tell you this much, my friend, I could have chartered a cargo aircraft for what I paid for in repairs. In New Mexico it changed for the better at a rest area. The car had blown a hose. As strange as it may sound, it was in the middle of the night, in the middle of nowhere. I was about to take the radiator cap off when this guy warned me that it was not a good idea. He knew his way around cars. Art, you'll need to hang onto your chair. He invited me into his camper to sleep, fixed my car while I slept, and made breakfast.

Art: That's outrageous. You have got to be pulling my leg. Then what happened?

Robert: If you think that's outrageous, get a load of this. This guy Zack never asked for any money or anything. Instead, he paid me a retainer. All he had was five dollars.

Art: I hope you'll write a nice legal letter on his behalf.

Robert: No, it's not like that. Here you go. It's all on the hardcopy. I have it here and the money.

He handed me an envelope. There were phone numbers on one side. On the other side was the list of service that should be taken care of as soon as possible for his car. Inside was a receipt; it appeared to be quite valid. The money was a coin. I dumped it on the desk just to see what he had.

Robert: I need a shower and change of clothes. I don't know which room I'm in.

John: May I show you the rooms?

Robert: Yes, please.

The first was nice but I wanted to see the second one. The second had a super nice view of the ocean with a walk out. I asked John to bring my bags here. Then I started for the showers. John had brought in a bathrobe for me. I just got into fresh clothes when I heard. Art called out.

Art: Bob, Bob where are you? Get in here, this is fantastic!

Robert: What's going on, Art?

Art: Did you look at Mr. Mulholland's five dollars American Money? Bob, listen to me. You remember that some people can surprise you? Well sit down and brace yourself. The five dollars you got as a retainer. I'll give you $10,000 for it. You name it-cash, money order, check. Here take my cards!

In the next two hours, this one coin in Bob's retainer would be valued at $50,000. I told Bob I needed to meet Mr. Mulholland. I also needed to get my board of directors and specialist involved. This may very well be the payday we have been waiting for. I was straight with Bob I knew he was here looking for a corporate job. The man walked in with the golden goose under his arm and didn't even know it. Our company, Greater Southwest Steel Surplus, may have its first major contract. I explained to Bob the importance of this meeting. The two of us went to work on a meeting in Las Vegas on March the sixth. It was arranged and everyone was notified.

I ask Bob to dress for a casual supper. We spent a generous portion of the night on the town. I took Bob to a small place I knew not far from home. It was a Blues and Jazz night club with live music. I told him it was my hiding place. He had a blast.

The very next day I decided it was imperative that we meet with Mr. Mulholland before everyone else. We needed to see firsthand if he had something truly dynamic. I carefully explained my position to Bob in the financial sense of the company's abilities. Bob agreed that having a bit of an edge may not be all that bad.

I had John charter a private jet to Vegas. Bob was carrying the phone number to reach Mr. Mulholland. By noon we were in route to his place of residence. I rang the doorbell. Zack opened the door and greeted us. Once inside, we took a seat at the kitchen table. A fast round of introductions was made.

Bob explained to Zack the purpose of our visit. We needed to obtain enough information to help us get him the best sale price. That said, this meeting should not be mentioned on the sixth. The talk was light and easy going.

"Zack, please forgive me, but we have a timetable. Just tell us your idea."

"Sure"

The flood gates of knowledge exploded. This, unassuming, average person, was the person that had given Bob a coin valued at

$50,000. Now he was explaining in detail his idea with all the parts in place. It was all there geographic location, design, engineering, material, size, metallurgy, time frame of process, and finally its disposal. During the forty-five-minute dissertation, I must have looked like the kid in a candy store. Then Zack stopped.

"Are you also an attorney?"

I told him Robert and I were classmates.

"Mr. Fellows can I pay you a retainer. All I have here is One Dollar American Money."

I must have looked like I had been hit with a brick that phrase-American Money.

"Of course!"

I said. As I made out the receipt for One Dollar American Money as a retainer. We said good bye and started back to L. A. On the flight back, Bob asked if I had looked at my dollar yet.

"Nope, not until I'm at my desk. It's a dollar, but it's a very old dollar."

∞

The first order of business was to check, in with John to see if anyone had tried to contact me. I was told he had spent the day on shopping and other tasks. The answering service recorded all calls coming into the house. Steaks were put on the grill. Bob and I would be dining in the den. We had set out the recorder to start studying the dissertation of Zack's. Bob reminded me of my retainer. I knew the coin was old because of its size. I sat down and dumped it onto the desktop with my jeweler's loop in hand I began examining it.

"I can't believe it, Bob! Mr. Mulholland just bought himself an attorney."

Bob was laughing a little.

"I remember someone saying something to the effect, some people can surprise you. What did he pay you, Art?"

"It's an 1854 gold dollar in very good condition, It appears it was made with a cracked die. I have heard of these, but this is the first one I have ever seen. I need to call Loren in Seattle."

The next twenty minutes on the phone proved one thing. It was very valuable.

"Bob our client needs our full attention."

"Art, you're not saying that retainer caught you off guard."

"In the business of rare coins, an offer is made sight unseen. The offer it's generally half the real value."

"OK so your retainer's true value is what exactly?"

"Three hundred thousand dollars!"

"A few nice legal type letters?"

"Bob, you can pick on me all you want. Never in my career have I ever received a retainer for that amount."

"We have some serious studying to get done before the sixth. Just like the old days at exam time. You up for it?"

"You bet!"

∞

March 6, 1984, 9:00 A.M. L.A.X.

Robert and myself along with Mr. James Howard the company banker and corporate investment analyst. Mr. Robert Nelson the company industrial engineer and metallurgist. Mr. Collin Webster the company physicist and geologist. Mr. Peter Clark and Mr. Richard Stone both major shareholders professional businessmen and presidents of their own company's. Mr. Marshal Bishop the company's head of security, consultant, and analyst to the U. S. government.

"Arthur, you've assembled a great deal of professional firepower here. What in heavens name is this we're doing?" Mr. Webster asked.

"Collin, we are going into Las Vegas to have a meeting with a most extraordinary young man. You need to hear his ideas. McCabe, would you continue please?"

"Gentlemen, Mr. Mulholland is a very unassuming individual. I have been paid a sizable retainer to assist in the promotion of his ideas. I have listened to the basics and believe that you will find his ideas most dynamic."

We took the company jet for the trip into Vegas. The Showboat provided transportation as well as a carefully arranged conference room. All was ready when we arrived. We called Mr. Mulholland to let him know that we had arrived. There was a brief break in the schedule. Zack arrived with his friend, Mr. Pauly. We gathered in the conference room and closed the doors. I introduced Zack and Jake to the group. The floor was all Zack's.

Zack: Good morning gentlemen. I hope you'll excuse me for not being a public speaker. I'll try to be as clear as possible. My idea is little more than a sophisticated garbage can. I should say what the purpose of it is. There is a growing amount of toxic waste in this country.

Industry and the government have stockpiles that are being handled all wrong.

For example, both when possible dilute their waste for shipping purposes only to bury it in sixteen-to-fourteen-gauge steel drums and at best lining the hole in the ground with little more than eight mil plastic.

Now we have hundreds of these sites across the country. Many of which are near major underground water tables being used by large numbers of people.

I believe that the best shape should be an oval or egg shape structure. An estimated size would be four-hundred yards in length by one-hundred-fifty yards at the center point width. The construction of the vessel should be done in three stages. First the bottom or base, next the sidewalls and finally the top or cap. The entire vessel is built in eighteen-inch-thick steel. My reason for such a thickness is that if our country came under attack it should be able to withstand a hit.

The easiest way of obtaining the steel needed for producing the pieces to build this would be obsolete ships. The transport of parts and/or panels would be done by rail to the job site. Because of the size, the vessel would be built outdoors as well as not far from its final resting place. The assembly, that is the welding to be done, has many variables. I see wire feed welding as the best option. The vessel and project itself, in my opinion should be done with no outside influence. It should not be open to anyone,-no media or safety inspectors.

Now the part that is still unknown the method of burying the vessel. First we thought a nuclear blast to cause the ground to liquefy. Next the possibility of an opening such as a mine shaft.

We have put together booklets with a bit more detail for you to examine.

Thank you, Mr. McCabe, Mr. Fellows I guess it's your turn.

"Thank you, Zack, Jake for sharing your ideas with us. I believe we will be going into a board meeting as all of us are here. Thank you."

Zack and Jake left the meeting. Bob and I took charge. For the retainer we had been paid, I was going to do everything I could to sell his idea.

"Gentlemen, I believe that this is something we should study a little more. I know that I have mineral studies from Area 71. I need to go over these before I can vote on this. I say we adjourn this meeting and meet again one week from now in Avalon to see if this is the deal we want. All in favor. OK, we meet next week." March 6, 1984, 11:35 A.M. Las Vegas, Nevada

WAITING-LIFE IS ON HOLD

As told by Jake Pauly

The weeks after the big meeting were fairly normal. Zack had the housework down to a science. My youngsters were doing surprisingly well in school. Myself, it was eat, sleep, and twelve hour shifts at work. The time I had with my kids was always great. Zack made it a point to try and have my time off left open. It sure took the stress off me. My son got a part time job at the stable. I was a little concerned about this, so I went to have a word with my son's boss.

I arrived at the stable and was greeted by Dave Holms. I introduced myself, then we had a conversation about my son. I was quite surprised when he told me that he and his wife were retired school-teachers. Also, he gave one hour with pay to do his homework. If more time was needed, it was without pay They were also there to give guidance as needed. Dave explained how he found that the right tool to motivate my son was simply being around the animals. I thanked Dave for the information and taking care of my son. I returned home feeling much better.

Zack's truck was gone when I pulled in. The house was all closed-up. It was strange he never went shopping at this time of day. I found a note on the fridge.

"Jake, Janet has been taken to the hospital from school. I'll call as soon as I know something. PS Your lunch is in the ice box. Zack."

My little girl is at the hospital. Zack will be with her. I best get going or I'd be late getting to work. All I could think about was Janet and another damn bill to be paid.

At work, I spoke to Mr. Allen I let him know that I was expecting, a call as my daughter was in the hospital. He immediately told the office staff that I would be getting a call regarding my girl's health and was to be put on a phone quickly. I went to do my job but was not doing very well. A little while later Mr. Allen asked me to take over in the shop, as he had business to do. I nodded and he left.

Forty minutes later he returned with Zack and Janet. Her arm was in a cast.

"Janet, how did this happen? Are you all right, who did this?"

"Daddy, I broke my arm on the playground playing kick ball. I made the turn at first base and tripped. Doctor Boyd said I'd be just fine, but I have to wear this cast for six to eight weeks."

I hugged my little girl and looked at Zack saying "Boyd?" He said, "The colonel."

"Take a long lunch, Jake, I'll see you later." My boss offered.

On the way to the diner, I ask Zack who was taking care of Jake Jr.

"I called Mr. Holms and he said that they'd pick him up at school."

Lunch was very good. It was a little funny watching my young lady eat tacos one handed. The rest of my workday went much better.

Getting out of bed the next day I decided I should find out the damages. I went into the kitchen for coffee. Zack was there waiting.

Zack: Morning old boy. Coffee?

Jake: Yes, thank you. Say, did you bring home the bill from the hospital?

Zack: Nope!

Jake: Damn! Those idiots will be sending bills forever.

Zack: Nope!

Jake: What are you saying man?

Zack: No bill, just a receipt.

Jake: Did you pay the hospital?

Zack: Yep!

Jake: How? I mean where did you get the money?

Zack: I took it from my savings. I know how the bills are around here, I'm just trying to help out.

Jake: Thanks brother. I didn't know how I could have paid it in the first place.

Zack: You know, I could put together a budget in such a way that in a few months you'd be in a lot better shape.

Jake: OK man if you think you can fix it, just do it.

Zack: Show me all your household paperwork and I'll go over it tonight and tomorrow. We'll see how much we can do and how fast. Say, you better get moving! It's almost work time.

∞

My son had told me about Zack and Janet's bath using a plastic bag on her arm. She'd called out for help and in the next breath yelled to not come in because she wasn't dressed. That had to be a real hoot. Helping her get dressed was hilarious.

I'm proud of the kids. Both of them for doing so well at school.

It was hard to believe, but the old man came up with a plan to get the household a good bit closer to being in the black as far as money goes. The bank was all in favor of a refinance loan with a generous grace period a lower monthly payment.

When tax time rolled around, Zack found a C.P.A. that would do in home tax returns. When I saw how much was coming back, I was shocked. That was all well and swell until I got the notice from the I.R.S. that I was being audited. I didn't sleep well for a week.

May sixth was the appointment date. We went in to the I.R.S. office to see a Mr. Johnson. He went over my return and began asking questions. The one that saved us was Zack being a student. Zack showed his ID card and the whole thing changed. There was something about him moving here along with me boarding a student. Before I knew it, I was getting back nearly twice as much money and Zack's amount went up as well.

∞

When it was time for Janet's cast to come off, Zack took her in to see Doctor Boyd. From what I got it was quite a procedure. The doctor remembered Zack from our time in the service. The one thing that was bad was the smell. Her arm smelled, really bad. The Doctor started cutting the cast off.

"Doctor, the yellow soap." Zack asked.

"The liquid. You apply it the second the cast is clear." Doctor Boyd answered.

Zack smeared the liquid surgical soap on her arm the second the cast came off so it would reduce the smell. An x-ray was taken then they came home with her yellow arm.

∞

May 12, 1984, When the tax returns arrived, I signed it and handed it straight to Zack. He went to work paying off all kinds of bills. The next day he surprised all of us. He had bought a microwave oven All of the bills, marked paid in full, were taped to the front of the microwave. He handed me three envelopes. The two for my kids each had a five-hundred-dollar savings bond in it. Mine had eight one-hundred-dollar bills in it. Only seven weeks into the budget and we are caught up with a little money ahead. I did have to explain how savings bonds worked to the kids. I think they understood that it's money for the future.

∞

On Sunday, me and the kids took a day trip to the hills. Zack was working in the garage as we left for the day. It was great just doing whatever a picnic, a hike just being together and having fun. When we returned home that evening, it was late. Janet asked if she could see Uncle Zack to tell him about her day. I told her to knock and not just walk in.

She knocked but came right back to me.

"Dad, I think Uncle Zack is sick; he's moaning in there."

I knocked on his door and peeked in. He was flat on his back in bed with his arms over his face.

"Are you bombed old man?"

"No brother, it's my eyes. The pain! Just shoot me."

Janet walked in as I was trying to get a look at what was going on with his eyes.

"Uncle Zack, move your arms."

He finally lifted his arms. His eye lids were swollen to the size of tennis balls. It was the most grotesque thing I had ever seen. My little girl was wiping the pus from his eyes with a towel. I called the hospital and within minutes was telling Doctor Boyd about Zack's eyes. The doctor said he would have a specialist standing by.

The next call was to the Holms' to ask if they could watch my son. Mrs. Holms said she would be right over to watch Jake Jr.

When Mrs. Holms arrived, for Jake Jr. I locked the house. Janet and Zack were in the back seat. I made good time getting to the hospital.

Once there Zack was put in an exam room. The doctor had a nurse take Janet to be cleaned up, as he did not know if Zack was contagious. A nurse took me to a washroom. I was given instructions on cleaning up, as if I were exposed to something contagious.

The nurse took me to the window of exam room three. My friend now had Doctor Boyd, two other doctors and three nurses. The two other doctors were removing goo from under his eye lids as nurses left with the samples. A fourth Doctor entered the room.

"Zack, what were you doing before this started?"

"Woodworking."

"What kind of wood?"

"Cedar."

"You have an allergy; treatment will begin shortly."

A pharmacist arrived with medicine to treat his eyes. I watched ten separate shots in each eye. It looked like the colonel was talking him through it all.

When they finished, Doctor Boyd stepped out to talk to me.

"Jake, your friend Zack is going to need to stay inside for three days. No driving and no sunlight. Other than that, he can go home in about thirty minutes."

I thanked him and went in to see how Zack was doing. His eyes were still very puffy, but he could open them a little.

"How are you doing, old man?"

"I'm beat right down to my socks. You might need to have some lunch money tomorrow."

"How are we going to pay for this stop?"

"Not we, it's as good as paid for already by the V.A., brother."

"Oh yeah I forgot."

Half an hour later, we were heading for the car and home. Janet got her uncle in the house then and told him to go to bed. I could tell he was beat. I got Janet in bed then checked on Zack. He was out like a light. I got the coffee ready for morning and turned in myself.

May 28, 1984, I took the kids to school. When I got back home, I walked into the house another surprise. Zack was up and had taken care of a lot of housework. His eyes still looked puffy. We sat down at the table to go over the budget until it was time to go to work. I left a note for my son to vacuum the garage clean so Uncle Zack wouldn't get sick again. He jumped right on it when he got home from school. As time passed normalcy in the house returned.

∞

June 1, 1984, 10:00 A.M. As June started, Janet was lining up her summer wardrobe. Jake Jr. was offered a seat in an animal husbandry class at U.N.L.V. Work was the same as always and Uncle Zack's eyes were back to normal. My lunch was ready, and I was off to work.

That night when I got home the kids were in bed. Zack was sitting staring out the back door.

"Someone in the back yard, old man?"

"No just lost in thought. Jake, maybe you should have a seat as well."

"Sure, man you look like you're a thousand miles away."

"Do you remember that meeting at the Showboat?"

"Yeah, why?"

"McCabe and Fellows will be here in the morning."

"OK so that means what?"

"My idea sold for five million dollars. They are coming here with a certified cashier's check tomorrow."

"I need a beer."

"Make that two please."

We didn't talk much after that. I could see how something like that would give a person a lot to think about. We finished our beers and Zack went about putting the coffee together for the morning. He had the place closed-up as I was going for the shower.

"You need to use the john, old man?"

"Yeah."

He was in and out and in bed in no time. I wasn't far behind.

June 2, 1984, 9:00 A.M. Zack and I were up early the next morning. The kids were still in bed. We had a quick breakfast and were sitting at the table spending five million dollars when there was a knock on the door. I answered it.

"Mr. McCabe, Mr. Fellows come in. Zack, you have company."

We used the kitchen table.

"Coffee anyone?"

Mr. McCabe: Zack, Jake, you can call me Bob, and this is Art. Now I suppose you'd like to see some money. Well, here you go straight from my briefcase to you.

Zack: Five million dollars. I can't believe it.

Jake: Let me see it brother...Wow.

Art: Zack, selling your idea had to be one of the easiest jobs I believe I've ever had.

Bob: Zack, Zack Earth to Zack Earth to Zack, come in Zack!

Zack: I'm sorry, it's just so weird. One minute you're worried about bills and then you're rich.

Bob: Good, you just said the key word, rich. Now you're rich. I've taken it upon myself to put together some things I believe will be helpful in the management of your new-found wealth.

Jake: You mean like a tax shelter.

Bob: It's more than a tax shelter. It's very complete and detailed.

Zack: So how should I go about the handling of my money, Bob?

Bob: Here's a list of the things you should do as soon as the check is cashed.

Zack: OK let see Insurance, I.R.A.s, T Bills, Charities, Pay Taxes Quarterly. Say, what if I wanted a trust fund for someone. Would that be a problem?

Bob: No problems with any trust funds.

Zack: Wow. What else can I do?

Art: Zack, the commission has already been taken out for Bob and my efforts. Now next item because you understand the size and details of this project. We would like it if you chose the people for the job site work. We are already a corporation, and I am permitted to pay you fifteen dollars per hour, that's twenty-four-hours a day for the offsite job of personnel manager. Supplies and equipment is being bought or manufactured as we speak.

Zack: Sure, I'll take the job. Bob are you the company attorney?

Bob: Yes, I am.

Zack: Art, then you must be the company design engineer?

Art: Well, you're close. I'm one of five engineers and a major share-holder, as well as being an attorney in the corporation.

Jake: Art, what is the pay going to be on the job?

Art: Jake, a person working as a welder would be making thirty dollars an hour. That's twenty-four-hours a day for an approximate time working on the first phase should be ninety days. At the end of that time period, you will have earned $64,800. So, we would like to offer you the job of assistant personnel manager. The same as Zack.

Jake: OK, put me on the staff.

Bob: Gentlemen, now there is something I must tell you that you might find unsettling. We are partially funded by the U.S. government.

Zack: What percentage have the federal folks gotten?

Art: At your end of the business, only ten percent. At our end, we will be dealing with close to forty percent involvement. Because of the security, the government has given rules and guidelines.

Jake: Sounds to me like there's going to be a pretty fair amount of paperwork.

Bob: I'm not saying it's bad, but to start it's a must. One reason is the earnings will be tax free, which means no I.R.S. and no pay checks.

Zack: Paid in cash.

Bob: I tried for paying in cash, but they wouldn't do it. But they did come up with a reasonable alternative. The pay will be direct deposit to a savings account at the bank of your choice. You would be paying tax on the interest making it to be a great deal less than the full amount.

Zack: Bob, as the company attorney, will we have your services like if we were working?

Bob: If you're on the job, I will be handling all your legal needs, from paying parking tickets to writing out wills. I am also ready for handling any household crisis.

Jake: It sounds good to me.

Zack: Say let's get to the bank so I can cash this baby in.

Art: Let's use the company car.

In no time, everyone was ready to go. My youngsters were on their best behavior. Art was driving and I was giving directions. At the bank, Bob went to get the manager to handle Zack's banking needs. Zack was sitting in a chair with a blank look on his face. I could only guess what he might be thinking. Bob returned with an older gentleman, and he asked us to follow him.

We followed him back to a meeting room. Everyone took a seat as he introduced himself.

"Good morning. I'm James Williams president of First National. I understand that a Mr. Mulholland has some business he needs my special help with."

Zack laid the check on the table.

"Mr. Williams, your bank has in the past been very fair and helpful with Mr. Pauly's banking needs and that's why I'm bringing my business here. I have a check for five million dollars. I have some business that I would like taken care of right off the bat, I mean first."

Mr. Williams leaned towards Zack and stuck out his hand.

"May I see the check, Mr. Mulholland?"

Zack handed him the check. Mr. Williams studied it then picked up the phone.

"Linda, bring the service cart and have security come to the meeting room. Thank you."

His secretary brought in a small cart that had a file drawer on it.

"Coffee or soft drinks." She asked.

The kids had pop and the rest in the room had coffee.

"Say this could take a little while. Janet, Jake, could I interest you in a tour of my bank?"

Both were all for that. Art asked if he might join in the tour.

Mr. Williams: Mr. Mulholland, if you'll sign on the back, we can get started on setting up your banking needs. The check was signed. Now sir, what would you like done first with your five million?

Zack: I have a list, but it may make better sense if my attorney handled it. Bob.

Bob: I'm feeling informal today.

Mr. Williams: Very well. Call me Jim. Informal is OK by me.

Bob had Zack's list. I had no idea what he was going to do. But in a half hour, I found out in a big way. I was more than surprised when I was told what Zack had done. He paid of my loans the house and the car. He got all kinds of insurance on everything, as well as everyone. In less than an hour Zack had spent or invested near two million.

Linda returned with Art and my kids. Jim asked how they liked his bank. He got very high marks. Art was the one who said he liked his bank so much, that he wanted to open an account for the business. A great deal of work was being done in Vegas so it made sense. Jim asked how much to start. Art just said twenty-five million. Jim said he would personally handle it. With the banking completed, we started for home.

The kids were chattering with Bob.

"Dad, look what Linda gave me. "He fished something from his pocket and handed it to me.

"Son, did Linda really give this to you? It's a twenty-dollar gold coin. You didn't help yourself to this?"

Art told me that Jake was telling the truth. I was about to hand it back to my son when Art asked if he might have a look at it. I said sure.

"Jake, the proper name of your coin is a Gold double eagle. It's the Liberty standing, Saint Gaudens; no motto, Arabic numerals 1908. A very nice coin to have, just don't spend it."

From the backseat I heard Zack say, "Bingo."

"What's that old man. Are you going out for a few games?"

"Nope, I kind of figured one of you to be a numismatist, coin collector. So Art, what did you come up with on Bob's retainer?"

"Zack, just one coin took me from fifteenth in the nation to second as far as major coin collectors." Art replied.

"Before you head back to L.A., take this with you for your spare time. I think you will find it interesting."

Zack set a small cloth bag on the table. Art and Bob took off, back to L.A.. Zack and I spent the rest of the day going over the application forms. There were plenty of forms to be filled out. June 2, 1984

PAPERS AND BODIES

As Told by Zechariah D. Mulholland

The first two pages seemed like any basic job application--name, address, education, etc. Page three was where it started getting a good deal tougher--list all addresses since date of birth. I knew I had them all written down somewhere in my military file. This was becoming a real challenge. The pages to follow were filled with questions about physical health starting from birth, diseases, sicknesses, broken bones. Jake and I spent almost the whole day trying our level best to get everything filled in on the questionnaire. After a long day at the kitchen table pushing a pen, we looked over one another's entries and ribbed each other about some of the answers.

We closed-up the paperwork for the day. The kids had decided on Pizza for supper. The idea didn't sound bad. We quickly headed out for supper. It was a great night out on the town. It was the end of a wonderful day.

June 3, 1984, 7:00 A.M.

Jake and I had started on our profiles. It seemed to be getting longer and in greater detail. The section on booze and drugs was four pages long. The yes and no questions weren't too tough There were just a lot of them. The essay questions were just plain terrible. The two of us kept going. The psychological part of the query was probably the worst. There were six long pages of what had to be the wordiest questions ever. Half the time was spent trying to find some of the words in the dictionary. The pages on phobias were where we both lost it. Everything was so ridiculous. There were only four pages left to go. We took the time off from the booklets of our lives' history and had some fun with the kids.

June 4, 1984, 6:45 A.M.

The next day it was coffee in one hand and pen in the other. The heading of this section was called Personal Essential Familiarity. The questions here became really disjointed. No two were alike in any way. My likes and dislikes, food, pets, music, weather, and people. Filling in all the answers took the better part of the morning. We agreed that someone that lived a real boring life would get a kick out of reading these over. It took a whole two days to complete the booklets.

I called Bob to find out where to send them. I was instructed to mail them to a P.O. Box in Atlanta, GA addressed Attn: Alice Krew. We decided to send the booklets next day delivery. It seemed to be the thing to do.

∞

Life in the Pauly house was back to its regular form. The kids were getting into their time away from school. Janet was working on tanning herself from head to toe. Jake was with Mr. Holms at U.N.L.V. taking a class. Work at Jake's job had dropped to maybe twenty hours a week. That evening the lot of us went out for burgers at Ron's Bar and Grill. It was a little family place with superb burgers and not too far from home. Ron himself took our order--milk and cheeseburgers for all.

I was enjoying my meal and listening to two guys talking at the bar. When we finished our meal, I excused myself from the table then went over to the gentlemen at the bar.

"What's the good word, guys?"

The greeting kind of threw them and broke up their conversation.

"Friend today's good words are pretty sparse. Unless unemployment is a good word."

The first fellow answered.

"Buddy we've been cut loose from a job that's been home for the past three years,"

The second piped up.

I gave it a moment.

"What do you guys do for a living?"

The first one returned with.

"I'll tell you mister we've been welding for so long it's all we know."

These guys sounded like the right ones to me.

"Gentlemen, I'm the personnel manager of a company that is in need of welders. Can you weld thick plate say twelve inches or more steel?"

"Yeah, it's been five years ago or so."

"Alright, I don't have the applications on me at the moment, but I will bring them tomorrow. Be here 10:00 A.M. tomorrow morning. OK?"

They agreed and the night drew to a close.

In the morning Janet headed out back to sunbathe as Jake took his boy to the Holms house for the day. By 7:30 A.M. we began planning on how we would find the people for the job. The newspaper was ruled out right off the bat. Finding the right folks for the job was not going to be as easy as I had hoped. At about 9:30 A.M. we started for Ron's. Jake and I were in suits, with briefcases--the works. We were early so we had coffee and talked about getting more people. The guys Joe Little and Abe Crow, arrived at ten sharp.

Ron brought more coffee.

Zack: Abe, Joe, we are personnel managers of a new company. We are in need of heavy plate steel welders.

Jake: The hours will be long. The job will be on site. You will eat, sleep and weld on site.

Abe: Sounds like a big project.

Zack: The size is big; at present we cannot give you any information along those lines.

Joe: Is the government involved in this?

Jake: The government is yes. The percentage as far as you being a welder is small.

Abe: I'm curious to know the pay and benefits.

Jake: Very well, you will have total medical insurance with no out of pocket, along with a two-million-dollar life insurance package and housing allowance. As for your pay, you will be paid thirty dollars per hour for every hour you're on the site. That's working or sleeping.

Joe: When will this job start?

Zack: From what I understand, it should be soon. A month or so.

Abe: The problem is that we have no current source of income.

Zack: I believe some part time work may be arranged.

Joe: Wow, this is sounding better by the minute.

Jake: Do you have a mailing address or a P.O. Box?

Abe: We have a street address. We're renting a house.

Zack: Good. Gentlemen, here are your applications. Please understand it is a must you fill these out completely. If you work at it steadily, it should take you about three days. These forms are very detailed.

Jake: If you have any questions or when you're finished filling in the forms, call the phone number on the back of the booklet.

Abe: OK with me, but at present we're short on cash for living expenses.

Zack: I see. Here's two hundred to tide you over until we get you to a part time job.

Joe: Hey, thank you. I've never been paid to fill out an application before.

Jake: Gentlemen, I wish we could spend more time with you but it's not possible. We must get to our next scheduled appointment.

We got up and everyone went on their way. On the way back home, I told Jake of an idea I had for finding a few more people for the company. He seemed to think it was worth giving it a try. At home, Janet was still in the backyard sunbathing. Jake was on the phone to Mr. Allen checking on some part time work for Abe and Joe. Mr. Allen told him to send them in anytime. I had my chores done and took a nap.

About 2:30 P.M. I was up and I was feeling lucky. I told Jake I was going out on a hunt for another body for the job. All he said was bring them back alive. I spent a good deal of time just driving around. I spotted a van up on a jack in a parking lot. A guy was fixing a flat tire. It took a good five blocks before I could get turned around. Pulling in the parking lot, it appeared this guy was down on his luck. I parked the truck and walked over to him.

"Hey friend, can I give you a hand?"

The half beat looking gent looked up at me and said, "Sure, but I can't pay for your help."

This guy was down and damn near out.

"If I don't do a good deed once a year, I start feeling bad."

The van wiggled on the jack. I continued.

"Say you got someone inside there?"

"Yes, my wife and my two girls," He answered.

"Maybe we could have them wait out here until the wheel is back on."

The ladies climbed out and waited quietly by the side. We worked at finding the hole then getting a plug to stay in place. Finally, the van was on all four tires, and the tools all put away.

I decided to make a pitch, the conversation started.

Zack: The name is Zack Mulholland and you?

Him: I'm Rodger Cook.

Zack: Rodger, from all outward appearances a person might guess you to be between jobs.

Rodger: Well, you're right on that one. We moved out here from Illinois and you just can't get a job.

Zack: Rodger, let me ask you a few questions. Maybe I can help you or at least point you to someone.

Rodger: I'm ready. Go ahead.

Zack: What kind of work have you been doing?

Rodger: Mainly farming.

Zack: So, you're accustomed to equipment like tractors, crawlers, end loaders and cranes.

Rodger: Those and more.

Zack: Good, have you ever had a class or some other type schooling in welding?

Rodger: Yes, in high school and six months in trade school.

Zack: I believe I can help. Here is what I would like you to do. In the morning call this number and ask for me. It's my home phone so please don't hand it out. I know of an application that maybe of interest to you. I'm the personnel manager of the company.

Rodger: Would 8:00 A.M. be OK?

Zack: That will be fine. I'll talk to you in the morning. Oh, and here is something in good faith.

Rodger: This is a hundred-dollar bill.

Zack: 8:00 A.M. That phone number.

Rodger: 8:00 A.M. It is.

With a quick good night, I headed home. I couldn't get Rodger's homeless condition off my mind. Night turned into morning fairly quick.

∞

June 7, 1984, 8:00 A.M.

The phone rang right at eight Jake Jr. won the race to answer. It was handed to me.

"Good morning Rodger...Yes thank you...Rodger, I'm spending the day here at home. Why don't you just come over and we'll go through some of the details."

He agreed, I gave him the address and directions and the call ended. Jake Jr. was getting ready for work; Dave would be picking him up. Janet the little sun goddess was out for her morning sun. Jake and I sat at the table talking about Rodgers living conditions. The Cook family showed up at the house at nine. Not bad timing for someone who didn't know the town. Janet came in to meet the twins, April, and May. The girls were begging their mother to go out to play. She OK'd it and they were gone like a shot. I got coffee for everyone.

Zack: I'd like to thank you for coming by today. I didn't feel like going anywhere.

Rodger: I should be the one doing the thanking. This is the first job offer I've had in a long time.

Lisa: Rodger hush, let them speak.

Zack: I think I can be of help to you if you will answer a few questions for us please. You said you are used to working with heavy equipment.

Rodger: Yes.

Jake: Good!

Zack: And you have had some training in welding?

Rodger: Yes, about a year's worth total time.

Jake: Have you done very much welding; or was it more of a hobby or personal use?

Rodger: Personal use on the farm, but I did a part time job in the winter at a quarry. I did a lot of welding there.

Zack: Like equipment repairs?

Rodger: Exactly.

Jake: Zack, he sounds good to me. I'm going out to check on the girls. Just keep going I'll be back in a minute.

Lisa: If my two are being bad I'll be right out. You just say the word.

Zack: What I have to say isn't the easiest thing for me, so please give me your trust and honesty. The way I figure you went bankrupt and the farm was repossessed. You sold some of your personal effects for gas money and moved out here hoping to find good paying jobs.

Rodger: Yes, that's it in a nutshell.

Zack: So, at present you are homeless with no mailing address.

Lisa: We've been living in the van for the last three months.

Zack: That's not a problem if you're ready to go to work. I'll just get you a place. It's only one phone call for me. I should tell you when you start the job, you will be away from home for roughly ninety days at a time.

Rodger: Yes, I'll take the job if I'm needed for ninety days. It will make it so my family can live with some pride.

Lisa: I can take care of the household while you're at work.

Zack: Good, we are all in agreement. I'll make the call and by 4:00 this afternoon you'll be home. If you'd like to see it, just walk around the corner. It's the third house up across the street.

Lisa: Rodger, let's go see it.

Rodger: OK, mother.

They had left to look at their new home. I was on the phone to the bank. Mr. Williams and I had a quick conversation. He said to be at the bank by 2:00 P.M. and he would have the paperwork ready to be signed.

Jake came in the back door.

"How are the young ladies doing out there?"

Jake just looked at me.

"Young ladies not quite. More like the three little pigs. They aren't doing anything, just playing in the dirt."

We decided not to fink on the girls.

The Cooks had returned. They loved the place.

Jake: Would you like to stay for lunch?

Zack: Maybe freshen up a bit, then we can head to the bank and go shopping.

Rodger: Zack, how long is this loan for, in years?

Zack: You will be able to pay off the loan in less than a year and still have money in the bank.

The girls came in from playing. Lisa came unglued and scolded the pair of them.

Jake: Lisa, may I be put in charge of the three dirt balls?

Lisa: You got it. Now you little monsters are in for it.

Jake: OK ladies, after a mud pack you bathe. So, all three of you get in the bathroom and take a shower and don't be afraid of wearing out the soap. Do you understand me?

Janet: Yes, Dad.

May: Yes, Mr. Pauly.

April: Yes, Mr. Pauly. Mom that man is a billionaire!

Lisa: You get in there or you'll be sorry, young lady. I am sorry Zack. Kids and their imaginations!

Zack: To be honest with you, it's millionaire not billionaire, so they're trying to build me up a little.

Rodger: So that's how you can do all of this for us.

Zack: Nope. Not really. You would get in a house. I simply moved the clock ahead.

The Cook family was invited to use Jake's home to get ready to go to the bank. I thought Lisa was going to break down in tears. It seems life for them had been a day-to-day battle for nearly everything. By 1:30 everyone was ready to go. Jake called the Holms to say we would be out but would call as soon as we got back.

On the way to the bank, it was pretty peaceful until a little voice piped up from the back seat.

May: Mr. Mulhowin, what's it like to be rich?

I was between shock and cracking up in laughter. Lisa snapped at her.

"May, mind your mouth, girl!"

Rodger was red faced. Jake had a big goofy grin. I figured that I'd better say something before the next question happened.

"Miss Cook, my name is Mul-hol-land just to remind you. As far as me being rich, I've never seen a dime of my money. Maybe we could have a look at it at the bank."

At the bank Mr. Williams greeted us and herded us into his meeting room. All the paperwork was on the table ready for me to sign. In about seven minutes I was a homeowner. I did ask if the girls and myself might have a look at my money. Jim had Linda take us to the vault. Inside Linda had one million dollars sitting on a table for viewing.

With the banking business done I got Jim off to the side and asked if Art had started his account yet?

"Fifty million."

I thanked him as we left the bank. I handed the keys and check book to Rodger. Lisa was now in tears.

Zack: Rodger, you and your family are going to be pretty busy the rest of the day shopping and all. Just spend wisely. Tomorrow morning you will be starting on your job application. We'll see you then.

At Jake's home they got in their van and drove the short distance home. Something inside told me I made the right choice.

∞

June 8, 1984, 7:30 A.M.

Jake had delivered the application to Rodger and got him started. Jake Jr. was on his way to work. The trio had assembled for their morning tanning. Jake and I were in a deadlock over who to get next. Janet came in for a glass of water.

"Dad, will you have a first aid room at work like I have at school?"

Jake and I looked at one another in disbelief.

"I'm pretty sure we'll have one dear."

A nurse was decided on. Jake had the right approach. We would just call Colonel Boyd. He'd know where to find the right one for the job. The call was made, and an appointment was set up to see the doctor. Jake called the Holms as I dashed to the Cook's house all the kid sitting was made.

∞

The three of us gathered in the Colonel's private office. We explained what we needed, asking if he had anyone he would recommend. The Colonel gave it a moment of thought, then gave us a name and phone number. Then said that she would be the best choice of all. We thanked the Colonel for his time and help then started back home. I had a feeling that this Miss Nancy Bergman would be the last person we needed.

At home, I got her on the phone on the first try. I told her how we had gotten her number and she said if it was Doctor Boyd that gave us her number, she would listen to our offer. I asked if we could meet with her, here or somewhere of her choice. She asked for Jake's address she said she could be here in about an hour.

We got busy cleaning up the house. We needed to change into something a little more businesslike. It was forty minutes and the doorbell rang. I answered, opening the door there was a five-foot five inch, powerfully built and attractive woman.

"Miss Bergman, I presume."

"Correct, but I prefer Nancy."

"Please come in. Thank you for your time. I hope this is not a waste of your time."

We settled at the kitchen table.

Zack: Nancy, after speaking with Doctor Boyd, I am confident with his choice.

This lady had schooling and studies that could fill a book.

Zack: I would guess you make roughly twenty-six to twenty-nine thousand a year?

Nancy: Twenty-four-point-five a year. How much would I be making per year with your company?

Jake: For one work period you will be paid just under seventy thousand plus benefits.

Nancy: OK, but what do you mean by work period?

Zack: I will answer your question, but first maybe we should give you a job description.

Nancy: Alright, I am interested in what my duties would be.

Zack: During the time on the job, you will be on around the clock and on call for all medical needs. You have five men working and sleeping that must be kept in top working health. As a nutritionist, food and the feeding schedule will be yours. You may use this group to do any other studies that you believe will be of importance. The length of time on the job, a period or phase, is estimated to be ninety days.

Nancy: It sounds like I would be the chief cook and bottle washer.

Jake: I know it sounds like we are looking for a maid, but it's quite the opposite. You will be in charge of the camp site not the work area.

Nancy: Cooking, cleaning, and nursing along with any studies or exams will be my duties. I don't see any problems with the duties. I need more information, is this going to be on a professional basis?

Zack: I believe what you are trying to say is are there going to be any requests made such as sexual in nature. No.

Nancy: Good. Everyone will be working and living as friends.

Jake: Exactly. That's the plan.

Nancy: Alright. I'm interested. Now where do I sign on?

Zack: Right here. Fill this application in completely then call the number on the back as soon as you've finished.

Nancy: OK. Thank You.

Jake: Nancy, Zack and I would like to thank you for the interest in the company.

We said our good-byes and she was on her way home.

Jake got on the phone to Bob in L.A. to check the equipment status. Bob told him he would be in town as soon as all the applications were received by Alice Krew. Knowing the forms were so over done with stupid questions, by the fourth day the phone started ringing. It was everyone saying Alice said they were to bring the forms here as the company attorney would be picking them up. I called Alice to see what exactly was going on. Once I reached Alice, I was informed Bob would hand deliver them to Atlanta. I did my best to explain because of the complexity of the applications they were very time consuming to complete. She then told me the sooner the better and that she was not in charge of writing the applications.

Joe and Abe were the first to call. I asked them to drop them off as soon as possible. They said OK. Then Rodger was knocking on the front door with forms in hand.

The youngsters were using the house as their track and field area. Jake and Rodger corralled the kids and directed them into the back yard. I threw the living room into something that looked like some kind of order. The kitchen was still covered with the remains of breakfast. Joe and Abe were now at the door.

Rodger was in swimming trunks, undershirt, and thongs. Jake had on a pajama top and cut offs. Abe was in a stained tee shirt, jeans, sneakers to match and a four-day beard. Joe won the prize a poncho, Speedos two sizes too small and sandals. I stood there in my cut off sweatpants, with the sky-blue Speedos in plain view. We looked just great. And all the while the little people freaking out in the backyard. Why should I be surprised when I heard the doorbell ring. I tried to muster the last thread of dignity, as I opened the door. I was pleasantly shocked Nancy in her best holey tee shirt, bikini bottoms, deck shoes and beach towel. Damn, we look good. So professional, as if we were already retired or on our last hours of depravity. I was trying to make the introductions, but we looked so damn funny. I managed to keep from laughing, but I didn't know for how long.

"Thank you, everyone. May I see your applications please? I would like to make the introductions by name and title. Joe Little, welder and more. Abe Crow, heavy equipment, and welder. Rodger Cook, heavy equipment, mechanic, and welder. Nancy Bergman, RN, cook, and the boss in camp. Whatever she says goes. Jake Pauly, welder, assistant personnel manager. Me, Zack Mulholland, welder. This project is my brainchild, so they put me in charge of all of this."

All the folks suddenly just began talking to one another.

I let it go in just minutes the entire group was beginning to sound like a team.

"Please follow me."

Jake knew it was show time. He pointed the way. I was seated at the drawing board and switched on the computer. The cover pages of the drawing pad were turned back as the computer came on. It was all right there in front of them--the drawings, the descriptions, the math and all the other details. Nancy's response was quick.

"You're a damn genius, this is the answer, but how many years of trash is it for?"

I wasn't sure what she was trying to find out.

"It's only designed to handle the most dangerous and deadly of toxic waste, so it's packed away then put to rest."

"How many years' worth?"

"How many years is an underground water table." I snapped. The real, truth was out.

I calmed down and continued.

"Now from the information I could acquire, there are several of these toxic waste landfills near large water tables."

It turned into Q & A time. The main one was when would the job start. I explained that a meeting was scheduled, and I would have more information from it. I had made some copies of parts from the book on heavy plate welding and passed them out. Nancy asked for literature on the subject of field medical supplies for emergencies, also diet guidelines for high heat conditions.

Jake found some books he felt would give some answers to Nancy. Then I gave Mr. Allen's phone number to Joe, Abe, and Rodger for some part time work.

Jake had gathered all the applications. About 1:00 P.M. the first meeting of those who would be known as KREW ended. Bob showed up at the door a little later. He opened his briefcase and put the forms inside. A taxi was waiting out front. All he said was.

"My jet is waiting next stop Atlanta, talk to you later."

It was June 12, 1984, 2:05 P.M

THE DAY OF RULES /
THE THOUSAND COMMANDMENTS

As told by Robert McCabe

August 1, 1984, 8:00 A.M. L.A.

I had completed assembly of the instruction booklets. I knew the group in Vegas was going to have a fit over these. I wasn't quite sure how I was going to convince them how much of a hold the government had gotten on the project. It seemed so incredibly simple in the beginning and now there was a book of rules. I managed to reach Jake on the phone and asked him to have the group meet at his house at 5:00 P.M. for company business. Jake said he'd have everyone at his place.

Art came in the den and began studying one of the booklets. He shook his head.

"This is a joke. Those fools in the government must think everyone on the face of the earth has had four years of law schooling. Are you going to be able to translate this over written mess?"

I was starting to have a sick feeling about even trying to explain this impossible to read piece of writing. I looked at Art.

"No, you and I can get through it, but they aren't going to understand a word of it. We have to get a hold of Bishop and see if a short form of this can be made up."

It took over an hour to get him on the phone. It took another two hours trying to convince him of the odds of anyone ever understanding anything in the booklets were none. It was a debate the likes of which I had never dreamed. Art asked Marshal if he would just hear me out. I opened the booklet to page three and began reading it back to him. After the best part of the page had been read to him, he reluctantly consented to a short form.

∞

We worked out the areas that should be abbreviated and the areas that must remain uncut, just simplified. The next two and a half hours were spent solely on the effort of abridging the stupid over worded book. Art and I cut the pages down to a reasonable size and made it plain and simple. Anyone would know at a glance what the rules were. The new rule booklets were assembled and then were packaged. Art had made all the arrangements for me to use the company jet. By 3:30 P.M., I was enroute to Las Vegas. I knew that this evening would be a turning point and the rules maybe a bit on the stiff side.

∞

In Vegas, a car and driver were waiting for me. The traffic was horrible with road construction. It took nearly an hour to get to Jake's. I was early, but not by much. Zack answered the door when I arrived. Odd, no one was here yet it was five minutes to five o'clock. There was a knock on the door and the whole group had arrived. With the group here and settled, Zack called the meeting to order.

"Folks this afternoon is our first official staff meeting and heading it up is Mr. Robert McCabe, our company attorney." Zack introduced.

I opened my briefcase and handed out the folders to everyone. I was comfortable with this group of people. I began the reading of the rules.

Robert: First I thank all of you for making it to this meeting. I will read to you the list of rules and communication codes. Please hold all questions until the end. These Documents, Lists of Rules, Regulations, Requirements, and Communication codes are deemed TOP SECRET by the United States Government. The release of any information in these documents in any form be it written, spoken, etc., maybe considered a breach of national security and will be punishable by imprisonment for not less than one year and not more than twenty years.

Section One

Item One: Your job is not to be talked about in any form with anyone. In the cases of dependents, spouse, and people of legal guardianship that may have need to contact you in the event of an emergency while you are working, a telephone number is being provided.

Item Two: Only one person will initial receipt documents for all incoming shipments.

Item Three: There will be no other communication equipment on the job site. Only the Communication equipment to be used is that provided. There will be no modifications made in any form on said equipment.

Item Four: There will be no firearms on the job site.

Item Five: You will have a code name for security purposes. On site you will use your code names, nicknames all your working period. In official communications will be the only other times code names are to be used off site.

Item Six: Leaving the job site will not be permitted except for the following: in the event of severe injury, illness, or death.

Item Seven: A complete medical exam will be required before and after every work period. No contact with family can be made in this time period.

Item Eight: There will be no modifications in any form of any working tools, machinery, or support supplies.

Item Nine: The following communication codes must be held for security purposes and no additions will be made.

Item Ten: All personal effects will be inspected entering and leaving the job site.

Section Two

The proper codes for daily communication, suited for all conditions.

1.	Atlanta A.K.	Hello, Good morning, Work is under way.
2.	Atlanta Good Morning	Goods, Mail, Supplies, Received.
3.	Atlanta Good Day	All is in order, all is fine.

4.	Atlanta Good Afternoon	Need Mail / Other communication.
5.	Atlanta Good Evening	Send Aircraft / Need Special Supplies.
6.	Atlanta Evening	Emergency, Mayday, S.O.S.
7.	Atlanta Good Night	Work Has Been Completed.
8.	Atlanta(use code name)	Need Outside Contact (family, etc.)
9.	Atlanta Open	Site is being Monitored, System On.
10.	Atlanta Closed	Site not being Monitored, System Off.
11.	Atlanta 1.2.	Channel Change.
12.	Atlanta Down	Need Security.

The transmission codes listed are for use on channel one only. Channel two will be for regular spoken communications. Channel one is a scrambled channel. Channel two is non scrambled channel, no code names will be used when using Channel two from the site. You will ask for Alice at all times. Your location code name will be Hotel or Hotel Krew, no substitutions. On the job site, the communication unit there is a key operated switch. This switch is to be used only for the most dire of emergencies.

Section Three

Defining names and titles.

1. Alice   Project's title / name of unit being built.

2. Hotel   The onsite living and working area.

3. Atlanta   Name of project headquarters.

4. Krew   Kiloton Rated Electric Welders / Title used by those working on site.

Now, are there any questions?

Abe: Are we supposed to pick out our own nickname?

Bob: Yes, that is up to you.

Rodger: Without firearms. Now I'm just guessing, but what if we have unwanted or dangerous wildlife in the area?

Bob: You have a good point there. I'll see if an addendum can be made.

Nancy: As I will be the person in the living area, that would put me in charge of the radio and signing receipts?

Bob: Exactly.

Joe: Will there be any restrictions put on our diets?

Bob: None. You can eat and drink whatever you want. Now, for the subject of health. Nancy will be conducting a medical study on everyone during the entire time on site. These studies will be turned over to the American Medical Association.

Jake: You are going to be taking care of guardianship papers for those of us who may need it.

Bob: I'm ready to handle all of everyone's personal business needs.

Zack: It would be a plus if we see the equipment to make sure we have what we need. To cut down on time lost in learning a new piece of equipment, assembly of things or hunting for needed items.

Bob: I'll make arrangements for a tour and any necessary schooling for maybe tomorrow. I believe it would be a good idea to start getting your shopping lists ready, food, drink, and medical supplies.

Abe: When are the code names supposed to be turned in?

Bob: If possible, tomorrow along with your bank's name, address, and savings account number. No account number, no pay. Well, Krew, if there are no more questions I'd like to see everyone here at ten A.M. tomorrow."

I got up and asked Zack if he could give me a lift to a hotel.

"Sure, is my camper not good enough?"

"Well yes, but have you put in a slot machine?"

"Nope, but I got a deck of cards."

"Nice, but not what I had in mind."

We took the car and started for downtown.

"Bob, I got to tell you that second rule is crap. If you want to stick to that one. I figure over a hundred days, if we have to stop and wait for supplies or parts the ninety days is off the table. And the rule sure sound pretty Uncle Sam to me."

I decided he should know.

"Zack, Uncle Sam himself is getting a cut. What's getting us now is the military for security."

He pulled into a parking place at what was one of my favorite hotels. I told him that I would take a cab in the morning. Once I was checked in, I went straight to my room then ordered supper and retired.

∞

August 2, 1984, 7:00 A.M.

After a light breakfast, I made all the needed phone calls. Then spent a little time at a slot machine. Just fooling around, thirty-eight dollars ahead was not bad. The taxi to Jake's was fast, real fast. I was early. To my surprise, everyone was already there. The Krew was in the kitchen, with coffee, and donuts.

We sat at the table as I reviewed the three by five cards handed to me in an envelope. Each card had been filled out with the person's name, code name, the name of their bank with address, and account number, then name of insurance beneficiary, next names of persons to have the company phone number. The cards had enough to get everyone set up.

Nancy handed me a folder. It was the list of medical supplies. She had a note attached, saying as she had no idea of food storage, she could not make a grocery list. This was surprising to me. All that was asked was here in less than a day.

It was time for a new round of introductions, I read the names back to them.

Zack Mulholland	Gentle
Jake Pauly	Pink
Joe Little	Spin
Abe Crow	Marker
Rodger Cook	Cable
Nancy Bergman	Ratchet

Ratchet and I went over the first draft of the lists of supplies. It looked fairly complete and in perfect detail.

∞

By 10:30 A.M., the Krew was enroute to the Air Base. Arriving at the gate, I handed the guard the instructions I had been given earlier that morning. We were asked to pull off to the side, stay in the vehicles and please wait. The please wait part had me a little worried. As it turned out, the wait was surprisingly short, roughly five minutes. A large step van parked in front of the cars.

Major Davis, Captain West, and Master Sergeant Amber greeted us. The Major explained that only two days of training on the set up and operation of equipment could be given. Before we could get to our equipment and area, each one of us was handed a large envelope then asked to put all our personal items such as rings, watches, billfolds, etc. in them and then we would be searched. The whole process was going fine, except for Marker's lucky bead, the Major checked it then asked a few questions and the bead stayed in place.

All hell broke loose. The guard frisking Ratchet must have been taking too much time or was being a little too friendly with his job.

She was hitting, kicking, and screaming. About the only thing we understood from her at the moment was.

"Touch me again Mister and you'll be a Miss."

Gentle, Pink, and Marker grabbed her and pulled her off the guard. The Major dragged the bloodied guard off the ground. Captain West checked him over and talked him back to the guard shack.

"So, this is the group called Krew. I didn't know you were an attack squad as well. I like it when people have some fight in them. It'll make my job a whole lot easier. How many of you have been in the service?" Sergeant Amber asked.

"Gentle, Army munitions depot."

"Pink, Army munitions depot."

"Spin, Marines, Chopper gunner."

"Marker, Navy, Welder aboard ship."

"Cable, Air Force SAC boomer and engineers."

"Ratchet, Civilian R.N. emergency room."

"Well, I believe I already have a working machine, a few drops of oil and a little adjustment and it'll run as smooth as silk."

The Major clipped our passes on us then we were taken to a hanger. As we entered the hanger, the first thing that caught my eye was some of the equipment had no Military markings, but everything was painted the same desert camo. I asked the Major about this and was told the equipment that had no markings was company equipment. As for looking the same, it just made it blend in when moving it. The training was in depth from first aid through equipment operations. The training ended at about 6:00 P.M. On the way back to

Pink's, I could see everyone was going over their mental notes. I stayed at a hotel closer to Pink's that night.

∞

August 3, 1984, 6:00 A.M.

I'd taken a cab to Pink's, house. His youngsters were going to Cable's house. We were waiting for Ratchet. She arrived at ten after six. I could see she had a long night and not too much sleep. I asked if she was OK. Her response was that she needed more coffee.

We made it to the Base in good time. Security went fast and we were in class ahead of schedule. The day started with testing of what was covered yesterday; everyone aced their tests. Then we broke into groups of two for more equipment studies.

Captain West and Ratchet were going over the shopping list for the kitchen, as well as the medical supplies for the hospital as he had added more items to the list. Major Davis was with Gentle and Cable discussing the camp layout using a map. Pink and I had a conversation going with Sergeant Amber in regarding clothing needs and the suits that would be worn while welding. He said a list would be provided with recommended clothing before we left the base. He added that the key to living in these conditions was to acclimatize as quickly as possible. This group was now equipped with the most technologically advanced tools for the task. The Krew now had all the lists and other information they needed.

∞

The List of Equipment.

	Quantity	Item/s	
1.	2	15,000 gal. Water Tank	Trailers
2.	1	Water Treatment with Heater	Trailer
3.	1	Fully Equipped Kitchen	Trailer
4.	1	Freezer Type Kitchen	Trailer
5.	1	Refrigeration Type Kitchen	Trailer
6.	1	Communication/Laundry	Trailer
7.	1	Hospital	Trailer
8.	1	Toilets/Basins/Showers	Trailer
9.	1	Hand Tools and Small Supplies	Trailer
10.	2	Living Unit	Trailers
11.	1	Power Plant	Trailer
12.	1	Fuel L.P. 5,000 gal	Trailer
13.	2	Fuel Diesel 10,000 gal	Trailers
14.	2	Welding Rig	Trucks
15.	1	Crawler	H.E.
16.	1	End Loader	H.E.
17.	1	Crane	H.E.
18.	1	Pick Up Truck Small	Truck
19.	2	Golf Cart	Lite units
20.	1	Steel Stock and Wood	Trailer
21.	1	Welding Gas	Trailer

Everything was here and ready to go. The Major called us together.

"People, we are moving all your gear pending notification and it will be your responsibility to set up your area. After the area is in its working order, your building supplies will be shipped to your area. To notify us of your being ready to receive your goods, use the key switch on the com. Panel, key the MIC and say (SYSTEM ON TEST, TEST) you will then hear (TEST SYSTEM ROGER LOUD AND STRONG). that is the end of the communication switch the key is put back to the off position."

The Krew took some more time in studying the spaces of their living quarters. After an hour had gone by, we were loaded in the van and taken to the gate and our cars. We thanked them for their time and left the base. The mood in the car was lighter than last night. I had decided to ask everyone to meet tomorrow before I went back to L.A. Ratchet dropped me off at the hotel then asked if she might stay a while to ask me some questions. We went to my room.

Ratchet: How did all this start, Bob?

Bob: It started the day Gentle fixed my car and paid me a retainer. The retainer part is a long story, but I will say it was a lot.

Ratchet: So Gentle or Pink are rich?

Bob: Gentle's the millionaire. Pink is his old friend who helped put some of his ideas together.

Ratchet: Why would a rich person want to work in the desert on a Top-Secret project?

Bob: Well, it's his baby. Who knows maybe when it's done, he'll act like a millionaire.

Ratchet: Ha, my boss a millionaire.

Bob: Make that Bosses. I'm a millionaire and everyone on the board is.

Ratchet: What, you too?

Bob: YEAH!

Ratchet: Well, do you have a boss?

Bob: Yes, but I can't give you a code name until it comes through.

Ratchet: Will we ever meet your boss?

Bob: As a matter of fact, yes, the day the camp is ready.

I was exhausted from the day's business. From there it was, eat and sleep. The next morning, I just took my time in the shower, shaved, and put my overnight bag together. I had a breakfast that was better than great. I spent a fair amount of time watching some sporting events on one of the TVs in the lounge. The company jet would be taking me back to L.A.

I got a cab to Pink's for our last meeting for a while. I asked the driver to wait as I gathered their lists.

"If you have the list of personal supplies remember it's for ninety days."

At the airport, the jet was ready to go. Art had arranged to have a helicopter pick me up to get me back to his place fast. Door to door in under one and a half hours. At Art's, John took my bag. Art came out of the den.

"Welcome back. OK, give me the details of the trip. What's the Krew look like and the equipment as well?"

"Art, the trip was excellent, and the Krew is the scruffiest lot you'd ever hope to see. I'll say right here and now if you thought Zack was an unlikely type with his idea, just wait till you see all of them at the same time. I tell you, Art, all of them are geniuses and they get along with one another. The equipment is top of the line. It's the most up to date goods you'd ever dream of, and I can run most of it. Now when will they start to work?"

Art and I moved into the den to continue our talk.

Art: John, bring up some cocktails. Thank you.

John: Yes, sir!

Art: Now, look at this.

Bob: Well, it's a model and all the equipment.

Art: This is to exact scale and the detail is perfect. Note the three panels laying down when they're in place. We make the call, and it starts.

Bob: I hate to be the bearer of bad news.

Art: What is it? What?

Bob: Your model is wrong. You need a bigger table and if the compass is correct to the structure, the equipment is way off and the locations are all wrong as well.

Art: Just how bad is the model off?

Bob: We need at least four feet on this side and this side about two and a half feet added.

Art: That much?

Bob: Yes, I studied the equipment and the layout.

Art: OK, we'll expand the model and do it right.

Bob: Say who's doing the modeling work?

Art: One moment. The cocktails. Thank you John. Please have a look at this.

John: I'm sorry for the delay. I was halfway into making dinner.

Art: John, Bob has been making very pointed remarks regarding the model you built It needs some important corrections and additions.

John: Sir, my model is incorrect?

Bob: Not incorrect, just too small. I'll draw a map with some dimensions.

Art: Well John, can you do it?

John: Sir, this isn't a toy is it?

Bob: It's no toy, and John, please don't breathe a word of this.

Art: Throw dinner in the refrigerator and call for delivery. We need to get this put together directly.

John: Sir, give me just a moment to put the house in order and gather the additional items.

Art: Well, Bob, now what do you think?

Bob: He's a craftsman all right.

John returned with a roll around chest. The additions were made, in less than an hour. The expansion was done. The painting, and landscaping was in place. He was smiling while he worked, as if he was being paid to play. Art and I worked on mapping the locations in greater detail. John was putting in the shrubs and we had completed drawing up the map. John would examine the map and set about placing each piece in its proper location. The work moved slow and steady for a lengthy amount of time. John stepped back surveying the model.

"Sir, I believe this is your model now, but there are still no roads."

"John as soon as we see the camp site in its true form, the roads and any other items can be added."

"Yes sir, I would be honored to care for any changes."

"You've got the job."

We packed up John's modeling goods and called it a day.

August 4, 1984

THE TIME BEFORE WORK

As Told by Individuals

(GENTLE aka Zack) I was staying busy with the household chores and everything else. The youngsters were getting ready to go back to school. They loved shopping for clothes. At the same time, I did some shopping myself. There was this athletics shop having a huge sale on all kinds of stuff. I got nine Speedos, ten complete sweat suits, ten pair of heavy gym socks, and a net bag for the laundry. After a few more sales, I called the others and mentioned the sales. I hadn't heard anything on the start date. I was working on putting my bag together for the job. I purchased the usual clothes, footwear, toilet items, two decks of cards, a set of dominoes, a large note pad, pencils, and magnets. The fun part was trying to figure out how much soap and tooth paste to get for ninety days.

I wrote a long letter to my folks telling them only that I got a job, but it was out of town. I explained to them that the hours would be long, but the pay was very good. I explained that they were my insurance beneficiaries. Next, I would call as soon as I'd be able to, but if there was an emergency to call the office at this 800-phone number and it would be relayed to me. I said I was pretty much over my homesickness. I enclosed a picture of the four of us here in the backyard. I got the RITZ cleaned up for storage so it was ready.

I was starting to notice that I was feeling a little nervous about all the top-secret business and that I had been made a boss. Trying to calm down had to be one of the toughest things I'd ever done. It helped a lot when I called Ratchet and tried to explain my position. She was really understanding and said it's just the new job jitters. I would be fine as soon as work started. I spent some time with the family, doing my daily routine. I was ready.

∞

(PINK aka Jake) My time was devoted to my kids and school starting in just a week. Zack and I must have walked through every store in town with them shopping for school clothes. On two occasions, May and April joined us. That was a true test of patience. I had gotten my travel bag together. Ten pairs of socks, four pair of sweatpants, four flannel shirts, six pair of cut offs, eight pair of shorts, eight tee shirts, shoes, and flip flops, bath goods and a six-band radio. The bag was packed and repacked several times. Each time I'd put something else new in or something I felt I couldn't live without. The packing of the bag for work was becoming a problem for me. At one point I decided to just sit down and make out a list of the things I needed to have and things I'd like to have. The list put a stop to two days of debating what did and didn't need to go. By the third day I had made my mind up on the things going and staying. Right or wrong, the bag was finally packed.

I knew I couldn't move the kids to another place. That would upset them and might mess them up in school. It was time to call in the grandparents. Calling my folks worked out pretty good. They said they'd have a neighbor take care of their place and they would be here whenever it was time. After the call to my folks, I got Mr. Williams at the bank on the phone. I let him know that I may be out of town for a while and to put my parents on my checking account. I was given a number to give them so they could be identified so there would be no mistakes.

I was busying myself with writing a list with all the information they would need as well as the do's and don'ts for the kids, the bank I.D. number, the emergency only 800 phone number. Bob had sent a basic guardianship folder for me and my family. The youngsters seemed to understand that me going to work and being gone was the way it had to be for now. I knew it could start anytime now. I felt prepared.

∞

(CABLE aka Rodger) Lisa and I were enjoying our time together before work began. We still had plenty of money in the checking account. Everything in the house, as far as the appliances went, were new or in good condition, so I didn't need to worry about stuff breaking down on them. The van was holding together, but not very well. I had a feeling it might quit at any time.

We'd got the girls registered in school and all their paperwork from back east. Lisa thought my clothing list sounded like I'd be working at a resort, but I explained that my real work clothes were being supplied by the company. Lisa and I set aside all the things for work. My clothes and personal items I'd need for the job. I felt that work would be starting soon. I was trying to keep from thinking of being away from my wife and girls. We'd never been apart. Even now, we were back on our feet, and it was time to pay the piper. I was sure everything would be fine

When the time comes, I'll be ready to go. My family and all the paperwork was in order. The parttime work with Mr. Allen had really sharpened my skills in welding and I was feeling good about it.

∞

(MARKER aka Abe) All I could think of was that first pay day. Man it was going to be great. I bet I spent that money ten times if I spent it once. Working for Mr. Allen was a piece of cake. That job could only be easier if someone else was doing it. I decided to keep up the rent on the house just for the sake of having a mailing address. Besides, the company was going to be kicking in money for housing. Shoot, packing a bag for work couldn't have been faster. I just pull a drawer out of the dresser and dump it in my flight bag quick and easy. I grabbed my junk in the bathroom and I was packed.

The insurance business kind of threw me, so I made up my mind to not make myself crazy over it all. The answer was simply to drop my address book on the floor and pick a number between one and eight and my insurance beneficiary was. Reese Crow, my cousin. Now that was done. Next was who gets the emergency phone number. Let's see Mom. Nope, she'd call if the light in the ice box quit. Dad, nope he'd call if his supper was cold. That leaves my sister Martha. She'd be the only person in the family that could keep from blabbing it to everyone. All my jazz is ready. If someone would say go, I'd be gone. This waiting around was beginning to get old in a big way.

∞

(SPIN aka Joe) I felt Abe was right about keeping the house. At least when we got off work, we'd have someplace to go to, rather than running around for a motel room. The rules said we had to have an address and there was the housing allowance. Abe and I have been traveling and working together for years. Packing a bag for work was no problem for me. Just take everything. Better to have it all than think you have it all. I made arrangements with the landlord to have the house cleaned and made ready for our return. He agreed to having it ready for us.

Being an orphan, the insurance could have been a problem, but it wasn't. The idea of making the orphanage in Lysite, Wyoming seemed to be the best way to go as far as a beneficiary. The emergency phone number just didn't apply, so nothing was done with it. Come on, people it's time to punch the clock!

∞

(RATCHET aka Nancy) One question was still in my head. Why would a good-looking guy who's a millionaire would want to work in the desert of all places? I made a call to Mama and told her I would be out of town for a while--probably three or four months. It was the same battery of questions from her. Who is he, what's his name, do I love him or is it just a friendship? I knew I couldn't say anything about the job. I had the phone number and telling her was going to be a real trick.

"Mama, I can't tell you where I'm going or when I'll be back. Now, I can tell you I won't have a phone, but the company has an emergency only line and they mean emergency only. Mama, I'm putting you and Dad on my insurance policy. Now please, don't ask me any more about this, because I can't tell you."

The rest of the conversation went surprisingly well, the family, the local gossip, and she never brought the subject up of what was going on again.

I asked a friend at work to watch my apartment for me while I was gone. That was taken care of. Good lord, what have I got myself into? Five men in the heart of who knows where for ninety days! Am I going to be safe? Have I been told what they want me to hear or what I wanted to hear?

My checkbook was the best it had been in a long time, plus I had my travel savings. I think the thing that would make me go out of my mind was bugs. I'm not going to have some nasty little thing crawling over me thinking I'm a damn flower, so I would need unscented stuff. I made a trip to my friendly pharmacist. He told me all about unscented soaps, and deodorants. I picked out the items that sounded the best. I had no idea it was so expensive to not smell at all. While I was there, I took care of the personal things I'd need. My list was soaps, deodorants, toothpastes, aspirins, and my regular brand of monthly goods. If I would have left it to the government to do my personal shopping, who knows what I'd wind up with. I did look strange at the checkout, but I didn't care.

The clothes to take were starting to give me a headache. After an intense search of my closets and dresser told me I needed to do some shopping. After a day's shopping, my trip bags were set to go. The apartment was ready I had a leave of absence all set up at the hospital. I was nervous about some of this, but it was my choice, and I was ready.

August 15, 1984, 7:45 P.M

THE CALL WAS RECEIVED--
IT'S SHOWTIME!

As told by Gentle and Ratchet

August 25, 1984, Friday 2:30 P.M.

Pink and I had just finished getting the dishes done after having a midday picnic and pool party. The phone started ringing. Pink picked up the receiver in the kitchen and told me to get on the extension.

"Krew, its Alice's Birthday. At 10:00 P.M. it's your time to gather at the desk in the private owner's terminal at McCarran. Have all the things you're taking packed and ready. Come by taxicab only. A red headed gentleman with wire frame glasses will meet you and say, Are you folks the camping Krew? You will answer, Yes, that's the game. He will then take you to your flight. No other talking, please. Not to anyone. At the end of your flight, you will be directed by your pilot where to wait for your next ride. Please stay in a group. You should be at the Hotel by 3:00 A.M. A desk clerk will be on duty. Have a nice day and a safe trip."

The two of us agreed it was Bob's voice, but it sounded like a recording. Pink got on the phone to his folks, and I ran over to Cable's house. He was standing with the phone to his ear listening to the message.

At the end of the call, he walked over to Lisa and said.

"It's time for me to go to work, dear. Is my bag ready?"

I guessed that he wanted to be alone with his family, and all, so I got out of there in a hurry. I managed to get through the door at home in time to be told the grandparents were on their way. He asked if it would be a problem if he spent some time with the kids. I said it was no problem and I only needed to make a few phone calls. Ten minutes later, I was headed for the door. Pink stopped me and showed me his reason for the family time. He'd gotten a heart shaped locket for Janet, and a clamshell type pocket watch for Jake Jr.. Inside each was a picture of Mom and Dad.

"I'll be back between six or seven to finish up in my room."

"That would be fine. Thank you, brother."

I took the RITZ for a drive. I wasn't feeling bad, but kind of a little alone. I decided to stop by Marker and Spin's place to see how they were doing. They were home hauling out what looked like a year's worth of trash.

"Say man, it's house cleaning time you hang around here and you'll be put to work." Marker greeted.

I was about to answer him when Spin came out of the garage.

"Well, all right the second shift is here. I quit. What's happening?" He joked.

The three of us went inside.

Gentle: What's going on here? Late spring cleaning?

Spin: Nope, just unloading the stuff we don't need around here.

Marker: Yeah, and I got the slumlord talked into fixing and cleaning this joint while we're gone.

Gentle: So, what's being done to the place?

Spin: You name it, man. This place needs it all. But for now, the jerk said he'd fix the shower and paint the place and put in some new carpet.

Marker: I just hope he fixes the holes in the walls before he paints.

We talked for about a half an hour. They were both ready to work.

I left, heading out to kill some time. I was trying to make up my mind about whether or not to stop by Ratchet's. I thought she might need a hand with some last-minute things. I'd never been to her place. I thought it would be best to call first. I stopped at a convenience store and called her. She said it was ok to stop by and gave me directions. It was a ten-minute drive to her apartment.

∞

August 25, 1984, 4:40 P.M.

I couldn't understand the reason for him calling me. I had almost everything in place. The instructions for my plants were all written down. I thought it would only be right to look fairly good for my new boss's visit. I went to pulled a brush through my hair. At least I didn't look like I just gotten out of the bed or been caught in a windstorm. My place looked fine. As for me, another five minutes in the bath wouldn't hurt, but he was at the door sooner than I thought.

Oh my, was this a social call or business? I opened the door.

"Hi, come on in."

He entered and seemed to be thinking over what he had to say.

"Ratchet, thank you for letting me stop by like this. I was just wondering if you might need a hand with any last-minute things. You know errands or stuff like that?"

Well, what a shock. I'd never guessed he'd ask me a question like that.

"Well, I believe I've got everything all set. I'm just finishing here with the dusting, and then I'm done. Have a seat. Thank you for asking."

He settled in my reading chair and began looking over the bookshelves. I dusted the last of my things. I continued to notice something was different. He was just being quiet and letting me finish up. I decided my mind was trying to play tricks on me. He was now standing and appeared to be studying the books a little closer.

"Would you care for some ice-tea?"

"Yes please. So, you're all ready for work now?" We sat down in the kitchen.

"The call came about 2:35, so I started straightening up the place. My bags have been packed for a week now. I noticed that you were really studying my books. Is there one you'd like to look through?"

"May I? You do have one I would like to leaf through."

"Sure, help yourself."

He was up from the table and over to the books in seconds. One of them had definitely caught his eye. In no time at all, he returned to the table. With the book tucked under his arm as he sat down.

"You probably won't let me borrow this one."

He laid it on the table. It was my dictionary--the one cut out to hide my jewelry. How did he find out? He's never been here before. I need to stay calm and ask him how he knew.

"Now that's a good trick, but how did you know about it?" He smiled.

"No trick. Really. Come here and I'll show you how simple it is."

We walked into the living room, and he began explaining how.

"Look at this room. Everything is in perfect order. Now look at the bookshelves. Top shelf antiques, next shelf reference, next your nursing texts and then novels. The dictionary is not a novel, so it must be special. When you were dusting, I simply thumped it to find out if it was hollow. See, no trick at all."

Wow. Am I that easy to figure out? He could have just as easily ripped me off. I had to say something without having my foot in the way.

"So, it would be less noticeable just to keep it in the reference area?"

That sounds really bright. If he starts having second thoughts about me being a nurse on the job, I wouldn't blame him.

"Yes, that would be OK, but I have an idea that you may be agreeable to."

Yeah, wear it all so I don't need to worry about being robbed. He may have a better idea.

"If you have a suggestion, I'd be happy to hear it." Great. He's got to be convinced now that I don't have a brain at all.

"You put your rings and things in an envelope and you're welcome to keep it in my safety deposit box."

I like that idea. It's really nice and thoughtful of him to offer.

"Sure, if it is no problem, I'd feel a lot better having my jewelry in a bank."

He needed to make a call to the bank, so I handed him the phone. He was talking to someone named Williams. The call was short.

"If we hurry, he said he'd take care of us at the drive up."

I was in my shoes and dumped everything from the dictionary into a bag. We were on our way to his bank. I'm kind of glad he stopped by. I still noticed that difference about him. I just couldn't put my finger on it. He's so quiet. He's afraid of disturbing something or someone. Maybe he's shy and this is being outgoing for him. It must be killing him being out in public. At the bank, he parked the truck and we hurried to the drive up. Gentle rapped on the window and the gentleman inside pointed to the side door. We stepped over to it and it opened.

"Mr. Mulholland, step in. How can I help you today?"

It was just too hard to believe--a bank letting a customer in the back door.

"I want to thank you for waiting for us. I'm sorry if I messed up your schedule. Oh, my manners! Mr. Williams president of the bank, this is Nancy Bergman, a friend of mine. She needs your help."

It's nice that I've been promoted to friend. A bank president waiting on us and waiting for us is the limit.

"Name it and I'll have it done up for you directly."

Is this bank president going to bend over and kiss his ring or what?

"What we need here today Jim is Nancy has a few things I'd like put in my deposit box. The problem we have is we're going out of town for a while."

He called him by his first name.

"Zack, your key please."

Gentle handed him the key and he was gone to the vault. In just about a minute, he returned with the box. It was opened. I put my jewelry in it then it was locked and taken back to the vault. Mr. Williams returned as quickly as before. It was simply unbelievable. If it had been me just trying to cash a paycheck, I'd have stood in line for twenty minutes. In less than five minutes, my jewelry was in a bank vault for safe keeping. I just couldn't get over how fast it all happened. The two of them spoke to one another a while.

"Miss Bergman, I hope you and Zack have a wonderful and safe trip. Stop in anytime."

I just couldn't stand it any longer. If I didn't ask him now, I'd never stop thinking about it. It was beginning to make me daft. As we were leaving the bank he asked.

"Ratchet, may I take you some place for dinner? I mean why make a mess in your kitchen now."

He asked me out and I look like this. He's kidding. Now wait a second he does have a point about my kitchen. Besides, he's probably straining himself just asking being the shy type.

"That would be fine. Do you have a favorite place?"

"Yes I do. Over on Rainbow. There's a pizza and chicken place I'm kind of fond of. The food is pretty good."

"Sounds good to me."

It was a short trip. When we arrived, the smell was wonderful. We were seated and the menu looked great. The waitress was at the table to take our order.

"I would like a small garden pizza and a large iced-tea."

She turned to Gentle. He smiled.

"The usual."

"You've been here a lot to get service like that."

"Well, yes, about three times a week."

Now ask him. It'll be a few minutes before we're served.

"Gentle there are a few things I'd like to ask you. One is why are you so quiet? And with you being rich, why would you ever want to work? How come I get a strange feeling around you like you're some kind of alien?"

He sat there. The tiny smile was gone. In fact, he looked like he was staring into a coffin. I think I asked the wrong thing. How stupid of me.

"Ratchet, I'm sorry if my being quiet makes you uncomfortable. It's just the way I've become since I got rich. I guess it's out of fear. You know, people could hurt me or a friend could be kidnapped or someone who is close to me. Being a quiet person is my defense. Working, well, I've always tried to stay busy I can't say making more money is a bad idea, especially in my case. Most of my income will go to taxes. Does me being a millionaire disturb you?"

I knew it. I'm having my foot as an hors d'oeuvre. Maybe I can smooth it over.

"So really you're not a shy person, but just protective. I see. The truth of the matter is yes, why can't you travel and have an office? Why don't you act rich?"

There I said it. If he doesn't like it, too bad.

"Nancy, I've only been rich a few months. Before that, I sold almost everything I owned to get here. It boils down to this. I've got the money. The money hasn't got me. If you want to try it, I'll sign all but a hundred thousand over to you in a heartbeat. The only other thing I'd want is having day or night visitation rights so I could see how you got along with being rich."

Oh boy, wait it can't be all that great. I wouldn't want a bodyguard or the worries of everyone I know being a possible target for money. No thank you.

"Gentle, I had everything all wrong. I wouldn't mind a few hours just for a shopping spree, but day to day I wouldn't want those kinds of worries.

"Thank you. Here comes our food."

He was a nice guy. The pizza was the best I'd had in years it had taste. It was cooked perfectly. I was feeling good about my new boss. It was early evening 6:30 or so, when we got back to my place. We parted company and I decided a nap was in order.

∞

August 25, 1984, 6:55 P.M.

The food was great, as always. I hope that Ratchet understood me. I wasn't mean to her. I didn't mean to insult her. I sure hope we get along on the job. That's odd--no cars in the drive. They must still be out. Yeah, no lights inside. I guess it's time to put the RITZ up until I get back. In minutes it was closed up tight. I entered the house and switched on a few lights. I guess they're still out.

The house was quiet as I headed to my room.

"Surprise!"

What's this? Everyone's in my room.

Jake's Dad broke the silence.

"Son, it didn't feel right to us that you didn't have any of your family here to see you off to work. You are part of the family and your legs are welcome under my table anytime."

"Well, OK." It was all I could say.

We carried on for an hour. It was great to be thought of in this way.

About 8:00 P.M. I asked if I could be excused. I still had some packing to finish up. I finished the last of it and was sitting on the edge of the bed when Janet poked her head in.

"Uncle Zack, can I have a minute?"

"Sure come on in."

She walked over and sat next to me on the bed.

"You're going to take care of Dad while you're at work, I mean like, so he don't get hurt?" She asked softly.

I drew a deep breath, and I knew the answer.

"Janet, I can't be by your Dad's side around the clock, but if I see anything that could hurt or be dangerous to him or anyone, I'll do my best to fix it. You have my word on it."

She kissed me on the cheek and said good night. My room was in order. The RITZ was ready. I was in need of some sleep. I told Mrs. Pauly of my need for a cat nap. She said she'd have me out the door on time, so I dropped off to dream land.

∞

August 25, 1984, 9:40 P.M

The taxi was out front. I had my tote bag and two big nylon duffle bags. The door was locked. I felt like I was going into some kind of change that I couldn't be in control of, but I was part of already. I got in the cab, bags in hand.

"Where to, Ma'am?"

I leaned to him and gave my request.

"Private terminal McCarran, its important I get there right away."

He calmly shoved the meter into the fare on position.

"Ma'am, enjoy the lights. You'll be there with time to spare"

Oh boy, I forgot the unwritten rule to never tell a hack I'm in a hurry. What a trip it was! My first flight of the night, and it didn't leave the ground. I think. I approached the counter at 9:50.

∞

August 25, 1984, 9:20 P.M.

Pink was saying good-bye to the kids one last time.

"It's an important job isn't it?" Mr. Pauly Sr. whispered to me.

The cab was out front. Mrs. Pauly was holding the door open for us.

"I wish I could tell you everything, but for now, yes, very important."

We piled in the cab. Pink gave the driver his instructions and we
were off. I figured we were running late.

"Say, this is about a five-dollar fare, right?"

"On or about. You fellas a little short tonight?"

I was beginning to get upset with the snail like driving habits. Pink
was studying his watch I could see he was nervous.

"Say Buddy, this may sound strange, but I tip by the minutes I
have to spare usually ten dollars per. Understand?"

He nodded his head and began to set a new land speed record. I
didn't mind the speed so much, but it was pretty hairy running the
six red lights. At the terminal door, 9:49PM, I handed the driver a
hundred and a twenty and told him to keep the change.

We started in the terminal. Cable, Marker and Spin were already
here. Pink looked back at the door. "Here she comes. Looks like everyone made it."

Damn, that woman had enough baggage for four people. We all
stood near the flight desk. Spin was ribbing Ratchet about needing
an extra plane just to haul her stuff. The minutes seemed like hours.
Everyone had sober expressions, except Marker. I'd guess he was the
class clown in school. He was just talking to anyone that would listen.

At exactly 10:00 P.M., a tall red headed fellow with gold wire
frame glasses came through a door behind the counter and approached
us.

"Are you folks the camping Krew?" His voice could be heard from
end to end in the terminal.

"Yeah, that's the game." Marker responded.

"Follow me please."

We grabbed our bags and took off after him. Very little time was wasted A brisk walk across the aircraft parking ramp brought us to a plain old grey DC-3. We climbed aboard and the red-haired guy strapped us in. I noticed that both engines started at the same time, and they sounded like they had been beefed up. This didn't sound or feel like any DC-3 I'd ever been around. Pink knew planes better than me. He was checking out as much as he could.

Everyone was trying to hear what the pilot was saying on the radio. We only heard twenty thousand feet and something west northwest. We were on the runway. Pink was listening to the engines, the look on his face told me he knew what kind of aircraft we were in. This baby was moving and in the air in seconds. Pink whispered to me.

"This thing is a modified old navy mail plane, made for aircraft carriers and war zones." Great! That tells me we can land on a football field and have room to spare.

The pilot had the engines running wide open. Everyone looked to be enjoying the flight. In less than twenty minutes, the engines were cut back, the landing gear was down. We were landing someplace. Two minutes later, we'd landed and stopped in the middle of nowhere. This was not making me very happy. The pilot pointed us to the side of the road. We were told to wait in the middle of the road, next to but not in, the intersection. All of us bunched up at the spot he had pointed to. He was back in the plane and gone in no time.

There was not a light or any signs of life in any direction. Spin dug out a flashlight and small telescope from his bag. He swept the entire area looking for anything that might give us a clue to where we were. Spin folded up his telescope and put it back in his bag. Ratchet was becoming noticeably disturbed in the choice of our waiting area. Cable was making the best of it.

"OK, here we are standing here on the corner of these terribly busy parkways, and we didn't get our bus schedule. Are we supposed to get the downtown or the uptown? Not very thoughtful of those idiots." Cable joked

That did it. Everyone was out of control in a burst of laughter. The six of us were in our own little world. Reality slowly worked its way through us again. In the dim light of the moon, I could see faces growing long and concern in their eyes.

We had been waiting over forty-five minutes. Marker picked Spin's billfold from his pocket and slipped something into his pack of smokes.

"You got the card."

Spin said under his breath.

"Ahh"

Marker hummed. Something was going on. Marker moved around a bit.

"We're being watched. Ratchet, I'm going to offer you a smoke. Take it. Spin will light it. Go across the road and make like you're going to the restroom. Pink, you take one and Cable, you watch the inside of the box. Nod if it turns red."

Ratchet did as he said to the letter. Pink never smoked but played the part. Cable nodded. I quietly said.

"What is it Marker?"

He was well-trained and knew things, being part Indian. We regrouped in the center of the road.

"Two hundred yards or more up this road, three people are watching us with infrared high power night scopes. They're pros. I thought I could hear more than us, so let's not give them anything to work with."

We stood quietly, Cable reached over and took the cigarette and held it to his face.

"Marker, what was in the pack that turned red?"

"An infrared reading card used for TV remote controls."

We continued our wait ten more minutes. Spin had a watch on the horizon. He grabbed Marker.

"Ooda," Spin hummed.

"Pink listen to the air behind you. What is it? It's low, no lights, ten miles out."

Pink listened to the air. It wasn't long he was smiling.

"Lear, Saber."

It was about a minute later that we saw the landing lights come on and we could hear it coming in. Why did we have to change flights in no man's land? It was a jet. It went past us and turned around. The plane had government type markings and it looked G.I..

"General's Bird." Pink said.

We filed into it and made ourselves at home. Everyone knew this pilot wasn't messing around. The engines only had three positions off, idle, and full blast. The one thing we were sure of was there were a lot of turns being made. The cockpit was completely isolated from us so there was no way of hearing anything in the front. Cable was trying to get some sleep. Ratchet had a string and was playing cats-cradle with Marker. Spin and Pink were having a conversation about where we might be. The flight had lasted a half hour. We knew we were landing when the copilot walked through checking the seat belts and baggage. Hey it's an airport. After landing, we taxied for a long period before stopping. The engines now fully shut down and we were backing up into a hanger. It was an Air Base, but which one? Stopping inside and the doors of the hanger closed.

We got out of the plane and grouped up; this is so weird. The copilot directed us to an office made to look like a waiting room with coffee, donuts, chairs, and rest room. "Now this is much nicer, why this must be the executive lounge." Cable joked. We sat around there for about an hour when our M.P. opened the door.

"Would one of you come with me and bring your luggage please?"

I got up, grabbed my bag, and followed him to another office area. Once inside, I was searched. My bag was gone through, then taken outside to a large helicopter. Nothing was taken from me in the search. So now comes the waiting.

Next to show was Cable. He said that nothing was taken from him. Marker came next, follow by Spin.

"Everyone OK? Might as well get comfortable Ratchet is next."

Cable was looking out the door like he was looking for something.

"What's going on, Cable?"

"Nothing yet. I figure the ambulance should be pulling up any second now. All it'll take is a guard making the wrong move with her. Remember."

We all were chuckling. It was like waiting for a firecracker to go off. Marker started a countdown.

"10, 9, 8," Everyone joined in."7, 6, 5, 4, 3, 2,"

She was screaming. We never made it to one. Three guards hauled her to the helicopter and we pulled her in. Boy, she was mad.

A few minutes later she had calmed down.

"I'm OK I can handle it; they checked my bags all the way through. I was doing fine through the strip search until that jerk touched me."

I chose, my words carefully.

"Ratchet, did you see if they took any of your stuff? How many guards was with you?"

"Yes, they took some things from my bath goods from my shoulder bag There was five of them."

Cable leaned to her.

"It's over now. Why is Pink taking so long?"

There were no answers. Eight more minutes passed before he arrived. He climbed in laughing.

"Lady, you've got a wicked back hand."

"What do you mean?"

"The one guy has a broken nose, and the other two guys got a good start on some black eyes."

She had a grin from ear to ear.

"Well, the one had on a wedding ring and the others weren't cute at all. If they were halfway good looking, I might have been nicer to them."

"When dogs fly. Here you sit with some of the best-looking guys on the face of the earth and you treat us like yesterday's newspaper." Spin mumbled.

Everyone was enjoying the stupid debate over most handsome, newspapers, and life without makeup. This went on for several minutes. I noticed the ground power unit was being hooked up, Major Davis stepped in the door.

"Good evening campers! Because everyone is in first class and the flight is under six hours there will be no stewardesses on this flight."

"I want to call my travel agent. I've been lied to. No stewardess this is an outrage." Marker joked.

The silliness continued as he checked our seat belts and bags. Ratchet won the silly award when the Major checked her seat belt, she let out a long moan and then growled at him. We were carrying on like a bunch of kids. The engine started and in just a minute or, so the flying comedians were on their way. It was a short flight--ten minutes I guess. We landed at the site. The Major got us out and away from the blades in no time flat before saying his good-byes. Then quickly flew off into the night sky.

Wait a minute. The keys, the middle of nowhere and no keys. Spin got out the flashlight as he, Marker and Cable were making a search of the area. Cable called to us come over to the other end of the line of equipment.

"What's this?"

An old looking gent stepped down from a semi.

"Howdy, Smokey, is the name and haulin freight is my game. I'm your delivery boy, mailman, and I got the keys for all your stuff. In the morning, I'll show you some of the changes on your gear. Your bunk trailers are there. You turn in and I'll be around in the morning."

That's it the message the desk clerk will be on duty Smokey.

The lot of us made our way into the living trailers and climbed into bed.

∞

August 26, 1984, 7:00 A.M. On Site

I awoke to the sounds of the equipment running. Come on get moving. Four more hours of sleep would be nice but it's time to get up. The guys had started moving equipment and were measuring and driving stakes. I found the kitchen trailer and began getting something together for breakfast. Whoever packed this kitchen did an outstanding job of it. Now if I can find what I want maybe I can feed these guys before long. Cable stuck his head in the door.

"Ratchet, forty minutes and we'll be pulling the kitchen in place." Then he was gone. The coffee was located, but there was no water, no gas, and no power.

I grabbed up an arm load of oranges from the cooler and started handing them out. Smokey and Cable were in semi tractors, so I threw theirs to them. Spin and Pink were building the deck while Gentle and Marker drove the last of the locating posts. Smokey and Cable pulled the generators into location, then the fuel tanks. Marker was hooking up the hoses and watching something underneath. By ten A.M. all the trailers that made up the camp were set. The deck had been finished as I watched as Smokey and Marker gently eased the deck into place. There was nearly no gap from the deck into any trailer.

The water was going in along with sewer lines. Cable was putting in the sewage pit as Pink and Spin were putting in the pipe. It was near lunch time, so I got busy trying to put something together. Sandwiches and sodas were the best I could do. As the guys would get something hooked up, in camp I was running around checking for leaks or the light switches and outlets. The LP was Gentle's job.

By 3:30 in the afternoon, all the trailers were leveled and tied together from the bath to the storage--seven trailers in a row straight as a string. A tent like top was up over the deck with ceiling fans and two swamp coolers. You could feel the difference the second you left the deck. Smokey said that he was leaving, as it was about five. He and Fats would be back just before sunrise as they were hauling the big top into camp. Before he got away, I did get his blood pressure.

Spin, Marker, and Pink were bringing all kinds of wooden lawn furniture for the deck. It looked odd, but for now it would be home. I was still working my way around the kitchen. The guys found a gas barbecue grill and had it by the deck, I think they were dropping a hint. We had steaks, Texas toast, and a salad with a glass of wine. There were no complaints. The guys helped with clean up, so that went quick.

∞

August 26, 1984, 7:35 P.M.

I was studying my people through supper. It was obvious we needed sleep.

"All in favor of knocking off early, raise your hands please."

Knocking off early won! I asked Ratchet if she had the meal plan worked out. She said it needed some more adjusting, but she would have it soon. I told everyone to hit the showers, then put away their things and go to bed. Remember you have an early start tomorrow. She closed up her areas and she was off to the showers. We got our stuff for cleaning up and waited for her to finish.

After twenty minutes, I walked into the bath. The shower was running and no one was in it. She had it running full blast on cold. I reached in the shower and shut it off. I asked her if she was near done. She rinsed her mouth.

"I am now."

"Come with me please."

She got on her flip flops carrying her bath goods as she followed me. We walked out behind the living units to the water tanks. She had a funny look on her face.

"Do you know why I ask you to come out here?"

"No, is there something I missed?"

"Ratchet, all of us are going to have a full plate. We are going to be so busy. The only thing is all of us need is see it to its end. Now please, put a hand on the tank."

She reached up and put her hand on the tank.

"Ratchet, that's why there's no cold water in the shower or the sink."

"I forgot the tanks."

"OK. We have to be careful with our water. I'm going to have Smokey give a talk about the water. You'd be a lot better informed believe me."

We walked back to her room, and she said good night.

I went back to the table to get my bath bag and towel. The guys were done in the bath, so I took my turn. Inside of an hour, we had cleaned up and gathered at the table to work on the plans for tomorrow's jobs. I got some wine, and it went around the table filling glasses.

Gentle: Spin, how's the woodworking coming?

Spin: If all goes well, I'll have it whipped by noon.

Gentle: Marker, have you rechecked the power system, plumbing, etc.?

Marker: Nope, not all the way through, but for tonight we should be OK.

Gentle: Good, but run through it first thing tomorrow and lock it in.

Marker: You got it.

Gentle: Pink, is all the survey work done for the big top?

Pink: Yeah, and Smokey is bringing in the poles, tent, and anchors in the morning.

Gentle: Cable, have you had a change to look over the rope rigging design?

Cable: I looked them over earlier, but there are some items that don't look quite right.

Gentle: I haven't seen the plans yet, so we can go through them with Smokey to see if he has any ideas.

Spin: Where's Ratchet?

Gentle: She better be in bed and asleep. Well, that wraps up the evening meeting.

Cable: Say Marker, you figure we're being watched tonight?

Marker: Oh, hell yes, since about 2:30 and are they stupid. Why if they were on a real reconnaissance they wouldn't be where they are. Bad location, bad. And if they make a little more noise, I'd show you them.

Gentle: How many and why is it a bad location?

He was scribbling a note then passed it to me. It read the words shot gun microphone and infrared as he played with a little piece of the infrared card.

Marker: There're two of them, maybe three. My people from the reservation of my childhood schooled us in the outdoors--where to sleep and the safe places. Up there (he pointed straight up the hillside) is not a safe place. The snakes will be out soon for food and the warmth on the rocks. It's sad, men not knowing the ways of the desert.

Spin: You are a lying sack of crap. You went to boarding school.

Marker: Snake bites, scorpion stings, tarantula bites, Gila monster bites and Vinegarroon. All very dangerous.

Gentle: So, if they were attacked by any of these, what are the odds of making it here for help?

Marker: A Tarantula bite good to fair and it can be treated. Snake bites you can't judge, but I'd say fair and they can be treated. The Scorpion stings are in two groups. The large ones will make you sick. It's the small ones they have the real poison. Both can be treated. A Gila monster they are bad. The odds are poor at best; treatment would have to start in minutes. The Vinegarroon bite has no hope. The person would be mad and near dead. In today's world you'd say make them comfortable for their remaining time.

Pink: Showtime!

We turned our chairs around, so we were looking down the valley. The shadows of the hills glided across the valley floor as the temperature began to drop. The wait time was brief. It was like a drive-in movie when the bulb burned out. From the hillside we heard screams.

"My neck my neck! Get it off!"

"How's that?"

"You missed!"

"OK! (Then three-gun shots.)"

"You get it?"

"I think so."

"Behind you. Lookout!" (Then three more-gun shots.)

"I got him alright."

"You damn fool you shot the battery pack."

"It looks like a snake or something."

"Damn, now they know we're up here."

"I got it."

"What's that, genius?"

"Hey down there, don't shoot. We're coming in."

"You idiot."

"They knew a long time ago we were here, Look at the bright side, maybe they're friendly?"

"OK, but if we get five years in the stockade you better hope it's in two different states."

Pink was smiling. Cable was chuckling. Spin shook his head looking at Marker.

"You, Big Chief Cow Pie!"

Marker was taking a ribbing. Our spies made it into camp and called for a ride out. In minutes, a helicopter arrived. We never had spies from then on. It was late so we turned in. Morning would be here soon enough.

∞

August 27, 1984, 5:00 A.M.

Ratchet was up and moving like wildfire. She'd found a chalkboard and had the meals for the day posted. Spin had taken a cart out to the edge of the camp. He had his telescope and was looking down into the valley. When he returned, he said two big trucks had just come into view. I check the time, wondering how long it would be before they got here. It was a good thirty minutes before they rolled in pulling at least one-hundred-foot-long trailers. The big top was here and was it big! We went for breakfast and a short break. Smokey and Fats went over the instructions of how it went up. It sounded simple enough The south end corners start pulling and that starts the center pole to lift. Then the north corners are pulled in place. Cable and Marker would be running winches as Smokey and Fats took care of the connection up on the hills. By 11:00 A.M. The big top was in place two-hundred-feet over head.

It was coming on to lunch time and something was smelling really good coming from the kitchen. We got into camp and wasted no time getting washed up. Beef stew, biscuits, and iced tea. With the heat and full stomachs, we took a break. Smokey and Fats were back in their trucks and heading back. I told Smokey that we may need more water. It would be no problem, but it would be later. Everyone checked and rechecked all our systems.

"Let's take a ride." Spin suggested.

"Sure, why not."

He pointed out how wide the perimeter road was along with all the extra space on the corners. As we continued the tour, we stopped at the southwest corner. We walked a few hundred feet.

"Did you feel it?" He asked.

"Yes, the ground changes like from just dirt to concrete."

The one that had me really wondering was when Spin stopped next to our welding equipment.

"What's missing?"

As I was looking at them, no gas tanks, and no wire, I didn't know what to say. Spin was smiling.

"Weird isn't it."

In camp I found Ratchet in the kitchen working on supper.

"You feel like making the first phone call?"

"Right after supper. Get everyone in here." We hit the showers and were ready for the evening meal it's fish, potatoes, and corn bread, ice water, and wine.

∞

After supper, Ratchet was at the radio, going over the instructions and her notes. Power on, standby switch, volume set at four, all breakers in, channel switch on one, emergency key in, and on. She keyed the MIC.

"System on test, test."

A few seconds passed then we heard a response.

"Test system roger loud and strong"

The key was turned off. She again keyed the MIC and continued.

"Atlanta A.K., Atlanta A.K., Atlanta Good Day.

"Hotel A. K., Hotel 1, 2,"Came the instant reply.

The channel switch was put on two and the conversation began.

Ratchet: Hi there.

Radio: Well, hi there. Is everything ready?

Ratchet: Yes, all ready.

Radio: Great I'll see you in the morning. Well, good night all.

Ratchet: Rest well.

The channel switch was put back on one.

Ratchet: Atlanta closed

Radio: Hotel closed

∞

August 27, 1984, 6:35 P.M.

Tomorrow the job really starts. The guys were in the wooden deck chairs at the other side of the deck. It's kind of sounding like another business meeting, but there was too much laughter. The kitchen was ready for another day, I got the meal list out for tomorrow. I was trying to figure a meal plan where I could get maybe seven hours of sleep. In bed by midnight was my only hope. The laundry was ready for the morning. I was ready to call it a day, shower, and bed. The unisex showers and toilets, I was still trying to get used to.

The showers were a treat--open air bathing and the sides were only shoulder high. Tee shirt, undies, thongs, towels, and my robe made me shower ready. I knew Spin was going to comment on my dress but for now I didn't care. Cable gave me the magic combination for the shower, and it was ideal. If it were possible, I'd be in here for an hour.

What the heck! Oh no! Something's on my foot. Now don't panic and don't make any sudden moves. This is terrible! Twenty-seven years old, second day on the job and killed in the shower by a wild creature. I'm not going to look down. I'd scream for sure. I've got to get help. Got to keep from making noise. Why isn't it moving? Throw the soap. Maybe that will bring help. Stay calm nice and easy does it Just lob it over. Now, if one of them will come here and see that I need help. Why are they taking so long? No don't start getting crazy. Help is on the way just stand still.

Spin peaked around the corner and disappeared. I couldn't hear them clearly. Help was coming. Hurry up guys, I need a hero now. Marker stepped into view. He was signaling me to be quiet. He eased over slowly. Everyone else was studying Markers every move. Oh no, he's laying down. He's going to grab it bare handed. Is he crazy or trying to show off? I've heard old stories of how Indians could catch fish bare handed. Why was he taking so long? I felt freed. The thing was off my foot, Marker had it and he was still moving slowly.

"You got it, oh thank you Marker, now kill it please." I whispered.

"Can't do that!"

"What?" I snapped.

"It's bad luck to kill one of these. Besides, she found you first and it looks like she wants to be with you."

He turned and showed me my monster. In his arms was a small grey and brown dog. It had a torn-up ear and was missing an eye. It was terrified. Marker was checking the little beast over.

"She must have been someone's pet at one time. She has been spade and looks about five years old. Poor critter has been abandoned. Well, what are you going to name her, Ratchet?"

I'm standing naked in the shower, and everyone is watching me. I now have a dog. Well, it's scruffy. Scruffy? No bad name. But it does look ripped up or diseased. Mange. I reached over the shower door.

"Marker hand me Mange and my soap please. I'm going to clean my little friend. Poor thing needs it really bad."

Ugly thing. Why did it take to me? I wasn't concerned with the little animals mysterious past. The two of us finished up our shower in privacy.

After a quick trip to the hospital, we joined the guys. I introduced them to the new member of the team.

"Well fellows I'd like you to meet Mange. "

The animal had found a home with us. Mange walked into the laundry and dragged a towel back. She showed us how at home she was. She spent a few minutes pushing, then turning it bit by bit into her bed. This small dog was smart. I had a spare comb and began combing her out. She was loving it.

∞

August 27, 1984, 9:15 P.M.

Tomorrow the first shipment would be coming in. It was going to be busy around here. I believed that everyone is ready. The business of no welding supplies is at the top of the list for me. Pink was trying to find a station for some news and weather. By 10:30 we started heading for bed.

ALICE, PHASE ONE, HOTEL KREW

As Told by Individuals

August 28, 1984, 6:45 A.M. Ratchet

Morning meal has been served and the radios are on. I've given everyone their first medical exams. All exams read good. Equipment is being moved into the field. Mange is surveying the area closely.

8:05 A.M. Spin: I've spotted Smokey at the far end of the valley. He should be here by 8:45. I guess, he's moving slower today. I asked Ratchet to marry me. No answer. Everything's in place.

8:15 A.M. Gentle: All of us have tested our heat suits. The suits, for being so complex with their water-cooling circulation systems and fresh air for breathing gear, were as easy to get into and out of as a pair of pants. Plus, inside the connection pack I'd found an air flow control along with the thermostat for the cooling system. These suits had to be developed by NASA.

8:45 A.M. Pink: Smokey pulled into the big top. One plate and six spools of welding wire were on a separate trailer. Smokey directed Cable to hook up the equipment trailer. While this was happening, Smokey tossed down a coffee. The two of them switched trucks, Smokey had started back out on the road and Cable moved our supplies into location.

9:00 A.M. Cable: Smokey's rig had to be the biggest I'd ever seen. His ride was so advanced, he could pull anything. It was all old school and high tech. An old master's rig with lots of power and it shifts so smooth. The trailer with the spools was disconnected first near the welders. Making a wide turn to get in the right spot to unload, I stopped. The saddle like jig and plate was unloaded then properly positioned in place. The crane lifted the two-hundred-sixty-ton plates easily. The wire was then set in its stands and on the machines. With all the goods in place, I stacked the trailers and locked them together.

9:45 A.M. Gentle: Smokey returned with the equipment trailer and some huge tanks of argon gas. I was informed by Smokey that we'd be having company about noon. I was also told that when two argon tanks were empty just put them on the trailer and he'd take care of it. Everything's in place, but it takes more than one piece before any real welding could start. Smokey departed about 10:30.

11:00 A.M. Marker: Everyone is suited up and all the fine adjustments are being made. The machines are matched at eighty-five percent power. The argon gas flow is set at eighteen cubic feet per minute. The wire feed speed had been dialed in at eight-hundred inches per minute. All the settings were made and noted. All of us ran test passes to get the feel of the size and speed of operation. The surprising thing with these new welding guns was they were so light for their size.

12:30 P.M. Ratchet: The noon meal had been taken care of and the guys are doing paperwork at the table. The general living areas had been swept and mopped. The laundry was finished and distributed. I was approached by Gentle asking if the evening meal could be changed to salads and burgers. I decided it sounded good to me and agreed to the change. In minutes, the Krew was in their swim trunks and out for some sunbathing with deck chairs in tow. It looked like the thing to do, so I joined in.

2:45 P.M. Gentle: Bob and Art have arrived by helicopter. A tour was conducted and the two of them were impressed with the complete layout of it. The Krew then received an addendum for shipments. Two to three plates per day would arrive along with all other supplies the first week. Then eight to ten plates per day until completion. We would be receiving goods all through daylight hours. The whole plan made sense to me. It sounded workable. Supper was great as always. The subject of getting a Vet to check Mange was brought up. One would be sent out to examine her.

7:30 P.M. Spin: The chopper landed and Bob and Art have left. It's quiet in camp now. Ratchet made the close-down call on the radio. I'm calling it a day. If I start now, I might get ten hours of sleep.

9:30 P.M. Cable: It appears everyone is following Spin's example and turning in early tonight. Ratchet and I took a walk around the area. It's just some quiet time. By 10:30 it's time to hit the sack.

∞

August 29, 1984, 6:00 A.M. Ratchet

The radio is on, the morning meal is ready. Smokey and Fats are at the far end of the valley and they're moving slow. The guys are up and moving to the showers. Breakfast was served, now the business of the day's work begins.

7:00 A.M. Pink: Cable and Gentle are moving the morning shipments of goods into place. We got four plates, mail, and info on when the Vet would be here for Mange. Fats has a look about him, like you'd want him on your side in a street fight. He must have been in Special Forces, or something on that order.

7:30 A.M. Spin: Marker and I, as we studied the setting of the plates. A fair guess would be near a ton of wire per joint. Pink and I are on the deck watching the action. We started out to the work area to see how the job of starting was going. They were fitting the first five pieces together.

8:30 A.M. Pink: The five plates were in place and tacked in solidly. Tacked is a poor term. When a person thinks of a tack, they think of something like a thumb tack or the size of a pea. These tacks are more like volleyballs in size.

11:55 A.M. Marker: Cable has got everything ready for the next four plates. Lunch was beef stew and dumplings. It was some good home cooking. Gentle's moving kind of slow, tired I guess. We made the first of the running shift changes. It went fairly smooth. Spin had a little trouble hooking up his air hose. It took a few tries. About 3:00 the next four plates rolled in.

4:00 P.M. Gentle: I was sitting in camp and noticed that something was not right. I called everyone into the deck Ratchet had been watching me as I kept making notes. I asked her to have a seat. She set right next to me.

"This is about you Ratchet."

"What did I do?"

"It's not like that. It's more like your health and all the rest of us as well."

"What are you saying?"

All of us were in camp and on the deck.

"Folks, I see a problem that will affect all of us. My guess is sooner rather than later and that is our sleep schedule. Right now, the way it's going, Ratchet may get only four hours at any time, if that much. So, this is how I see it. Cable on days in the crane and help around the place as needed. Marker and myself will be tacking mainly and welding on days. Pink, Spin, the two of you will be burning wire. I have the pattern for putting all your welds in. This should be very workable if Smokey has some flood lights with generators. Ratchet, this gives you an early start like 5:00 A.M. to make a breakfast and supper. Then all your other work in camp and as far as lunch that is noon as well as midnight, they could be box or premade. This will get you to near eight hours of sleep per night. If we don't get our sleep schedules together, soon none of us will be worth a damn. Pink, Spin I'm asking you to stay up all night do whatever play cards have cart races then turn in around 8:30 in the morning. As for plates and supplies after six Cable, and Marker can flip a coin. It turns out Art told Smokey three loads a day, so we got a little head start. Any questions?" No questions.

7:00 P.M. Marker: Pink and Spin must have a lot of energy to burn. They've been running around here like kids. I just wondered what they'd be like in the morning.

8:30 P.M. Ratchet: I was a little shocked by Gentle's concern over our rest periods, but he had a point. It only made sense to get on a schedule. I did find out how to call Smokey. I checked on flood lights. He knew just what we needed. I was tired. I didn't even notice Gentle being in the shower next to me until I stepped out. It was bedtime.

∞

August 30, 1984, 5:00 A.M. Marker

I had a good night sleep. It was warm outside so I figured lighter clothes would be OK. Ratchet fixed me up with coffee and said breakfast would be out soon. The night shift was still going. I found that hard to believe. Cable was at the table going over the list of plates we would be getting and checking their locations.

5:30 A.M. Gentle: I was near speechless when I sat down at the table for breakfast.

"Cable, is the crane ready?"

"It sure is why do you ask?"

"You're going to need a sweat band on your head. Smokey and Fats are on their way loaded with two trailers four plates per trailer."

"Really!"

Ratchet sat down with us and I asked her if she could get the night shift off to bed without help. She smiled and nodded. I'd finished breakfast and went out front to the telescope to see where they were. It looks like it will be after six when they pull in.

6:15 A.M. Cable: The plates were hanging over the sides of the trailers. Both of them just unhooked their trailers and left them. What I didn't see was they'd brought another truck to move them around. It was like a quarry dump truck, but no dump box. Marker was familiar with the drive systems of it. So, in an hour, Gentle and Marker had suited up and were tacking. The second load of the day came in just after 8:00 and they were gone. At 9:00, I suited up and took Marker's gun. He gave me a rundown of how much and where. They took a break for food.

There's a very weird condition that happens to the guys we call it arc hypnosis, A.H. for short. To explain this is not as easy as a person may think. For one, A.H. is very different from person to person. Arc hypnosis is the point of the person's repetitive movements become second nature as less concentration is needed only that of staying on-line. Then they go into a dream like state. Bringing a person out of A.H. is tricky. Out here it's a little simpler just to shut off their machine.

11:45 A.M. Ratchet: I had lunch ready all three of them went straight to the showers. I didn't comment on them heading to their cubes in the nude. As they were having lunch, Gentle asked if Smokey had said how many more trips they would be making today? He told him two. Marker asked how it went putting the night shift in bed.

"Well, not all that bad. They had supper and two glasses of wine and a shower. Spin walked into my room and got in bed. I was able to move him. Pink found his way just fine and was out the second he laid down."

At 12:30 they were back in the field. I got a call the Vet would be here around 2:00 P.M. for Mange.

2:30 P.M. Gentle: The next load of plates came in as I was sizing up how much we had and would have into the morning. For the moment it looked like twenty-four plates could be put down by the day shift. That was very doable in a ninety-day time frame. All I could see was how to get the last eight plates in for the night shift. Cable was telling me the numbers were off as far as wire, gas run time. He believes we are leaking a lot of argon. Well, if it needs to be fixed, do it. Before we went back out, I asked Ratchet to call Smokey to ask if one load of plates could be held back as we needed to do work on the machines, but we may need water. She said she had a list started.

3:00 P.M. Ratchet: The requests were out of the way in no time. Smokey and I had a nice chat. All the supplies--water, fuel, and such--would be handled in the morning. Once that was done, I had a little me time. I'd go for a run. I needed a water bottle and something real light to wear. My swimsuit should be OK. Forty-five minutes later, I had made a very unpleasant discovery. I smelled so bad, I got into the shower while still in my swimsuit.

6:00 P.M. Cable: What a day it's hard to believe how much is done in a day. I can see why Gentle wants the equipment at peak performance. Well, we have more than enough steel for testing. The night shift is up and moving slowly. As I understand it, there is a sequence to the welds to keep its shape correct. That's one of those things I don't understand yet.

7:00 P.M. Pink: Gentle filled me in on where to start and how much goes where. We got it made. Just burn wire. This is going to be easy money. We checked our machines and got to it. At about 2:30 we noticed the machines were getting soft. It was losing power and not running as hot. The daytime folks needed to know about this.

∞

August 31, 1984, 4:30 A.M. Spin

This is great. Just weld everything is in place. Just pull the trigger and go. Pink said we're driving the welding rigs back to camp--something about an argon leak. Well, it does seem like were going through a lot.

6:00 A.M. Marker: The night people parked the welding rigs next to the camp. We started by taking off the covers to check the internal connections only to find nearly everything was loose. The power line for the machine could be slipped out of place by hand. Not good the argon lines were simple. Every connection leaked. So, it turned into a major repair from the generator to the machine then from the argon tank to the machine on both of them. Ratchet had a new makeup brush she donated to the cause for tracking down the argon leaks. Cable was going for a speed record in repair It's like he knew where to go next with no manual. By 1:00 we were back in the field testing the machines. With all the work on them we found ninety-six percent on the power was doable, the wire speed was turned up to twelve-hundred inches per minute, and the argon dropped to fifteen cubic feet per minute. The welds look like they were done with a butter knife, nice and smooth.

2:00 P.M. Cable: I hope we don't find more of that crap. That's poor craftsmanship. Gentle is really wanting to get as much tacked in as possible for the night people. I was doing my best to keep up with the two of them. The plates were fitting together perfectly. By the end of our shift, twenty-four plates had been tacked in place.

6:30 P.M. Pink: I was told the machines had been turned up a little. If anything, they felt more balanced now. Spin went over the layout for tonight and was ready to get going. At 10:30 that night, we discovered how smart Mange was. The dog came out from the camp and was barking for all it was worth. We were looking at the camp, but nothing odd was there, Spin figured it out. The dog was telling us we were about out of wire. I could guess it was the spool made a different sound and we stopped. A wire change and it was smooth sailing to 5:30. We fueled up the equipment and our day was done.

∞

September 1, 1984, 4:30 A.M. Ratchet

The temp outside isn't too bad. I'm going for a lap around the place. If I can, I should only be out twelve minutes tops. Mange stayed right with me the whole time. By the time we got back I could feel it was going to be a warm one today. I got a quick shower before starting work in the kitchen. I hope Spin is quite. His needling me for a date was sweet, but it was getting old. I've noticed how some of the guys have their quirks. Marker is well-organized and a polite person but isn't able to get going without coffee first thing in the morning.

5:30 A.M. Gentle: A quick trip to the telescope says 6:15 and we're up and running. Cable had the crane fueled and checked out. They pulled in as I had guessed. The trailers dropped off and hooked up to empties, then had a fast breakfast. On the way back out to their rigs Smokey told me all the plates, wire and argon were in the supply yard.

I was then told they had a mess on their hands. The numbering of the parts was way out of sequence and we might be sitting a few days. Well, not much we can do about that, but for today we would have plates. I guess we have twenty-four more hours of work to the next break. It really hadn't mattered at five days; we were ten days ahead of schedule. The 9:00 load carried more good news. We would be getting forty-eight plates today, so they could have that little extra space for their rearranging. There were no complaints from here.

The camp was developing a routine. It was an odd way of life, but the pay is good. The shift was trouble free as Cable hustled to unload the trailers as fast as possible. Maybe two days of work, we finished our day as the night team was getting ready.

6:15 P.M. Pink: We got tonight and tomorrow then we might have some down time according to Gentle. We checked the area and decided it was time to burn wire.

∞

September 5, 1984, 9:30 A.M. Ratchet

I'd just got off the radio with Smokey. They were finished fixing the messed-up supplies. They said they had mail, stuff for the kitchen and were bringing a surprise for us. He then told me to have one of the guys put in an outlet on the day shifts trailer. Marker checked and said everything about it looked good. All the rest of Smokey's conversation was that it would be 1:00 or so when he'd be here.

The guys were on the deck just listening to the radio. The sweat was dripping off them. They were just sitting motionless. It looked weird. I was in a swimsuit and it felt like I was in a sweat suit I walked into the shower got wet and then drove out to the telescope. Yes, Smokey is in the valley! I checked the little thermometer there. It was one hundred eighteen degrees. No tanning today.

It was right at 1:00 when he rolled into the big top. He had a huge trailer. He took the longest time lining it up to park it. There was all kinds of stuff strapped down on it. The huge trailer was unhooked. The side door made it look like a camper. It was a big refrigerator. We got all kinds of fresh produce and a generous supply of wine. There was mail for everyone. I was instructed to go to my room.

I did as asked. They didn't say that I couldn't listen at my window. The main thing I got was the importance of a screwdriver. About a half hour later, Gentle knocked on my door and asked very nicely if he could blindfold me. I said OK. I handed him one of my bandanas I was gently blindfolded. He was very polite about every move with his hands on my shoulders. First I was taken into the shower. He said for a rinse and then walked me across the deck and down the steps. I was not ready for what happened next. Gentle was on one side and Marker on the other. Cable was behind me. I heard Smokey tell them to pick me up then put her down. I had no idea what was going on yet. I felt safe and it was cool near cold water. Smokey slipped my blindfold off. It was like a hot tub, in a way, but cool. I smiled at Smokey.

"Thank you."

He smiled back.

"I've got to get back to the supply area. If Fats gets in the kitchen, I'd need to come here to have supper."

I didn't believe a word he said I was cool sitting in this tub.

∞

September 6, 1984, 5:00 A.M. Marker

Sometime last night, our guys from the supply camp rolled in and out without a sound. I respected that. What I don't understand is that two people were awake and moving about the place. I checked to see if they were on the road. Yes and they were full.

6:00 A.M. Gentle: Smokey and Fats were going over our new shipping schedule. It sounded heavy, but still workable. I knew all it would take was a few days of steady work and we'd have our routine back.

WORKING /
LIVING BEHIND A WINDOW

As Told by Gentle and Pink

September 10, 1984, 6:30 A.M. Gentle

Pink and I were talking at shift change about how the plates had been fitting, along with all the dimensions being so close for its mammoth size. The steel never cools enough for precise measurements, yet the overall plus or minus was under an inch. Ratchet has the camp well in her control. She is everything in camp, like a friend, along with chief cook and sock washer, bandage passer, and the all-around coordinator. She does all the support she can possibly do, yet I think if given the chance she would take a shot at welding. One thing she has been harping on is dehydration. Our urine samples are not what they should be. She's calling them syrup samples. We were all put on an increased fluids intake for the time being. Everyone is doing as they are told and drinking almost twice as much.

Tomorrow we start the run to the outside ring at the south end. The shipments of plates and supplies are now like clockwork. The rest periods for the Krew are still very adequate for everyone. Mange the wonder dog is learning new tricks without being taught. The most recent was when Ratchet went into shower. The dog would take its towel into the laundry and leave it. Then wait for her to drop the freshly used one in the laundry that towel became its new bedding until the next shower. There was no explanation for this four-legged wonder. Day or night we all knew at least one order would be given to us by a dog. We could expect that.

The daily reports to Atlanta were now the same from day to day. Cable has been receiving the side fixtures for the outside ring. The last row of plates to be put in place would end phase one. We're sitting pretty good for wire and argon. A good ten-day supply would be my guess. Marker is into getting all the sleep he can on his off time. When it's time to go he's ready. He has a good working attitude and pays attention to everything around him. He even claims he can stop welding at any time and be able to tell you without looking how much argon is left in the tank within ten pounds.

∞

September 19, 1984, Midnight Pink

I've noticed Gentle is really getting into the project to the point that he's no longer a boss figure. He just goes along with the day-to-day stuff like the rest of us. He tries to keep a time frame for nearly everything. If time can be saved or made more productive, he's all for it, even more so if it means making a task easier.

Spins has been doing OK, but I've noticed he seems to be tiring somewhat by the end of a shift. We had a talk about it. He agreed that maybe he should have Ratchet give him a good medical going over.

Cable is the man of time and space if you said what time and what space that something will be in that space at that time. Not being a psychiatrist or having any training in the area, I can't help it but seeing what looks like homesickness starting to set in. I know I'd love to be home right now, but the job is here and so am I. I had a feeling Cable might try something crazy like walking off. My best guess was to have him get on the radio and try to get a call through to his family. I hope it works so he'll feel a little more at home here on the job site.

∞

September 24, 1984, 6:00 A.M. Gentle

My Krew is working like a Swiss watch. There's a quiet insanity that is very visible in camp. To explain, nudism is the accepted form of dress or undress from 6:00 A.M. to 8:30 A.M. then from 11:00 A.M. to 2:00 P.M. then for the afternoon sunbathing time 4:00 P.M. until sunset. I wish I knew how or who started this. I don't mind everyone running around naked. The grand remark is we're saving water by having less clothes to be washed. The 6:00 P.M. staff meetings are lots more open now. So far no one has gotten weird or made any sexual advances. Being the leader of this group is easy I simply let them do what makes them comfortable and happy then everything else drops into place.

Hobbies are becoming obsessions for all of us along with games. Pink is working on a needlepoint pillowcase; Ratchet has been running almost daily now in the nude. Marker and Spin are working together on making deck chairs out of the unused lengths of welding wire. They're real cool looking. Cable is the artist. He's a wood carver And myself, well, I'm just sitting and watching the countryside. There's a checkerboard set up on one of the tables. It's a game that everyone is in on from shift to shift, day to day. The shifts seem to be going much faster now, but twelve hours is still twelve hours.

∞

September 27, 1984. 6:00 P.M. Pink

With everyone on the go around the clock, the word of the day is still easy does it. It's finally gotten to the point. That we just don't realize how hard we are really working. My guess is it's just become natural. I suppose for the amount of money we're making; it balances out. I was thinking last night I'm one of the highest paid welders maybe on the whole planet. I can't talk about my work. I can't even take a picture of this thing. Well, I think I can make my own souvenir of this place, this time, the people, this place, this place. Well, no one really knows where this place is. Time is the funniest thing we have. It reminds me of the painting by Dali--the one of the clocks.

There's a power here. We work this power as if we were sorcerers brought here to perform the most incredible bit of magic ever. Magic, not sorcerer rather magicians, yes like the mark of the magician from tarot cards the infinite line. Power, powerful, power is so many things, so many signs. The only one that makes sense for us is the one that is lightning. Next a bolt of lightning right through the center of the infinite line. That sounds about proper for who we really are.

Let's see, jewelry is a good way of showing membership in an organization. The military, lodges, and businesses have logos. We should have a logo that is ours. I'm going to show this emblem to the Krew to see if it's just the right piece.

I pitched my idea to everyone, and it was unanimous. It was loved by all, plus they had ideas for pieces and offered help in making the molds. Gentle made a call to Bob with the shopping list and asked him to deliver the supplies himself.

∞

September 29, 1984, Noon Gentle

If the calendar isn't lying, we been out here a month. Bob delivered all the supplies and then some. He'd brought extra chain along with jeweler's tools. He stayed a full day and slept in the hospital that night. The thing that got me laughing was when Ratchet went for her morning run in the nude. She walked across the deck asking Bob to time her. It was an all-a-round good time while he was here.

I was pleased with knowing we would have some memento of this place and time. Maybe someday we could tell the story of what happened here. But for now, it was the excitement of making the molds. If anything, this has done wonders for the morale around here. Everyone is putting a little time in on the molds. The whole project would take time, but I knew Pink would have the absolute perfect pieces when he'd finished. One of the last operations making the molds was cleaning and polishing them. This process made a soot like dust that made a mess. Still, they stayed at it.

∞

October 2, 1984, 5:00 A.M. Pink

I worked a deal with Cable to relieve me at five this morning so I could do the first pouring today. I had everything ready to go when Gentle found me and he gave me the news. A dust storm was heading straight for us. Those things can be a real problem on the machines. He told me to just keep going and he would take care of buttoning up the camp. By nine, the pouring was done for today. I sealed up the shop and headed out to see what I could do to help.

Ratchet caught me coming across the deck. She said there were buckets of sand by the storage unit that she needed to put on the whirl-pool cover. Gentle was in the field with Cable. He had tied the center pole to the crane for more support. Marker was covering the swamp coolers while Spin was on watch out front. A little after ten, Gentle asked us to get something to eat, hit the showers and head for bed.

6:00 A.M. Gentle: There were no shipments. A fast word with Smokey told the story that the storm was two hours away, so they were closing up shop at the supply yard. He did remind me if anything happened to the base radio to use the radio in the pickup. Spin was with the telescope, and he was heading into camp at full speed. Looking out the front, the sky was sand brown and coming this way fast.

The grill was the last thing to be lashed down. In our favor, was that the living trailers were equipped with an intercom system. It had only been tested, but never used. Well, we'd know in a minute. The wall of dust was right outside the big top when we dashed for our trailers. I ran to check doors and made it inside just as it hit.

Ratchet was already on the intercom.

"Yes ma'am?"

"How long will this last?"

"No clue, but I've tried to make a good start for us."

"What's that good start?"

"Just go to your cooler in the back."

It took her a minute to check it out. "Gentle, thank you, but what's in the five-gallon bucket?"

"Well, it's about a gallon of water and an inch of motor oil, It's a poor man's chemical toilet."

"Thank you."

The wind had to be blowing a solid fifty miles per hour the airborne dust and sand was indescribable. Everyone was inside trying to get some sack time. I've seen all kinds of storms, even dust storms, but none like this. We've been pinned down a good fourteen hours and not much change. Unreal. This has just got to break soon, if only to save the spots on our playing cards from being completely worn off.

Even if the wind stopped this minute, who knows how many hours of clean up and repairs we'd have. A loud crashing noise came from right outside.

"What the hell was that?"

Marker suited up and stepped out. The wind had died down some, but there was still dust flying. He had made it back inside. We helped him out of his suit.

"What did you find?"

"I'm not sure about the noise, but on the side of the steel and wood storage there is a bunch of corrugated metal. The satellite dish and the antennas are gone."

"No radio we're cut off from the supply camp?" Cable asked.

"Nope, the pickup has a radio. It's got to calm down out there a lot more before we do anything."

∞

October 5, 1984, 5:00 A.M. Gentle

The winds started dying down during the night. The storm broke and it near broke us. We made it. We were looking at a mess and only the radio in the truck for communication; everything is loaded with dirt. We still have the supplies to get back to some sort of normal. The cleanup is moving along smoothly. So far no one's found any other major damage. We've been at this almost six hours now and it looks like we'll be at it for at least another two or three before we're done. Ratchet and Marker handled the camp cleaning. The rest of us were checking and cleaning our equipment. The carts had been taken from the container so the pickup truck could be brought out to call the supply camp.

Smokey answered on the first try. He gave us instructions on where to dump our extra sand and not to drive on the work field. He told us that there was some of the road that had been drifted over pretty bad. If all went well, they would be starting this way in about two hours. We put together a list of items needed for any repairs. After the call, we continued going over as much as we could, cleaning and checking for damage.

Cable had turned his attention to our main generator after gathering everything. It was shut down as he did a full service on it. Spin said he got the call from Smokey and gave him the list of the things we really needed.

Early lunch was on the fly. We all grabbed something to eat and went back to work. It was coming on 5:30 in the afternoon. We were shot. We looked like a pack of kids who had spent the day in a sand box. Pink announced Smokey and Fats were coming up the grade and moving slow. There was no argument when I called it a day.

"Hit the showers."

Ratchet took the lead as her and Mange got their things to freshen up. When she was done, we took over the showers.

Our supply guys were in camp and looking as beat as we were. Smokey explained that the two of them would be spending the night with us so they could get the field cleared out first thing in the morning. We turned on the hospitality once their trucks were parked for the night with a power line to each of them. They made themselves right at home.

Ratchet had steaks on the grill, and it was a feast to say the least. After dinner we pitched in to help Ratchet get out of the kitchen sooner so all of us could settle back and just relax with a glass of wine.

We learned a little about our supply guys. Years ago Smokey was a Marine and was Special Forces, but not a Green Beret. The thing that came as a surprise to me was he held a doctorate in geology. Fats had spent years in the study of rocks, as he held a doctorate in mineralogy. Ratchet had to ask why they worked out here. Fats looked and simply said.

"I can't tell you now, but I promise in the future you will find out."

The evening came to a close at nine as Spin and Pink were into a game of checkers.

∞

October 6, 1984, 5:00 A.M. Gentle

The night shift had an early supper and were turning in. The supply guys were up and moving coffee, breakfast and they were working on their trucks. Their trucks were equipped with some huge blowers. We made sure everything in camp was closed up. Once they got in position and turned the blowers on. In a half hour, the work field along with base and plates had been blown clean. Smokey and Fats were on their way back to the supply yard saying they might be able to get two loads after one o'clock.

Marker and I worked on getting the radio back in operation as Cable began moving plates in position. At 10:45 A.M., we were running. The time we had banked took a hit, but we were still on the plus side by eight days. Pink had gotten back to working on castings. The shifts worked on the pieces again. The question came up of what should be done with the molds. We didn't want to destroy them, yet we didn't want them found or taken. Ratchet had the best idea of all of us. Simply to hide something, just put it in the open. All that needs to be done is put the molds face to face then fit a frame around them to make a sign.

∞

October 8, 1984, 7:00 A.M. Pink

The jewelry is near done. As for the molds, we have a very nice little sign next to the kitchen door saying GOOD MORNING in a steel frame. It appears we're caught up on all the odd jobs around here. One indicator is everyone's gone out for some sunning. But for now, for me, rest and relaxation includes enough time to settle back to write a letter to my youngsters.

∞

October 10, 1984, 9:00 A.M. Gentle

Smokey and Fats got their bracelets this morning and loved them. For now, it's burn wire. Marker came up with this wager that we could outrun Cable with us tacking versus him setting the next plate in place. It was close, but it turned out Cable was waiting on us on nearly every plate. Ratchet came out to the field. Cable has been teaching her how to operate the crane. I can say this she's doing really well. Marker flagged her to set the next plate in. I watched as she carefully maneuvered the crane in place. Not too bad, not too bad at all. Only three minutes longer, but she did it with no help. Ratchet gave us a ride back to camp for a short break. Other than lunch, it was setting plates in place, tacking, and moving onto the next one.

Through the course of the day, my thoughts would go back to the look on Art Fellows face when I dumped the bag of coins in front of him. Now that was great. He is probably still trying to figure out how I got so many odd ball old coins. My coin collecting went back to when I was four, maybe five.

It was one of the few times I can remember ever talking with Mr. Murrey's grandpa. That guy was old. He'd tell some of the wildest stories about the first cars in the area and doctors and doctoring. When he got started on his stories, look out! Half the town could've heard him.

The one I remembered him telling me was the one that paid off. He told me about back in the days around the time he opened the store. In those days, he was on the lookout for counterfeit money. So, whenever he saw anything that even slightly looked like funny money, he took it out on the bridge in the middle and threw it in the river so no one else would try using it in his store again. Even as a kid I had a good idea of where to look.

It was the summer, after I got out of high school. I made my first attempt at the river. I had an underwater metal detector, the scoop shovel, and two battery packs. The river level was down to near three foot where I wanted to start. I was in the river a solid two hours and had nothing but junk.

But on the bright side on my first trip to the river, I helped almost a hundred leaches to shore and did that hurt. Mom got the saltshaker from the stove and went to work on me. I was in a lawn chair on the back porch. Mom had enough lotions and stuff on my legs. I didn't dare use the shower in the house.

My dear sweet father was still half laughing as he looked at me.

"Get your gear. Let's go prospecting."

Dad knew I was hurting, but I was sure he wasn't kidding. I got the gear and put it in my truck. Dad came over with hip waders and a pair of knee-high waders. I noticed he wasn't laughing, but still had a smile.

"Son, from what you told me you did everything perfectly, but missed on one thing."

My Dad was up to something as we drove across the bridge and up the road.

"Son, now I'm taking you to the old bridge. From granddad Murrey's stories, you've been at the wrong bridge. Now you can see if they are really true."

Wrong bridge? I was near eaten alive and now he tells me.

"The bridge he told you about was the old bridge and that's where we're going." He turned on this old farm lane then turned back to the river. It wasn't as far as I thought. Now all that was there were the concrete bridge pilings.

Shortly after we parked, I got in the hip waders and started. The first two hours I got about a hundred feet downstream of the old bridge. Coins, all kinds of them! Over six days, we harvested seven five-gallon buckets of coins and two truckloads of one pint whiskey bottles. We went back and in six more days and came back with three more buckets of coins. The story was true. Dad had a smile that was beyond belief. Mom and Dad took care of the coins while I was in trade school and when I was in the service. I brought a few with me. If Art shows up again, I'll just see how much a numismatist he really is.

What's that? Mange is barking, OK one of us is about out of wire. Yeah, both of us, it looks like.

∞

October 13, 1984, 6:00 P.M. Pink

The plates have been coming in like clockwork. All the jewelry is done and the pieces for Bob and Art have been shipped out. It's time to get going One more trip to the john and suit up. Well, alright, we're full for starting wire and gas. Just pull the trigger and go.

It's been found that both machines must start at the same time or you have your hands full hanging onto the gun. It's called arc blow. There is the signal and go now, settle in, and burn wire. I've been thinking about maybe dating. I believe I'll have a chat with Ratchet. She might have some great ideas.

∞

October 21, 1984, 8:00 P.M. Gentle

I'm happy to say that the past several days have been perfect for working. The days have been warm but not the oven heat we've been dealing with. The nights are starting to become real cool almost cold. The cooler weather is a plus for the equipment and so far, no break downs. Ratchet is on a new kick here lately. Her and Mange are into making a noon walk on the perimeter road in the nude. It's not catching on too well, but the sunbathing was doing just fine.

Spin's health is still being watched by Ratchet. Everything is normal and he comes off shift spent. Cable is calling home at least every three days. He's a family man and he knew on the front end he was going to be away. If five minutes here and ten minutes there keeps his head screwed on, it's OK by me.

∞

October 28, 1984, 6:00 A.M. Pink

The last two shipments and all the plates will be in place. Then it's all straight welding for both shifts. Gentle believes we can be done with phase one in ten days and on our way home.

∞

November 2, 1984, 4:35 A.M. Gentle

The morning was cool, like sweatshirt weather. I then made the first radio transmission for the day. I don't know how it happened or even when for sure. At 4:20, Pink found Spin passed out still holding the trigger. Spin wasn't moving. Pink rushed him into Ratchet. The call was made to Atlanta on the secure channel.

"Atlanta good evening, Atlanta evening, Atlanta Evening, Atlanta evening"

Only a few seconds passed,

"Hotel 1,2."

I threw the switch and keyed the mic to let them know we were on channel two the reply was instantaneous.

"Hotel who is this and what's the trouble?"

"Alice, this is Gentle. We got trouble one of us out here needs one of those flying ambulance and I mean now."

"Gentle I'm on it."

Ratchet stuck her head in the door.

"No need Gentle."

My next communication was notably slower.

"Alice, make that a hearse."

"Gentle, who's dead?"

"Spin."

"Gentle, I'll notify Bob."

"Thank you."

All of us knew our places and jobs, but for a few hours only Cable went about getting things done. The machines shut down and the equipment parked. Marker took it the hardest. He walked out to the road and sat down. He didn't move or make a sound for hours.

Pink was pretty shocked so I held off on asking any questions. Cable sat down next to me and wasn't saying much. Neither was I.

Ratchet was still in the first aid room making out a report. It sounded like she was talking to herself.

"Guess this makes you the executor." Cable mumbled.

I knew he was right.

I checked with Ratchet just to see if she was OK. She said she was alright but couldn't understand what had happened. I watched and listened as she reviewed all the records on file for Spin. I asked if she could put them in some kind of order to be shipped with his body and effects. It was plain to see she was having a tough time. She was trying to do her job and was losing her fight with holding back the tears. On the way to Spin's cube, I stopped with Pink for a second.

"Listen for the chopper for me, please."

"Done."

Cable and I went into the trailer where Spin's cube was.

Something was wrong. I could feel it, a sense. Turning to Cable. I could see that he was feeling something or trying to find something. His eyes were scanning the place.

"Cable, you notice anything different in here?"

Opening Spin's cube, nothing looked out of the ordinary. Stepping in, I turned on the ceiling light.

"Cable, get Marker in here to see if anything here is missing or looks weird. Please."

Cable was out the door in seconds. Pink called in the trailer

"Gentle, the radio just said the chopper is going to be an hour before it gets here."

"OK, thank you."

An hour? Why so long? Marker made his way into the trailer and down the narrow hallway to the cube.

"Marker, you knew Spin better than any of us. Can you tell me anything of how or why?"

Marker looked around the cube for a bit before speaking.

"Look Gentle, I think I know what happened. A few years ago, he got real sick. We were working a job at a chemical treatment plant. The place was a death trap, with bad welds, leaky joints, and valves. Spin was working in a transfer bundle at ground level and I was in the rafters anchoring hangers. I didn't hear his machine running and looked down to see what the problem was. He was out cold in a puddle of goo. The company nurse said he'd have something like the flu for a few days and it would clear up. He was sick for five days. I believed that nurse. I stayed with him for the time he was laid up. We lost our jobs and the company denied ever contracting us for work. Well, I noticed if he'd catch a cold or flu, it was major for him. So, when this job came around, he wasn't going to let anything screw it up. He paid off a doctor for a good medical exam."

"You've known he could become extremely ill all this time?"

"I knew whatever it was, was killing him."

"Marker, don't breathe a word of this to anyone until I say it's OK."

"Yeah, OK."

We started the unpleasant task of packing up all that he'd brought to the job site. Clothes, boots, a few books, wallet, knife, pliers, writing paper.

"Just a minute. There're entries in it, Gentle look here."

I quickly read over some of the pages. It was a will and last wishes. There were letters to people. I closed it up and set it on the bed. It would be the last thing packed. Now gutted of Spin's effects, the cube was empty. The door was closed at the end of this distasteful duty. Although the time before the helicopter arrival was short, it seemed like minutes became hours.

We sat on the deck, each with our own quiet faraway look, the blend of shock and sorrow. Except for Ratchet. She was sobbing freely. Before long, the helicopter showed up out over the valley, just like Atlanta said. Upon landing, Bob was out of the craft and into camp like a shot. Seeing us sitting there in mourning, I guess he decided to go easy on the questions and answers stuff for the time being. I called Bob over to sit with me. After he got comfortable in the chair, I reached into Spin's bag and produced his writing paper. I handed it to him.

"I believe this to be his last wishes and letters to be mailed."

Taking it from my hand he studied the pages carefully.

Ratchet had started getting it together.

"Ratchet, may I have all your records on Spin, I would like to see him before we load up." Bob asked.

They left for the first aid room and I joined them. Bob looked over Spins remains in an abbreviated manner. Bob began asking questions. Ratchet gave the same answer for nearly all of them.

"It's in the files."

With everything said and done Joe Spin Little was placed in a body bag and sealed up. All of us escorted him and his effects to the helicopter. Before we knew it, the helicopter was leaving the far end of the valley. This day has been the worst I've felt in years. I couldn't ask anyone to get back to work. It would be wrong. All I could tell them was tomorrow 6:00 A.M. we're having a meeting.

∞

November 3, 1984, 6:00 A.M. Gentle

The Krew started making their way to the deck for the meeting. We needed ideas of how to get the job done on time. Ratchet had coffee and breakfast ready. She supplied a notebook to keep track of ideas. Pink, Cable, and Marker were seated. Ratchet had the food on the table with a pot of coffee.

Gentle: All right, let's get started. We need ideas. We need ideas to make a working plan from.

Cable: I think we should check with Atlanta or Bob to see if they might have a replacement welder.

Marker: We could try six on six off. If it's timed right, spool and tank changes would land at shift change.

Ratchet: Well guys I've a few ideas.

Pink: OK, let's hear what you got.

Ratchet: Put me on a gun. If I took someone's six-hour shift, then someone would get twelve to eighteen hours of down time. I've been working on getting a chart put together for fast meals that I can set up in advance, so I can fill in on field work.

Gentle: I'd say from everything we've put on the table so far nothing sounds unworkable to me. OK so far, we call for help, six-hour shifts. Smokey and Fats, I need to talk to about supplies and other items. Ratchet, you realize running one of the guns looks easy only because all of us have been welding most of our lives. If you've never done it, looking easy and being easy are worlds apart. Now I'm not saying no to you welding, but it's the learning it. It's not putting on the suit and pulling the trigger. Am I making myself understood?

Marker: Look, if Ratchet wants to weld, I'll get her started. All of us are going to help her with simulated starts first thing.

Gentle: OK with me. Pink, get Atlanta on the radio about some help. Ratchet, how much more to go on your chart?

Ratchet: About an hour.

Gentle: OK, we get together at lunch for updates.

Marker had finished a service inspection on one of the welding trucks. I had a feeling he was going out to do repairs on Spin's last weld and felt it best to leave him alone. Cable and I were doing the service work on all the equipment. Pink was in the radio room a long time. Ratchet was doing so many things at once it was hard to tell. What all she was doing.

Noon the meeting was under way.

"No help from Atlanta. Smokey and Fats will make sure we stay stocked up. The work starts at midnight. Ratchet, I guess it's on to the next step. Are you ready to suit up for some time with a gun?"

Ratchet had a serious look on her face. The guys started back to work.

"The suit!" Pink whispered.

Oh no, she has to be fitted. That's a two-person job. No wonder they got out of here. They didn't want the job thinking they would get the same treatment as the guards. This is easy. I'll just tell her what I'm doing.

"May I see what you have in the way of work clothes, ma'am?"

We went right to her cube. No sweatpants. Good a plain sweatshirt and heavy cotton socks.

For some odd reason, my brain shut off as I said, "It's alright. You can get into my pants."

"What!"

"I mean I have pants that you can use."

"OK and undies?"

"Cotton is best or what has the most cotton."

"Got it now, what?"

"Get dressed. I'll be right back so you can get into my pants."

"Sure."

I was back in no time. Ratchet was sitting on her bed laughing. She finished dressing and we went to the dry goods trailer.

"Now to find you a lady's size medium."

"Why are you so nervous?"

"Look, suits have to be fitted, and it gets personal. I am going to have a hand in the suit as a gauge for the right air space."

"So that's why the guys got out of here so fast, saying you're the boss and I'm married. If you get too friendly, I'll tell you. OK?"

Things were going at a fair pace. The boots were now like slippers. The pants legs were a handful. After an hour of fighting, I reviewed the manual low and behold her suit is a different model. A fast read and the problems are no longer problems. In all of twenty minutes, the suit was on and looked good. The gloves even had some adjustments. Her hood is really nice, more glass even an overhead, and it fits. The main thing that was different was the suit had to be flooded--that is filled with coolant. I was still a little nervous, I guess.

"Gentle, why are you so damn nervous when I'm around? Did I say something?"

"I don't know why I just have never been able to since."

Marker showed up.

"Come on Ratchet, the school bell rang. Get on and let's go."

The two of them headed out for her first welding lesson. I hope she gets the starts right or she's going to be hurting. It was going to be Cable and I doing the midnight to six shift, so we napped on the deck. At ten, all three of them were back in camp. It was Ratchet. She was barely moving.

"What happened? Ratchet, talk to me now?"

"Heat. I can't move my arms my legs. Pain."

"What do you need?"

"Me out of this suit. Please!"

I carefully bent her over so she could grab the strap for the zipper. Her arm was hard and stiff.

"She's locking up! Pink, start a shower on low hot, Marker, you ready to get the suit off? Cable would handle the laundry and watch the hot water."

She managed to get the zipper down and she popped out drenched in sweat Her clothes were soaked. With her suit off, we moved into the shower now that she was stripped.

Pink and Marker worked on her legs, as I was balancing her on my knee and trying to work on her arms. How the hell did she get so overheated? We worked on massaging down her knotted muscles. It took a while to soften her up so she could stand on her own. Once she made it to her feet, I soaped up a washcloth did her back and handed it to her

"You finish up."

As I was leaving the showers, I found I had a problem. My left knee was giving me trouble. Maybe her jumping and wiggling around popped something out of place. I made my way around to find Cable. It was a short search, as he was still in the laundry getting caught up.

"Cable, where is Ratchet's suit?"

My knee was now starting to become noticeably sore. I began checking the suit for damage or a clue why it wasn't cooling. I was about to tell her that we needed to fit her in another suit when I looked at the cooling line connection. The control was the problem. This thing is backwards to ours. Marker walked in asking if I had found anything. I pointed to the control.

"Damn I could have killed her. It works the other way. I was shutting it off."

Cable was looking at my knee.

"Man, you can't go out like that."

"In the freezer on the top shelve is some large ice packs. Get me two please."

Marker got the knee packed up as Ratchet left the bathroom.

Marker made the comment both of us should be in the whirlpool with a few blocks of ice for at least an hour. Pink said he would take my place tonight. Wrapped in a towel only, Ratchet was looking at me saying.

"Be right back."

"Ratchet, in my cube on the top shelf over the bed is a white rolled up rag would you get it for me, please."

She wasn't gone all that long as she returned in a two-piece swimsuit and the rag in hand. She put it on the arm of the deck chair.

"Hey lady where do you think you're going? Get over here."

"Ok and thank you for the first aid."

"Look, here this is your color of bandana. This is the first thing you put on when you get out of bed, the necklace only the welders wear."

"You and I have a date with the whirlpool. Get up Mister, or do I have to carry you?"

"Nope, but I might not be too graceful."

With just the right amount of moaning and groaning, we made it into the whirlpool. Marker released two five-gallon blocks of ice.

"Gentle"

The cool water was beginning to kick in.

"Yes?"

"Do you think we could die of hypothermia in here?"

"Not likely. The air temp is at about ninety degree. Simply put, just rest your hand on a block, count to thirty, then grab your other arm. If your hand feels cold. Your OK, if it feels the same, you're in trouble."

"I'm sorry about your knee." I smiled then shook my head.

"My over confidence bit me. That's all."

We continued until almost midnight. We made our way to the deck. Ratchet checked on my knee.

"I'll take your shift in the morning."

"OK. You'll be with Marker."

I started for bed when Ratchet stopped me.

"You sleep with that leg elevated or you're going to have some pain in the morning."

I figured as a nurse she wasn't joking around. It wasn't long until I was in bed, the leg propped up, and I was out.

∞

November 9, 1984, 7:00 A.M. Pink

I got the twelve-hour slot on Ratchet's rotation. She's got it figured out to every third shift someone gets the down time. All that's asked of whoever is still in camp is check the meals and do some laundry. It's only about an hour and a half of work. After that's done, rest maybe eight hours of sleep. Ratchet is turning into one fine welder. Good clean work. She's just a little slow for my taste, but she stays with it. She was out with Gentle. If I know him and how he can instruct how things are done, she'll turn into one fast welder.

Mange has been all over the place looking for who knows what. I guess the strangest thing about her is her searches. They look like they're in zones. She has one just the other side of the water tank. Maybe she'll let me in on her secret.

∞

November 21, 1984, 9:15 A.M. Gentle

The last weld has been finished. The machines are being shut down by a check list. I'm going for a shower and a glass of wine. In camp I fulfilled my wish to me. Then all my attention was turned to my Krew. Pink knew of the letter, but never pressed for its contents. For that I'm glad It may not set well.

"Everyone, hey, your attention please! Thank you. We can do this now if it's alright with you?"

Marker: What you got there?

Gentle: I got this letter a day ago from Art and Bob. Here's what we do before we leave. Now bear with me. It's not all bad, weird, damn weird. Here's the map. Because new equipment is coming in, we have a list of odd jobs to get done. Then we are heading home.

The list was passed around the table. Ratchet copied down our to do list so we could check them off as we went. At that point, all of us got our second wind and got busy working through the list. By lunch we put a sizable dent in the list then we treated ourselves to an extended lunch.

2:00 P.M. Pink: Ratchet and I were breaking down wire spools we only had forty or fifty to do. I was noticing Ratchet had been staring at me a good deal this afternoon.

"Something on your mind girlfriend?"

"Well, yes. You've known Gentle a long time. Who was he or what was he before all of this?"

"Why do you ask?"

"Oh, just curious I guess. He's so different."

"OK, Ratchet my dear, I'll tell you the story behind our Mr. Gentle, but you swear never, I mean never say a work of it to anyone."

"I swear."

"The two of us met just after high school. Before that he was honor roll, letterman in sports, and had a high school sweetheart. We bummed around now and then. We went to college, well two years of trade school, and we worked a night job at a gas station. Then he went to a real college and did four years of studies in two. He made his money in buying and selling cars, coins, and there for a while, manure.

When it was time for the service, so we joined on the buddy plan. He saved my life a few times and I saved his. At the end of our time in the Army we didn't see each other for about six months.

I got a call from him, He asked me to be his best man. I had wedding plans too. A few trips back and forth and it turned into a double wedding. It was a great day, but it was the last time I saw him until last March. I called to wish him a happy first year anniversary. The phone was disconnected. I called his folk's house. His mom answered. That's when I got word of him being hospitalized.

His wife had skipped labor pains. She laid down on the living room floor and had a baby girl. The ambulance got there and took them into the hospital to get checked out. Some drunk or stoned woman ran the ambulance off the road killing his wife, his newborn baby girl and one of the medics who was someone I knew. The ambulance driver and two medics lived through it.

The cops caught the woman and put her in jail. From what I was told he drove straight from the cemetery services and rammed the police station with his car. Then went totally insane. He beat three cops to the ground. He busted down the door to the jail area. In less than five minutes, he'd done $30,000 in damages trying to get his hands on her. No one knows how they stopped him.

It turned out the woman never made it to trial. She hung herself. He was hospitalized for a year. He's had a hard time around women. Several years ago, he would've never touched you. He'd just walked away. You're lucky you know him now."

∞

5:00 P.M. Gentle My instructions read.

"On the day of phase completion and attached shut down check list. Make radio contact 6:00 P.M. your time. The time of personnel pick up will be given then."

My laundry is done, folded, and packed. Ratchet has just made it back from her run. It's surprising how funny a sweaty nude person looks.

"How many miles?"

"Three, five I don't know. I feel great."

"The laundry is done. I left it on your bed."

"Thank you. Right now I'm heading for the showers."

All of us were in bad need of getting cleaned up and started filing into the showers. We were on our way home.

It was coming on to 6:00 P.M. time to make the call I keyed the MIC

"Atlanta Good Night" A few seconds passed.

"Hotel 1,2." I switched channels.

Ratchet: "That's not Alice it's not the same voice."

"Atlanta."

"Hi! Who am I talking to?" We looked at one another.

Marker: "She sounds like some ding-a-ling."

"Atlanta this is Gentle, did you understand the message?"

"Oh sure." Another pause.

"I'm sorry I guess I should hold the button down when I talk." Again a pause.

"Atlanta who is this?"

"Gabby."

"Oh Gabby, our departure time, please."

"I'm on the phone."

Cable: "I hope she is not talking to her boyfriend." It was becoming an almost laughable conversation.

"Hello, Gabby, I don't mean to be pushy BUT."

"Give me a second please."

Pink: "Maybe she is tracking down the Major."

Ratchet: "That could be."

Marker: "Well folks, a Gabby second is now equal to three minutes."

"Hello, hello, Gentle are you still there?"

"Yes Gabby. What do you have there?"

Pizza."

"Pizza! Gabby the time, the time we get picked up."

"Oh, OK That will be 9:35 P.M. your time. Be packed, have a jacket."

"Thank you Gabby."

"Why have a jacket?"

Pink: "Can I talk to her?" I handed him the mic.

"Gabby, this is Pink we need jackets because helicopters don't have real good heaters in them."

"Really, I'll be. Well, you learn something new every day. Pink yep, you're on my list."

"Who else is on your list?"

"Well, there's Gentle, Pink, Ratchet, Cable, then they blacked out a name and Marker. Did someone get fired?"

"No that was Spin. He died."

"I'm sorry."

Pink got Gabby to call Cable and his homes to let them know we would be back late tonight. Ratchet got on the radio for an hour plus chat.

Looking out down the valley, the shadows had stopped. The sun had set. We will be home soon. I asked Marker to tell everyone the story behind Spin's death. He agreed to tell them. It was interesting watching their faces in the dim light. It was like looking at a personality not just a person. We sat in silence, in memory of our friend. The night sky was absolutely clear and the temp was dropping. It was feeling like upper forties.

We loaded our bags into the pickup truck then checked the camp one last time. Ratchet had a towel for Mange, who knew we were going away. She was carrying her water bowl. Shortly after 9:00, we drove out front to wait. I noticed Marker wasn't watching the horizon. He was watching the dog. The only sound was the generator running back at the camp over a half mile away. Mange was lying next to Ratchet when her head came up. Her ears turned forward as she looked straight down the valley. There was something heading this way. Cable turned on his flashlight. Marker was in the truck. They drove out to set the flashlight as a locator. Well, whoever was flying seemed to understand, flew right over the flashlight, turned around and landed.

The cabin lights came on. There was Major Davis. Once the blades had nearly stopped, he got out and started our way.

"Good evening! Someone call for a cab?"

Pink: "Why yes! Oh Major, did you set the parking brake?"

"No, but I can assure you I got high marks in helicopter 101--my home correspondence course you know! Alright folks, if everyone is ready to go, I've got only one rule for you tonight. The curtains are to be closed the first fifteen minutes of the flight. Let's load up."

The Major picked up a bag in each hand. Ratchet carried Mange, who was wrapped in a towel. The bags were strapped to the rear bulkhead then we climbed in. The seats were large plush things, super comfortable. Mange curled up in a seat with a towel and was asleep before the engine started. We were buckled in as the Major pulled the blinds then our door was latched. There was a brief wait as he checked his controls and made ready to take off. He looked back at us, just before closing the door to the cockpit.

"A short flight folks. Only about ninety minutes."

Looking back at the faces of my workmates, my friends had the look of relief blended with exhaustion. The cabin lights dimmed as the engine powered up. The flight was smooth and didn't seem all that long. It appears I was the only one awake when the cockpit door opened. I asked the Major if I could join him up front. He said sure then gave me directions on how to get in the co-pilots seat. The view even at night is amazing.

"So, tell me Gentle, what was it really like out there, you being in charge? That's some pretty impressive work your people have done."

"Thank you. Major, I'd guess by now you've read all of our files and memorized a good portion of them."

"Yes."

"Look, I've never been in a leadership job before. Some of it was okay, but some of it I could live without you know. I might feel better or do more if I had some kind of training."

"I can help you with the leadership skills. There's a refresher course for upper rank officers coming up. I'll get you a seat if you like."

"Okay, just as long as I can have a few days to rest up."

"No problem."

"Major, there's something I got to say now. I'm not trying to be difficult or disrespectful, but my people and I are called Krew. That's with a K. That stands for kiloton rated electric welders. That's what we are, all of us, and proud of it. It would be nice to hear it once in awhile."

"No problem, you handle that very well you are going to fit in the leadership class like it was made for you."

The conversation began getting lighter in content. At this point in the day, I had lost track of when I had a full night's sleep. I just couldn't remember. He turned into a valley, in a minute we were in an airport, but where? We were all up and moving. It was kind of cold here--well below freezing. As we started unloading our bags, a bus parked next to us. The Major handed the driver a note.

"Yes sir, Major Davis, I'll have it taken care of. Thank you."

Once on the bus, our next stop was the terminal where the driver made an announcement.

"Lady and gentlemen, I apologize for this inconvenience. There has been a mix up on your departure time. Your aircraft is being serviced as I speak. I expect this delay to be short, not more than one hour. Again, I apologize. The V.I.P. lounge is open, food and drink no charge. Thank you."

Pink: "Excuse me sir, our bags stay here or come in with us?"

"Please leave the bags. I'll have them loaded for you."

Marker: "Thank you."

This was much nicer than a road in the desert. At least we'll be warm. All of us took a few minutes to stretch our legs and gave Mange a chance to pee. Inside, we found some chairs by the window. We settled in for the wait. There was red wine for us and water for Mange. We were not alone in the lounge. Everyone else looked to be businessmen. Two of them were heading our way. We had a brief conversation, as our jet was towed to the gate.

Not long after boarding the executive jet, our flight began. Sleeping was the order of business Now not knowing the time, as I was totally disoriented. We awoke parked in a hanger. Looking out the door, there was a limo parked. All of us were exhausted as we piled into it.

"Good morning everyone. I have a list of addresses here to deliver you to. Miss Bergman may I start with yours?"

"Yes, please straight there so everyone can get home sooner."

"Of course, ma'am."

The driver was a no joke kind of guy. We were passing cars in town like he was flying. Nancy was quickly home at her apartment. I said good night as the driver carried her bag to the door.

From there Rodger was next; Lisa, April, and May were out front the second the limo stopped.

"Rodger, try to get some sleep, man."

He just smiled.

Next was Abe. He wasn't doing too good. His longtime friend was no longer with him.

Abe: "I wonder if they already had Joe's funeral?"

"I'll check for you, Abe, and call you tomorrow. I'll let you know what I can find out. OK with you!"

"OK." Abe unlocked the front door and stepped in.

Jake and I were the last stop. Bags in hand, we made it through the front door and there sat everyone, TVs on and them asleep.

"Dad? Dad!"

"Jake, son! Mother, wake up. Kids, look who's home."

The party started. I could only hang on a little longer before I'd drop. I excused myself from the party and returned to my room. The only thing left in me was the need to sleep and sleep some more.

TIME BETWEEN

As told by Individuals

Nancy Bergman: I've been home four days. Thanksgiving kind of slipped passed me. I called my parents to wish them happy holidays. Otherwise, about all I've been able to do is eat a little bit and sleep. I'm almost feeling human again. Mange is staying with me. I've never had a pet. It's not as bad as I figured. We coexist quite nicely. I feel pretty good today, so we are going for a walk. I've only had one call from Zack since we've been back.

Abe Crow: It's just too quiet here at home. I'm not handling Joe's death well at all. I've known for years it was killing him, but for whatever reason I can't seem to accept it. I'm calling Nancy, Maybe she knows a head doctor. Zack has been trying to find out about a funeral or something, but nothing yet.

Rodger Cook: Being home now at Thanksgiving, it's the holiday that I'll remember the rest of my life. I was the center of attention somewhat, but I tried not to be too puffed up. We had a true family day of TV and food. Zack and Jake with his kids stopped in for a few minutes before going to Jake's folk's house. Of all the things on the face of this earth to be thankful for, a flat tire is high on my list.

Jake Pauly: We were so glad to be back the few hours of sleep we got was not near enough, so naps were needed. Jake Jr. is doing super in school and Janet is turning into a young lady. Mom and Dad have out done themselves. I thought they did a pretty good job with me, but now my kids are doing better than ever. Zack called home earlier and talked to his folks for a good while. He's had no luck reaching Robert. I'm tired, but Zack looks drawn. I'm worried a little about him. I was surprised how well my kids handled the holiday with no mom. As for myself, I've had a few rocky moments, but Mom did a good job of keeping me in line.

Abe: I've talked to Nancy, I told her I needed a shrink or something. She lined me up with some grief specialist at the hospital. She claims the guy is one of the best. Maybe he can help me. Zack stopped by with news. Joe is going home. He said he'd get back to me with the details. Just a funeral for him. He deserves that much.

Zack: I've gotten caught up on some sleep, but I could sure use more. Saturday, I finally reached Robert. I said we needed to do something and soon. As far as a burial to end the questions of what became of Joe? I was informed that an autopsy had been done. He had nerve damage of the lungs. The cause was unknown. It was one of those things that wouldn't have showed up on any standard exam. Art added that Joe's body was being prepared for the funeral service by a very prestigious firm in L. A. and would be ready on the 29th. I asked the time and place. It been arranged to be in Lysite on the 30th for services and burial to follow.

I first went to Abe's place and told him that Joe was getting his funeral. I gave him all the details. Even though he was still sad, he did appear relieved. I then stopped at everyone's home with the news about Joe. My next stop was at the Base to see if the Major might be able to provide us a plane and pilot hoping he would take the job.

"Can do," he said.

I asked if a chair was still free in his class? He assured me that there would be. He then remembered that Joe, being a veteran, was entitled to a military escort for services. I agreed it just seemed right.

Abe: Now I can at least say goodbye. Maybe go home a few days. See some family.

Rodger: Joe was a friend. It's only right that I go. My wife and girls are pretty understanding about it. It really makes me wonder why he worked to the very end.

Robert McCabe: The papers regarding Joe's death are in order. I have set up a trust fund so the insurance can be deposited then allotted yearly over the next twenty years. Art has arranged all the transportation and lodging for this trip. I only knew Joe only from the few times I met him face to face and then through the records, will, etc. I knew him and I will miss him.

Major Davis: All arrangements, are made. He will have a full honor guard, along with the flight and housing. These are tough people. This shouldn't have happened.

∞

Friday November 29, 1984, 3:00 P.M. Zack

All of us are at the hanger at the McCarren airport. Overnight and suit bags were in our hands as the jet was brought out. The Major was at the controls. In minutes we were on board and soon to be in the air. The Major said about two hours to Riverton. The flight was quick.

Arthur Fellows: We made the trip in good time. Robert spoke highly of the Major as well as Joe's home, as he questioned its location. Our arrival in Riverton was a pointed reminder to me. Cold is the reason I choose L.A. to be my home. Both of us shared the feeling of loss.

Robert McCabe: I found the funeral director at home by phone that evening. He explained in detail the service that had been planned. I understood everything I was told. I questioned him with my problem of locating the guardians or the orphanage. He said he would have some answers for me in the morning.

Saturday November 30, 1984, 9:00 A.M. Joe Little's Funeral

Zack: Joe being an orphan has made things not so easy on Robert. He said it's taken care of now. The funeral home provided the limos, to pick us up at the motel for the drive to Lysite.

Robert: I spoke with the funeral director a while ago. He gave me the phone number of the people who raised Joe. I called. It turns out this couple have been raising throw away babies all their life. They'd had more than thirty children. Joe was their first. He was left on the doorstep. These people took him in and according to the lady I spoke with, said it still happens now and then at times. The reason that finding these people has been so difficult was that the house was unsafe for them to live in. After they moved it had been torn down. As it was in a rural area, the address had been dropped.

Jake: I'd guess the insurance will come to some good use for his folks.

Abe: No doubt it will. I was there once. They didn't have much then. Not much food or clothes. The house was in bad shape back then. The toys were hand me downs. I remember a letter from Joe, his first letter from basic training. He said that was the first time he'd had new clothes from head to toe. He even got in trouble for dressing to go to Sunday dinner in his dress class A uniform. Some officers jumped his case outside, asking the reason for him wearing his dress uniform to a meal. Joe answered them simply that he'd never owned a suit before.

The rest of the trip was quiet for the most part. We arrived at a small chapel at the edge of town. A lady walked to the limo. A sad looking person in her face and her appearance a person who had done without for a lifetime.

"Hello, I'm Maud White. My husband Bill is in the chapel. I want to thank you for bringing our boy home to rest."

Rodger took care of the introductions once inside. Maud returned with introductions of their fourteen children. We visited the coffin in single file. We then took a seat. The pastor gave a very nice service. At the end of it the honor guard formed a line in front of the coffin as it was sealed shut. The flag was then placed covering the entire top side. The three Sailors, with the three Marines, carried the coffin out the door at the back of the chapel. The grave itself was a half-buried vault. The movement of the honor guard had to have been rehearsed. It was precision to see. After setting the coffin on the two planks there was the folding of the flag and the playing of taps. The planks were removed, Joe was lower by rope to his place of rest.

The cover of the vault set in place. It read "Joseph Little April 4, 1951, to November 2, 1984" At the top of the cover was the Marine emblem. Just below the dates was the Krew logo and at the very foot of it in small letters "In God's light there are no shadows." It looked good. Everyone had returned to the chapel except Abe. Hot cocoa and coffee was served as the reading of the will would be done shortly.

Arthur: "Mr. and Mrs. White, I have here the Last Will and Testament of Joe, the child you raised. It states of my personal effects tools and all welding gear is given to Abe Crow. All other effects are to be shipped to the home of Bill and Maud White, to do with as they wish. As for the matter of money my bank account and that from insurance, it is to be paid to the Whites. As the insurance is paid to a trust fund you will receive a check yearly around April 4th for the sum of $100,000. for the next twenty years. This money is for the care and schooling of the children and as retirement fund for the Whites."

A check was given to them for the amount $48,240 as it was his bank account.

There was a question and answers meeting between the Whites and Robert I thank goodness Robert was here. He handled all of it, as well as providing them with a booklet of guidelines, planners, and budgets. It was quite obvious these people had never had much and what they had went to the children.

Bill White: Mother, we are going to have a real Christmas this year.

Zack: By 1:00P.M. the goodbyes were said with a few tears and we began our trip home. The rest of the day went by very quickly. In no time at all, it seems we were home. Abe stayed behind to visit family and friends. Bob and Art took off straight to L.A. Now at home I'm planning on calling my folks and work on getting some more sleep time in. It's like I'm not getting enough.

∞

December 3, 1984, Jake

Zack and I have been called to a meeting in L.A. at Art's place on the 7th. Just the two of us. It must be big is all I can think. Zack has started to become a little more himself here the last few days. It seems just getting sleep was all he really needed. As for myself, I've made an effort to stick to a simple routine and it's working for me so far. Janet and Rodger's girls have become good friends. My boy is doing great in school and is convinced on being a vet. Well, time will tell.

Zack: I got a call from the Major. The officer's leadership class is going to be on the 12th and if Jake can make it, a chair is reserved for him. I'm presently trying to figure the reason for this meeting Robert has scheduled. As far as the Krew, we're ahead on the timetable. The last I heard tools and supplies were ahead also. Well come the seventh, we'll know. Here at home Jake is planning to restore his old Ford truck. I needed something else to think about.

∞

December 7, 1984, Robert

Everyone has arrived at Art's home. The agenda is morning coffee in the den for everyone to assemble their thoughts and review documents and relax some from their trip here. The meeting will start at 8:30 in Art's meeting room.

8:30 The meeting begins

Robert: Gentlemen, we are here today because of revisions in the plans.

Marshal Bishop: After many attempts in using a nuclear device to aid in burying the vessel, I've been told no. Under a part of the testing plan we are one, three miles now from the next closest point of testing.

Art: Bishop, are you saying from the time we started the government decided to move the damn borders and not tell us.

Marshal: That is correct. Please let me continue. Two, there will be one test made and it is scheduled for Mid-January, at which time surveys are to begin over the new range time allotted for this next year.

James Howard: Marshal, you got any good news, because I don't need any more of this. The very thought of scrapping this now is unthinkable.

Marshal: Yes, Collin would you?

Collin Webster: Before we panic, I have solved most of the problems we face. If you will please note the map John is putting up. At present, because of the landscape along with the need for security, moving the vessel to a new location is not cost effective in anyway. After examining some dated research documents by the government and current geological with a mineralogical testing, I believe we have an answer. Next John, the aerial photos thank you. Here we see the camp site. Now here at this point, in this mountain, there is a vein of very high-grade manganese. Mr. Bishop.

Marshal: Because the vane is on controlled land, I have obtained rights for mining along with the closure of the four valleys surrounding both sites, the how it will be done, Mr. Nelson.

Robert Nelson: Using the elevation map, thank you, John. We see from the site to this point here the lowest point in the valley. In this near eight miles there is a drop of only five hundred feet, but please note in the first half mile there is a fifty-foot drop. The rest of the distance is a long gradual down grade. The line from the site to the mouth of the mine at the valley floor is a straight line. Now Zack, Jake, this is an item you will both find a plus. From the site to the supply yard is a solid shelf of bed rock large enough for a small switch yard, as there will be rail service to the site as well as the road.

Jake: Sir, please understand what you see on the model here appears askew in scale. I remind you, it's big.

Robert Nelson: Mr. Pauly, I do understand. Now, I will explain how the vessel will be moved. John, if you please.

John wheeled in a second table with more model pieces on it. The model's big top was removed on the second model.

Collin Webster: I realize you are questioning how the base will be moved. First a hydraulic system will be positioned. Mr. Clark.

Peter Clark: With the base now in this location my company will come in and lift the base as tooling is already on site, Mr. Stone.

Richard Stone: The base now lifted. My people will then construct a rail and dolly system with saddles for the base. In this same time period, the tower crane's base or footing is to be installed. The estimated time to complete the dolly system, the crane base, and the rail system to supply the site is thirty-five days.

Art and John position the pieces on the second model.

Arthur: Zack, Jake, what you see here is what you will be going back to. What do you think?

The two of us moved in closer to the model studying it.

Zack: Jake, do you see it?

Jake: Sure do.

Arthur: Do we have a problem, gentlemen?

Zack: Is the tower crane set up for the second and third phase?

Arthur: Yes, it is.

Zack: Art, do you have something in mind for the welding platforms?

Arthur: Yes, it is part of the tower crane system. John have you had a chance to do work on the welding towers yet?

John: Sir, I do have a few pieces started. May I ask if I might have some time with Mr. Mulholland and Mr. Pauly. It may benefit the group.

Arthur: John, it is your model and I believe Zack and Jake would be honored in assisting you. Roughly how much time will you need?

John: I believe an hour would be a fair estimate, Sir.

Arthur: John, you're in charge. Zack, Jake, please give as much information as you can in assisting. Gentlemen, we are breaking for now so additions can be put in place. Let's move to the den.

Zack: OK John, where would you like to start?

John: First, it would be best if we move this back to my apartment.

We wheeled the newest model down the hall to John's quarters which in itself was spacious.

John: Zack, Jake, I have a question. You live and work here. Can you show and tell me of life there?

Jake and I reach for pencils to use as pointers the tent top was removed from the camp, and we began.

Zack: John, stand here. Oh, how much do you know about the camp itself?

John: Very little I would say.

Zack: John, this is the grand tour in scale. The tour: this is the small items storage. This the refrigeration unit, the kitchen and the freezer unit are all connected together. Here is the first aid unit, the radio room and laundry. Then we have the bath. Our living space or common area, our sleeping quarters, here and here. In this spot is our whirlpool to cool off in. Now, my chair is here. I sleep here, and this is where I sit to eat. Abe eats here, sleeps here, and his chair. Nancy eats here, sleeps here, chair here. She jogs at about noon on the road, here most generally, in the nude. As all of us do from time to time.

Jake: Sleep here, eat here, chair here, and I jog at sunrise. Rodger sleeps here, eats here and chair here, he walks day or night. Mange our dog, eats here and sleeps wherever a towel is dropped on the deck. Next, right here, is the spot Joe Little's career in welding ended.

Zack: The days can get up to one-hundred-twenty degrees and nights it can drop to the thirties. Not many bugs. A rattlesnake lives across the road. Not much else. Just dust.

The three of us went to work on the model. John knew what he was doing. Jake and I were busy studying the plans for the things we would need to have in the end.

"John, would you tell Art, that we might run a little longer. We have a revision that must be seen to."

John was back in the room in under a minute. He was back with Art.

Arthur: What's the hold up? Have you found something in the plan?

Jake: Yes, Art, a few small changes may make a world of difference in how much is spent and how time can be made. We need twenty or so minutes more to have the model ready.

Arthur: Give me give us your best. We need to know.

Another full fifteen minutes of work and the model is ready. John went to the den to say the meeting could restart as we rolled the model into the meeting room.

Robert Nelson: Yes, brilliant.

Peter Clark: Seeing this, we can have this built in thirty days or less is my estimate.

James Howard: I see some cost cutting ideas, yes.

Collin Webster: The shelf is wide enough to handle a roadway and a rail system. This is very doable.

Richard Stone: An extra rail inside, of course. The space maybe close, but it will be safe.

Marshal Bishop: Zack, Jake, I have something I must tell you now. Because of all these changes there is one more you must know. We, that is Atlanta, will be handling the hiring from here on.

Zack: So, I'm a foreman now. Is that it?

Marshal: Yes and no. Please hear me out. We have examined, cross checked, and profiled all of you in Krew then used that as well as trying our best to use common sense. Atlanta is working as we speak finding you more help.

Jake: Marshal, you, and I both know looking at just the money side of it, that there will be a flood of dead beats. So, what happens when we have one that's a slug or can't do the job?

Marshal: I give them a new home.

Zack: WHAT!?

Marshal: A lovely place, one problem only one key and it's mine. If anyone screws up on you at the site. You now have the power to give them a P.O. Box in Kansas. One call and they are gone.

Jake: Art, not to be a wet blanket, but are there any loose ends you know. a wild card? Is everything here?

Art: No, the tower crane is docked in Denmark. There are storms out at sea. I'm told when it breaks, they will be at the canal in three days.

Zack: John, may I have a moment of your time?

John: Yes, Sir, how can I help?

Zack: John, when I was looking over the plans, the engineering firm was only initialed. I ask because it looks very well drawn up.

John: I am sorry, the gentleman I do not know. He was on in years, grey hair he still looked quite healthy. He did have a liking for sherry. Mr. Fellows had the one he was interested in, I served it and he loved it. Sir, I believe you use the term rotgut it was the worst I have smelled.

Zack: John, thank you. It's something to go on.

There was a picnic indoors for lunch then by mid-afternoon the group started for home. Marshal had left just after lunch.

Zack: Art, do you wager--that is gamble?

Art: Nearly every day. Why do you ask?

Zack: Marshal is a bad bet. Here's a penny saying I'm right.

Art: If this is real you make a strong statement and bet.

With that Jake and I went to an airport and were home by 5:30.

December 9, 1984, Zack

Before leaving Art's the other day, I managed to talk Marshal into at least reviewing the applications and getting Atlanta's phone number. After what seem to be an endless phone call, Gabby said she is having the applications hand delivered to Jake's house. I think I should look them over. I still want to pick my own people or some of them, I know Jake still wants to.

∞

December 10, 1984, Nancy

I'm looking for Christmas gifts. The list is going pretty easy. My folks and Zack are the only ones left. I've made up my mind what to get for my parents, tickets for a cruise ship. Luckily the first agent I talk to made a lot of sense, so it was easy to pick one out. Zack on the other hand is a problem. He's got enough money to buy anything. Wait, Jake might have some ideas. Five minutes on the phone paid off. Bandanas and coin cachets. Well, it's time to put the Christmas cards in the mail and head to the shopping plazas.

∞

December 10, 1984, Zack

Marshal just called to say he would agree to any decisions I make on the applications and to return them to Atlanta as soon as possible.

He must have his hands full is all I can figure. Jake and I began the task of reading applications.

Jake: Look is there any reason we should have all the fun.

Only two hours of this and I understood him.

Zack: No, give me the phone.

I got Rodger then Nancy on the phone, asking if they could break away and lend a hand with the apps. Both said they could be here soon.

I tried Abe's place and got no answer. He must still be visiting up north.

The two of us quickly went through applications and sorted them by jobs. Rodger walked in and took a seat.

Rodger: OK, where do I start?

Zack: Look through these carefully. If you like what you see put it on the table. If you find something that's odd or wrong show me, please. Without a word, Rodger dug into the stack in front of him.

Now we were gaining ground. Roughly an hour later Nancy showed up.

Nancy: Hi. What's all of this homework?

Jake: That's it. You got it on the first guess.

Nancy: Which pile is mine?

Zack: This pile here is yours. Like I told Rodger. If it looks good put it on the table. If something looks odd, show me.

We got to work going through them one by one. Rodger was pointing at some of the apps he'd been working on.

Zack: Everyone, Rodger's got some that's questionable. OK man, tell me and show me on paper. I trust your judgment If the person doesn't look or feel right into the box. Otherwise I'd like to think on it. Alright, one at a time.

Rodger: Age too old.

Zack: Sixty-two, box.

Rodger: Age too old and no contacts in employer.

Jake: Fifty-seven need a list, box.

Rodger: I can't tell what this one is doing. He filled it in but it's not right, look here and then here.

Zack: OK, I see, liar, box.

Rodger: Three of these dead beats, dead beats, dead beats.

Jake: Why?

Rodger: Right here. This company I know them. If you work, they keep you.

Jake: Box, box, box.

Rodger: This one is odd, That is, I can't put my finger on it.

Zack: Alright, which part of it?

Rodger: All of it, it's too perfect, I'm just not sure.

Jake: Let me see that.

Zack: OK, Nancy, would you and Jake look this one over please.

Nancy: Sure, my turn, I've done all the doctors that are here.

Zack: Let's have it.

Nancy: Bad schools, good grades.

Jake: Box.

Nancy: Good schools, Bad grades.

Zack: Box.

Nancy: This one moves too much.

Jake: Explain please.

Nancy: OK, this one does long distance moves from state to state. Average time in one place is fourteen months. My first guess is malpractice or fraud.

Zack: Box.

Nancy: Age.

Jake: Too old.

Nancy: Too young, not enough work experience.

Jake: Box.

Nancy: This one I want.

Zack: Reason for that one.

Nancy: The schools are OK, grades OK, worked in E.R. and has other good backgrounds. Same area for four years. Can take leave of absence. Works in a clinic.

Zack: No other doctor apps.

Nancy: No, I only saw five.

Jake: Sounds like we've got a doctor to interview.

Zack: Jake your turn at bat, Go.

Jake: Dead beat and dead beat.

Zack: Why?

Jake: Check the time employed.

Zack: Troublemaker's box and box.

Jake: No skills.

Zack: I got to see this.

Jake: Here you go.

Zack: Next I'll look at this in a minute.

Jake: These six I do not want at all.

Zack: Reason.

Jake: Union.

Zack: Say no more. All into the box. We don't have the time to deal with union foot dragging.

Jake: I need to check this stack one more time to be sure.

Zack: So, what is it you've got there?

Jake: If I didn't screw up this here is three troublemakers, nine union, and two idiots.

Zack: When you find them, box them.

Our studies continued from notebook to notebook then from person to person.

Rodger: Hey, hey I just set one down. Where is it?

Zack: What have you got?

Rodger: Matching entries I know it is.

Jake: Hell, I got two already.

Rodger: Matching this?

Jake: Yes, yes. Times are the same, employer, reason for leaving and more.

Rodger: Here it is. Look at the ship to and the received dates.

Nancy: Zack, look at Jake's. No skills, this is a schooled cook, high grades and is working as a cook now. I found this just a minute ago. Navy communications, hobbies; cooks and bakes, now working in a food service job.

I checked the time it was still early enough I might catch Marshal at his office. I excused myself from our meeting then went to my room to talk to Marshal in private. Surprisingly, I got him in only a few rings.

"Hello?"

"Marshal, Zack here."

"What's going on?"

"Look we studied the applications and I want to do the interviews."

"You're sure?"

"I'm sure. I do have use of the company plane, right?"

"Of course, you do."

"I'll start the interviews on the 14th."

"That will be fine. Who do you have?"

"We found a doctor, a cook, a communication person, and five welders."

"Very good Zack I'll see to having a pilot there for you and Robert."

"I'd like to see these people before calling Robert. I'm the one they'll be living with."

"You're right. Call me after the interviews, I'll talk to you then."

"Goodbye."

This is excellent. It's my chance to meet everyone. I asked Nancy to call the ladies on the list to inform them we would be in there between the 14th to the 19th. Jake called Rodger's Mr. Perfect, while I had questions for the four matched welders.

Jake: Hey Zack, you've been staring at those for a good thirty minutes what are you thinking man.

Zack: I've got to call one. I'm trying to pick one.

Rodger: I can help, high card gets the call.

Jake went to get the cards then did a few fast shuffles.

Rodger: A four, a nine, a deuce and a jack. There you go. The lucky winner is?

Zack: Mr. Martin Crus. As soon as I'm done eating.

After supper I stepped outside to collect my thoughts. My friends stood at the door.

Rodger: What's on your mind, Zack? You know, if we can help, just say so.

Zack: I know, I have an idea of how to get some answers.

Dialing Mr. Crus' home phone number, my line of questions was clear, now it rang.

"Hello?"

"Hello, Martin Crus please."

"Junior or Senior?"

I gave the date of birth.

"That would be junior. One moment."

"Hello?"

"Hello, Mr. Crus. My name is Zack and I'm calling in regards to the application you sent to Atlanta."

"Yes, I sent one."

"Mr. Crus which of the four of you found our company?"

"Well, that would have been Terry, Terry Singer."

"Alright Mr. Crus, your application looks so good. We will have to speak to Mr. Singer first. Is he at home presently, would you know?"

"Well, I think so."

"Thank you. We will be calling you back before the 14th. Goodbye."

"Goodbye."

I dialed Singer's number.

"Hello."

"Hello, Mr. Singer, please."

"That's me."

"Mr. Singer, my name is Zack."

"Hi Zack, what can I do for you today?"

"Mr. Singer, I'm calling in regards to a rather large application you sent to Atlanta."

"Oh that, yes sir. I'm sorry. I thought you were a salesman."

"No, No, I'm the guy who is missing some paperwork on you."

"I filled in that whole book."

"Mr. Singer, it looks good really, but I can't seem to find your letter."

"My letter! Honest, I read that whole thing sir. I didn't see anything about a letter."

"Well, my secretary has made more work for me again. Alright, I have a simple answer to this mess. I would like you to write a letter saying where or how you found our company."

"Yes, I can do that."

"Oh, the sooner it gets to me, the sooner we can get to interviews, money, benefits, etc."

"I'll start now."

"If it's alright with you, I'll have it picked up at your home. Please call this number when it's ready to go."

I gave him the number.

"Sure thing."

"Goodbye."

Well, I did get picked on for playing mister big shot, but I needed to know.

Nancy: Why do you want to know how they found us?

Zack: To tell you the truth, they are already a team. I just can't see one person doing all the leg work for all of them. If I'm right on this one, I'll feel pretty damn good.

As we were packing away the applications to be sent back to Atlanta, I had a feeling something didn't fit. I called Art just to check. I had his number in my room. I told Jake I had to make a call to get some information. Then I called Art.

"Fellows' residence."

"Hello, John is Art in?"

"Zack, one moment please."

"Hello, Zack, I understand you're working on the applications."

"That is correct and I'm just double checking on use of the company plane. As I have, that is, we have interviews. I want to get moving on them."

"Now that sounds promising. You said double check. How is that?"

"I asked Marshal and he OK'd use of a company plane."

"I see. Well, Marshal, is in charge of transportation, but from now on call me for use of the company aircraft. So, you're going to take care of interviews I'll tell Bob."

"Art, I would like to do my interviews first. Please remember we are going to be living together."

"I see what you mean. How many will be traveling?"

"Well, it would be eight or nine. We haven't heard from Abe yet. I'm hoping it might be alright to goof off a little--sightseeing, tours, maybe a theme park for the kids."

"That's a wonderful idea. The families would love that, and it's only right. I'm sending a bigger plane to Vegas for you and a company charge card. When will you need the plane?"

"Early morning on the 14th please."

"Before I forget, I would like to see you here sometime after your interviews."

"It's on my things to-do list."

"I'll see you then. Bye for now."

∞

December 11, 1984, Jake

Who the hell is calling at 6:30 in the morning?

"Hello?"

"Hello, Mr. Zack please."

"And who should I say is calling."

"Terry Singer, sir."

"Mr. Singer, hold the line while I get him for you."

"Sure thing."

Zack is never awake before 8:00 if he can help it. Well the guy called.

"Zack, Zack, get up."

"What is it?"

"Singer is on the phone for you."

"Now geez, is this guy human?"

He dragged himself to the phone taking a breath.

"Good morning, Mr. Singer. How are you today?"

"Fine, sir."

"Good. Is your letter all set?"

"Yes, sir."

"Please, not so formal it's Zack. Someone should be there soon to pick it up. I have some things I must get to, but we will be seeing all of you very soon, so thank you. Goodbye."

"Goodbye."

"Hey old man, my kids are ready to play jet setters."

"It's going to be fun. I'm going back to bed."

At five pm the letter arrived.

∞

Zack,

In mid-1984, I was working as a welder in the industry. The first and nearly undetectable clue of our study began. Part of my job at the time was inventory including, price and availability of shop supplies including the steel stock. Some friends and I were going through the trade publications when it was first noticed. The numbers didn't match up. Some weeks after that, it was brought up in conversation with one of our many salesmen. He said it was correct. I decided I would ask about the big discrepancy in the numbers. His reply was, I don't know but, I'll see if I can dig up a name. The general idea of everyone was to get a company name, check into the stock market, and make a little money. A month passed and our salesman showed up saying he got the company name--Greater Southwest Steel Surplus Holdings, based in Atlanta, GA. Correspondence went to a woman named Alice Krew. Well, we had the name, address, and phone number. We started checking for stock prices and came to a dead end, an unlisted business. So, we tried calling the Atlanta number. All we got was the answering machine. We tried calling at least twenty times. The shop was sold and we lost our jobs. On our last day of work, we tried the number one more time. A lady answered, we said we were looking for work she got our addresses and all. That was November the 3rd. If you have any questions, please call.

Thank You.

Terry Singer

∞

"Jake, you busy?"

"Nope, be right there"

"You're going to like this"

"What you got there? Oh the letter."

"Read it. I want to see the hair on your neck stand."

"That good?"

"Better read"

The time is coming for me to ask Mr. Marshal Bishop a question or two. Jake eased through the letter and handed it back. He had a look of true concern.

"Well, needless to say, old friend, we got to rat hole this letter."

"Right!"

Putting the letter in my billfold I knew I had to lose it or burn it. It's future business so it went to my safe deposit box.

SCHOOL TIME /
FIRST FACE TO FACE

As told by individuals

December 12, 1984, 8:00 A.M. Jake

The Major met us at the gate. We followed him to a small brick building. No name or number on the building. Odd. Normally there's at least a number. Inside it was open, one room, two restrooms, chairs with a large table and not much else.

"Zack, do you remember seeing a place like this when you were here?"

"Not in person, but I remember seeing it in a book I think this was an armory at one time."

"That's right, you must be Mr. Mulholland and Mr. Pauly," came a voice from behind us.

There were a dozen officers behind us. A one-star general spoke, "Gentlemen take a seat, and we'll get started today we have special guests with us by invitation. Major Davis would you do the introductions please."

"Yes sir, gentlemen this is Zack Mulholland. He's a college man served in the army ammunitions depot, an inventor, now the leader of a group of highly specialized craftsmen in their trade. This is Jake Pauly single father, years of trade education, also army ammunition depot, second in command. From this, I can say I have seen the work they do as well as their staff. I cannot give details, but I can say in harsh working conditions, extremely physical work, they excel."

I noticed no one had name tags only rank.

"Excuse me, General, No name tags?"

"That is correct. You work without names. We are working inside your rules."

Major Davis: "Fellows, you are the center of attention here. It was necessary I give the rules to secure your invitation."

Zack: "Major, so we are the subject of this class. I thought this was do's and don'ts, a speaker, maybe a movie."

General: "Gentlemen we are here today to learn from one another. If you'd like a minute to gather your thoughts, step outside a minute. It's OK."

Both of us were out the door.

"Zack, what do you think man?"

"I got a lot on my mind."

"So dump on them."

"Yeah."

"Talk about your power thing and keeping things going, death. We should get some kind of feedback from it all."

"Dump."

Returning, we were seated.

"I think we understand how this works now. Zack, hit it."

He slowly stood and began walking around the table.

"First, I'm sorry. I just seem to think better on my feet I guess, because I don't have a desk. I'm the boss. I'm in charge. I've got power--a lot of power. Major, nothing leaves this room. Correct?"

"Correct"

"All of you are now my employees. Your pay is great. Your benefits are great. You will be out of debt in three months. How can this be? Simple, just do your job. One of you is having a problem, won't work, won't help out, is disrespectful to others and is believed to be screwing up equipment. I want to be fair; I want to be a friend; I have to be the boss."

An older colonel: "Alright you caught me. You're a slave driving idiot and the staff you got are stupid, no skills, clowns."

"Man, you signed on. You knew the rules before day one so, what's the problem?"

"I don't like the job I don't like any of you."

"OK you're out of here, but let me remind you, you signed legal government papers and forms. I hope you remember what they said."

"I don't care."

"Your ride will be here in ten minutes."

General: "Zack, may I?"

"Sure"

"This is a humane and controlled problem. Now, how controlled is the problem?"

"I have sent him away to regain order and on his request. Now because he's signed papers of non-disclosure, if he is caught talking about the job, he loses everything."

A colonel: "He would be arrested, tried, and jailed."

"No just jailed. It's all in writing in the beginning."

General: "How much power do you have?"

"I can have any one of my people vanish, never to be seen again."

Major Davis: "Excuse me Zack, can I have the floor"

"Go ahead"

"Gentlemen, what he is telling us is true. On his job site Zack is the law. Because of a time frame, he cannot be bogged down with labor problems."

Another major: "Zack, you show very good leadership skills. Now I believe your question to us is when to turn it on and how much."

"Sir, you hit the nail on the head. I'm not dumb, but I don't know if I'm smart enough. I guess I need a check list or a warning light."

General: "Look, if leadership were something from a book, I could make anyone my equal, his equal, your equal. Being the one on top isn't easy and usually a great deal of work."

A colonel: "Something to think about, fellows. You two have to know when the other is needing a break so he can give thought to a problem. A person needs time to reflect before he makes any big decisions. I feel that is very important."

We had an hour or so of questions and answers. I tapped Zack's shoulder.

"I have a question. A show of hands will be needed. How many of you have physically carried one of your own who is dead?"

Only two of the officers had not done that job. Somehow it was like now we were talking like equals to one another.

A colonel: "On your job, what have you found to be most effective when dealing with your people?"

I was staring at Zack as a big stupid grin was taking over his face. He was trying not to laugh.

"Sir, have you ever heard the line if it's not broke don't fix it. Well, it's a little like that. I guess you may find it funny. I only have two rules that needs to be followed. Do your job of course and no sex. I say, this because sex gets in the way, so to speak. However, because of living in high heat, as well as working in heat that has been measured to one-hundred-eighty-five degrees and higher on the job, clothing is from very little to none."

General: "So you're living in the nude at work?"

"Maybe I should try putting this another way. If it were possible to have you live in extreme heat, I believe at some point you would find less is better. All of us are naked from time to time. The camp itself has all the standard areas: sleeping, dining and bath but none are connected. That said, you shower over here, and your sleeping is over there. We move between them nude. It's normal. Our nurse jogs three to five miles daily in her birthday suit."

Major Davis: "Everything you are hearing is the truth I have witnessed this myself. It's how they live. Zack has there ever been any problems with Nancy running or being in camp nude?"

"None, never."

Colonel: "I have a question for one or both of you. Can you describe an average workday?"

We stared at one another.

Zack: "Colonel when we started, that's like the first sixty days, well that would have been the closest to what I'd say to be average days. Or at least as average as I had figured them to be anyhow. Jake, pick a start time."

Jake - "6:00 A.M. dayshift relieves nightshift."

Zack - "12 hour shifts."

Jake - "And work starts."

Zack - "Between 7:30 to 8:30."

Jake - "The morning shipment pulls in."

Zack - "Mail and newspapers."

Jake - "Equipment person unloads freight and locates it for continuous work."

Zack - "Stopping work just long enough to lock new items in place."

Jake - "Then back to work till roughly 10:30."

Zack - "Supply restock 30 minutes to complete."

Jake - "Noon Stop for lunch, eat, drink, relieve yourself."

Zack - "12:30 back to work."

Jake - "1:00 second shipment arrives."

Zack - "Unload, place, lock."

Jake - "1:30 to 5:30 work."

Zack - "5:30 third shipment arrives."

Jake - "Unload, place, lock."

Zack - "6:00 P.M. nightshift relieves dayshift."

Jake - "Work till 8:00."

Zack - "Last shipment arrives 8:00."

Jake - "Unload, place, lock."

Zack - "Work till 10:30 restock."

Jake - "Work to midnight."

Zack - "Midnight chow thirty minutes."

Jake - "12:30 to 6:00 A.M. work."

Zack - "Seven days a week."

Jake - "Nonstop."

Major Davis: "Was that rehearsed."

Zack: "No that's how the workday goes. That's how we live."

Jake: "A break is a windstorm, an equipment failure, a death."

"Nonstop."

General: "In your off time or rest periods, what do you do then?"

"Help in camp, check equipment, relax a little like hobbies and sleep. That sums up all a person's down time."

The next few hours were more questions and answers. By 5:30, the class was ending, as everyone started for their cars and home. Zack was fairly quiet on the way home. I could tell he was going over the class in his head. I let him be. I stopped at a café, just a little Mom and Pop place to get takeout for supper. It was just burgers and fries. I knew everyone's favorites, so it was pretty easy. We got back home, had supper. Zack turned in early. He was still thinking about the class.

∞

December 13, 1984, A.M. Zack

My first call of the day was Robert. I explained to him the importance of having as much of the paperwork done as possible at the time of the interviews. I was told that it would be tricky, but he would be in town later with Art to go over the forms. I then called Nancy to see if she could be here for paperwork training, I asked about her shopping for her folks. She carefully informed me what looks easy isn't all that easy. I told her Art would be here and maybe I might be able to recruit some help from him. She agreed, saying why not.

Following the call to Nancy, I began calling everyone on our list of interviews to give them a heads up on roughly when we would be in their area. The doctor was first on the list. She was quite a talker. The cook was next on the list. She was a very pleasant-sounding lady on the phone. The communications cook was next in line. She said she would need to take notes on the time, as she was a shift worker. The next on the list was Mr. Perfect. He had a shared phone line which I thought strange, but he said he would be available anytime for us. I then figured on making it simple. I called Mr. Singer to let him know we would be starting his way soon. I asked if he could inform the others of us coming for the interviews. He said he would make sure everyone knew we were coming.

My next order of business was giving Jake a hand working on his truck. Before I could get to the garage, the phone started ringing.

"Hello?"

"Hello Zack."

"Art, I understand you're coming this way today."

"That's right. I hope I can get a minute of your time later."

"Sure, will you be here for supper?"

"It's possible, but for the moment, please don't make any special plans."

"OK, Art. I'm guessing you've got some kind of news for us or me?"

"Yes, so please be at home. We need to talk. I'll see you soon, Goodbye."

"Goodbye."

That was different--Art checking to make sure I'm going to be here.

It was time to give Jake a hand in the garage. Around 4:30, Jake took a phone call. It was Bob and Art. They had just gotten into town. They were coming straight here. Jake went to see if Lisa could watch Janet, then called Mr. Holms asking if he could watch Jake Jr. The kids were taken care of. Nancy arrived earlier and Rodger was on his way here. I felt all of us should be in the know as far as the job goes. The two of them made it here at 5:00 and we got started. Bob and Jake were putting out file folders on the kitchen table.

Art asked if he could see me in private. I directed him to my room. He put his briefcase on the corner of my bed then had a seat in the desk chair. I was seated on my bed. He took a large envelope from the briefcase and handed it to me. He was holding a smaller item. It was a photograph, but I couldn't say what it was I was looking at.

"Art, a little help. What is this I'm looking at?"

"That was a 1985 Corvette once owned by Abe Crow."

"Abe is dead?"

"I'm afraid so, Bob got this just before he called."

"You know this means I'm shorthanded now."

"Zack, I'm in your corner. You and your people are the key to this project."

"I need a miracle now."

"For two cents, I believe I can come up with a miracle."

I slipped a hand in my vest pocket and flipped the coin onto the desk.

"Keep the change."

Art picked it up.

"I need to use the phone please."

It cost me three cents. I need a miracle; the only thing was my three cents was in the form of an 1873. As I was leaving so he could have some privacy. He handed me the other envelope. I knew what it was the second it was in my hand.

In the kitchen, things just stopped when I walked around the corner. All of them looked at me, waiting. I open the envelope and dumped the contents on the table. Abe's bloodstained necklace. I was fighting, trying to keep it together. The rest knew what it meant. I put the necklace back in the envelope and asked Bob if we could have a while before starting on the paperwork. He agreed. Everyone needed a break.

Art was calling me from the back. Everyone headed out to the backyard to think and remember our friend. In my bedroom, Art handed me a piece of paper with two names and two phone numbers.

"One miracle. Here you go."

Something inside told me he did it. Two more people out of thin air.

"Art, please understand, I'm not trying to be a pig, but do you have any magic left today?"

I was rolling a coin across my knuckles. This brought all of Art's attention to one thing, the coin.

"I need help with a very special Christmas gift for some people that work in the shadows, you could say. What I'm hoping you can help with is New Years in Hawaii and a two-week vacation for Mr. and Mrs. Pauly and Mr. and Mrs. Bergman."

Art's eyes were fixed on the coin as he listened.

"Art, maybe this will help with fuel."

I dropped it in his hand.

"OK, one more miracle. Of course this is all first class?"

"Yes, please."

"As good as done. They will have the time of their lives."

"Will that take care of some of the cost?"

"Zack, have you lost your mind. This is an 1866 plain half dollar. It's nearly priceless."

"OK its priceless, big deal. You haven't seen the cream of the crop yet."

"We need to get to the kitchen and get started on the paperwork."

"Zack, one more thing. Marshal's being watched. You were right. He is doing a lot of travel in the company planes and not turning in trip reports."

In the kitchen, I had a sad group as Bob and Art went through the very legal looking paperwork, half of which I don't remember signing. It took the better part of an hour and a half to get through them, but we got the hang of it. Bob wrote out everything for each form.

The two of them blindsided all of us. We were getting a much bigger plane to collect the new people as they were interviewed. What I thought to be a two-or three-day trip, was now closer to five. I was thinking of John's model and had to ask Art if there would be training for the tower crane. His answer was most unexpected.

"Don't worry. I got it covered. I'm doing the hiring for that. It's nobody's business but mine. They're your people."

Wow, Art is on top of things. Bob was telling Nancy the people she would be interviewing in detail, with an emphasis on the doctor. I had to ask if there was a problem, she just smiled saying no not at all.

It was coming on 8:00 P.M. Bob called for a cab to the airport. Before Art left, he said our pilots name was Jean Sloan. The meeting had ended. We had lost Abe. We were growing but the cost was getting a little heavy. Two damn good workers in every sense of the job and the Krew were gone. I thanked everyone for their time in moving the job forward. I believe all of them could see I was hit hard by Abe's death. The day ended. I found the radio theater station and was listening to it as I fell asleep.

∞

December 15, 1984, 6:00 A.M. Zack

From what I'd been told, yesterday was shopping madness for the ladies, which turned into packing mania. Everyone is here, somewhat awake, and ready to board. Jean, our lady pilot was ready to go. The ground crew got our bags loaded quickly. This plane was much bigger than what I was expecting; it was for thirty people and first class. It was luxurious with no cheap seats. With all of us on board, Jean gave the safety speech and then she was in the pilot's seat. In no time the engines were running and we started for the runway. Jean gave our estimated flight time as three hours.

We hadn't even left the ground and Jake Jr. was already out like a light. Lisa was holding Rodger's hand. Let's just say that she had a death grip on it. Nancy was reading a newspaper and looked like she was enjoying herself. The trio of young ladies had their faces glued to the windows and were chattering. At thirty minutes into our flight, Jean called me to the front. She had me in the copilot's seat and pointed out the two gauges that she wanted me to watch so she could go to the lady's room and have a fast chat with the Cooks. Nancy was staring at me. I knew that if I kept looking back at her, she'd get me laughing. Jean had taken care of all she had said and was back in her seat. On my way back to my seat, Nancy whispered, "Auto pilot" as I passed. I just smiled and kept going.

Back in my seat, it wasn't long, before I dozed off. Janet woke me when we were about to land in Atlanta. When we were on the ground and had taxied to our parking place, Jean had the engines shut down, the cockpit shut off, the door opened. Everyone assembled near the plane Jean told us that a tour bus would be taking all of them on the grand tour of Atlanta.

Jean and I waited with the plane as the bus drove off sightseeing. I ask Jean what stop would be best next for us. She told me Norristown, PA. It sounded good to me. She would check the weather. Jean wrote down the phone number for the pilot's lounge. That's where she would be after the plane had been serviced.

A car arrived to take me to the office along, with two boxes of applications and one large briefcase. I asked the driver how long before we would be there.

"Twenty minutes or so."

Just enough time to recheck the apps before getting there. The driver parked in front of an older looking brick building. It looked a lot like a warehouse. One door in front and no windows. I pushed the doorbell.

"Hello who is it?"

"This is Zack with a delivery for Alice Krew."

A few seconds later and the door opened. There stood a woman maybe four and a half foot tall, bright red hair, big green eyes, and white as a ghost.

"Ma'am, my name is Zack and I am returning this paperwork to you." She reached up and tugged on my shirt to lean forward then whispered in my ear.

"I'm Gabby."

I was in the right place. The driver helped carry the boxes in and said he would be back in two hours. I thanked him and he was gone.

"Come in the office, Zack, and bring the files of the people you'll be interviewing."

"Sure thing." I grabbed the briefcase and followed her into a rather large room.

"Excuse me for asking, Gabby, but this doesn't look like an office. What is it really?"

"Well, it's the office and it's my home for now."

"Your home? If it's OK with you, I'd like to hear more of your arrangement."

She pulled a chair over, well, I should say the only normal size chair, to the side of the desk.

"Zack, you're the only person I've seen in almost two months."

We talked for a while.

"Would you like to go out and get some lunch?"

"I can't. I can't leave the office. It's the rules."

"Call Marshal I'll talk to him."

She did as I requested and minutes later, we were headed out the door.

"This may sound silly, but you do have a key to the place?"

"Right here" As she pulled her necklace out and showed me a key.

"Maybe I should try it."

It worked just fine. We were on our way. In the day light, I made a startling discovery. Not only was she small, she was very woman like, only small. There was a pizza place a block and a half away. The two of us made tracks for it. Our lucky day, they were open. She said the food was really good.

"How would you know if their food is good?"

"Delivery, silly. Everything I get is delivered to the entrance. It's all paid for by credit card plus, I leave a tip on the bench. You name it, they deliver. It works."

"This place looks nice. What's really good here?"

"I know just the thing."

The waiter came over, she pointed to the menu and said, "A platter please and a seven-inch cheese pizza."

"Gabby, what did you order?"

She had a smile that was amazing. I had a feeling she ordered her favorites. It wasn't very long and our food arrived. There was two small plates, the pizza with a platter. It was a sampler. Well, she was hungry and so was I. The food was fantastic. The platter was all but licked clean with only two pieces of pizza left.

"You know, I can't take this on the plane."

"It's OK I know where I'll keep it."

She was patting her stomach. I took care of the bill and she got a small box for the pizza. Before we left the pizza place, I asked if I could use the phone.

Our waiter looked at the phone number dialed it then handed me the phone.

"Hello, Jean Sloan please."

"One moment."

"Jean here."

"Jean its Zack. Question. What's the weather like around Norristown?"

"Not all that good really tonight. By noon tomorrow it should be safe I'd say."

"Jean, you and everyone get a hotel for the night. A nice one. You and the group just relax for tonight. I'll be spending the night at the office. I should be back with everyone about 9:00 A.M. How would that be for travel?"

"That's a good time. I'll take care of the lodging and all, no problem. You just take care of business."

"Thank you, Goodbye."

"Goodbye."

We started back to the office, as we passed the front of a furniture store.

"Gabby, let's stop in here and look around. What do you say?"

"Alright, do you have something in mind?"

"I think so, but I'll know it when I see it."

We went in and started looking over everything. It was premium quality goods no junk. I walked over to see what it was she was admiring. It was a really nice desk chair.

"Try it on to see if it fits."

"Alright, I will. Oh this is better than it looks. It's a perfect fit."

"Well, you know when I get back this way, I might need a place to sit."

"I like that, I think we should start on finding your perfect chair now."

I had a clerk come over to see if the chair she was happy with was the only one in stock. He asked if we wanted this model or the executive.

"What executive?" She said.

The clerk took us to the real high-end section. There was one that looked like the same chair. Gabby had a seat.

"What is the difference?"

The clerk pointed out the controls under the seat one side was to recline the other was to make it a cot. Gabby looked up at me.

"This one is it, just give me a pillow and blanket."

I was still scanning the choices and there was plenty here. I found a charcoal grey that looked good to me, I pointed it out to the clerk.

"Sir, are you sure this is the one you want."

"Yes, and we need these delivered in the next half hour or no sale."

"How far out are you?"

"One block"

I walked to the front door of the store and pointed down the block.

"Right there please"

"We can do that, sir."

I'd found a beautiful older style ledger and set it on the counter. Our chairs matched in style, but there was a size difference.

The bill was paid and the odd procession started down the block; a man and woman with two men per large box. Two boxes, four men total. We did look weird, but it was fun and the guys from the store had a great sense of humor. Gabby was laughing like mad. The chairs were placed in the entry of her place, and I tipped them for their help. The smile on Gabby's face was unreal. She was thrilled as we carried the chairs to just the right place in her home.

"Gabby, what is your real name?"

"Abigail."

"So Abby turned into Gabby."

"Yeah, not my doing, but that's what it turned into."

With the chair in place, we started working on the applications. It was 10:00 P.M. and I was shot. She had gone through the apps and made notes for each one of them.

"Abby, I need to get some sleep. Just leave me in the chair. I promise I won't be a problem in any way."

"You need a pillow and blanket. I'll get them."

I was out in no time. I awoke to her wedged up against the front of me sound asleep. Her pillow was under her head and she's holding my arm like a blanket. The alarm was going off. She reached over to shut it off.

"Good morning. Did you sleep OK?"

"Yes, Abigail. How did you manage to sleep with me?"

"Well, you were shivering, so I patted you on the hip and slipped under the covers. You're a perfect gentleman. Even asleep, you held me like a pillow and stopped shivering. You never moved. I was asleep just like you and was warm."

"Abby, I don't want to be a pest, but I do need to clean up a little."

"Oh, the showers are over there, but I did get up earlier and freshened up your clothes, except your vest."

"Thank you. I'm afraid of getting in a plane and smelling like meatballs and pizza."

"I even have a new toothbrush you can use." She got everything I needed to get ready for the day.

"Abby, I'm going to miss this place and you."

"Don't talk like that. I know you'll be back."

I got cleaned up and ready for the day. Abby was cooking something. It smelled like meat. She'd made up breakfast. She had no kitchen table, so we ate at the desk, which was fine. I was checking the time; my ride would be here soon. I needed something.

"Abby, may I have something of yours?"

"Like what?"

I reached in my pocket and took out my bandana.

"How about a trade?"

She got a faded yellow bandana from her dresser and handed it to me. It went into my vest pocket. I rolled my worn-out blue bandana and tied it around her neck. We held one another until the car arrived to take me to the airport. I kissed her goodbye.

"Hurry back and be safe," She said as I climbed into the car.

The trip from the office to the airport was fast. At the airport, Jean was filling me in on our best plans for travel. She explained that we needed to be out of Norristown by 4:00 P.M. So we didn't get caught in bad weather. On board, Jean didn't waste time. The second the door was closed we were moving. The flight was only an hour. Nancy and I were talking on the way. I was doing my best to make sure she worked fast with the doctor. In the airport, she had Mary Jo Door on the phone in the first minute of arrival. The doctor said she could be at the airport in ten minutes.

We got with the airport manager to get a conference room. The manager had a small meeting room available. Jake and I waited near the entrance, as both of us knew the description of who to watch for. It was just like she said. Ten minutes. A car pulled in the lot and a rather tall woman was coming to the door.

December 16, 1984, 10:00 A.M. Nancy

A knock on the door of the conference room, opening it.

Nancy: Hello, you must be Mary Jo Door come in. Please have a seat. Let me introduce myself, I'm Nancy Bergman. I've looked at your application and well, I like it.

Mary: Miss Bergman, it's Doctor Door.

Nancy: So, you're a doctor. I'm the nurse. That said, we need a doctor. Any question?

Mary: Miss Bergman.

Nancy: Call me Nancy, please.

Mary: Look Nancy, I have plenty of questions. One is, where is Mr. Mulholland? It was my understanding he would be here.

Nancy: He will be here shortly I'm very sure. I know he's busy, now, Mary.

Mary: It's doctor.

Nancy: OK Doctor, you pull twenty hours a week, you make a salary of $80,000 a year. You draw from a group stipend. Because of work hours being on the low side, you are passed over by hospitals. Your stipend is barely enough to maintain continuing credits with no funds for research studies. You have a $50,000 life insurance policy that's half paid for. Your health insurance is a sixty/forty plan with a $500 deductible at a cost monthly of $290. You have no dental, no optical. You have a $250 a month car insurance that is three months late. Now, I chose you for many other sound reasons. Please understand this, we are very informal. We have no time for titles or egos. We do respect one another on the job. We have to. There's nowhere to run to or hide. There is no his and hers rest rooms. Privacy is your cube. Your sleeping area is six foot wide eight foot long, with no TV, and a few radio stations. The days are hot, the nights are cold. There is wildlife in the area, poisonous and non-poisonous. The pay is more than I've ever seen. The job itself is in hell, deadly heat, in the middle of nowhere, and you can't leave. Mary, would you like to hear more about yourself or the job?

Mary: Nancy, you're good. I forgot all about my car insurance. Let me see if I've got this straight. I'm the doctor in this company. Titles aren't used.

Nancy: No titles, nicknames, because of radio communications.

Mary: I'd have a nickname only.

Nancy: Correct.

Mary: For security reasons.

Nancy: Correct.

Mary: Nancy, you got my attention. Call me Mary, not Mary Jo. My father named me, and I just haven't got the heart to have it changed.

Nancy: Great Mary. Really any questions?

Mary: You're an RN?

Nancy: Yes.

Mary: How much did you make this year?

Nancy: I think you're asking me how much I've made with this company?

Mary: Yes.

Nancy: I signed on in August. I worked eighty-seven days straight, no break. It all totaled in pay and paid benefits about $100,000. Mary,

I must remind you that's eighty-seven days in hell. One man died on me. I did all the standard tests. He was gone.

Mary: So, you stopped for the funeral?

Nancy: We stopped operations one day. It was to regroup, to get a new plan for working, service the equipment and restart. Oh, his body was shipped hours after it was reported. You can't leave the job site.

Mary: This is sounding like a job I can do.

Nancy: Great. I'll get Zack and you'll be on the payroll. There is one thing I do need to ask. Is it possible for you to pack a bag and leave with us in two hours?

Mary: I believe I can do that.

Nancy: Even better. I'll be right back.

Zack was sitting reading a newspaper.

Nancy: Come Zack, time to see your doctor.

We returned to the meeting room quickly.

Zack: Miss Door, I'm Zack Mulholland. Thank you for being here in a timely manner today. I understand you wish to be part of our band of crazies. Nancy picked your application as one saying that we had to meet you. Nancy do you have all the papers?

Nancy: Sure thing. Mary, once these papers are signed, you are on the payroll, which is why I ask if you could travel with us today.

Mary: I'm ready. Let's get started.

For the next twenty-five minutes, we were giving the meaning and purpose of each page. Soon the last page had been signed.

Zack: Welcome to the team, Mary. Now if you're going with us, please hurry with your packing. There is a weather system. We need to outrun it or we could be stuck here a while. Nancy, do you have the relocation sheet?

Nancy: Right here.

Zack: OK new person, please get packed.

I borrowed Jean's coat and quickly learned why Mary paid that much for car insurance. She drives fast. As it turned out, she was even faster at packing two large suitcases. It took under an hour while I was reading the housing benefits. Mary was on the phone.

Nancy: Calling a cab?

Mary: Better, a cop a friend to watch the place. His wife has a key. Plus we'll get a ride in the squad car to the airport.

Mary wasn't kidding. A police car was out front in minutes and we were back at the airport. I handed Jean her coat and thanked her. She said we should be boarding in ten minutes, as she had heaters on the engines and in the cabin. That pilot of ours had nailed it. In fifteen minutes, we were in the air. Once we got to our cruising speed, Zack joined Mary and I, as we gave the no sex rule and then remarked that we hoped she wasn't shy. The look on her face was priceless.

∞

December 16, 1984, 3:30 P.M. Jake

The trip into St. Louis went pretty good with just a few bumps. Lisa didn't freak out; I'd say she's starting to get the hang of flying. I couldn't imagine trying to do this on a bus. Mary is really a cool person. She has the girls spellbound by being a doctor. My boy was asking how old he should be to start dating. I may have to have the father to son talk, the birds and bees thing sooner than I thought.

Jean said she had made our reservations at a very nice hotel near the airport. Tomorrow if all went well, we might have four more members.

∞

December 17, 1984, 6:30A.M. Mary

I woke up this morning to Zack patting my foot.

"Mary, Mary, time to get up. Time to get moving."

"Zack, how did you get in here?"

"Nancy, let me in twenty minutes ago. Now don't take this the wrong way please, but you are very nice looking asleep."

"I've never been complimented for sleeping."

"Yes, your mouth was hanging open. The drool was all over. Oh, in case you forgot, you're naked."

"You're right. I forgot"

"Now, let's get this day started, please."

He left the room. Nancy had the water running for me in the shower. Holy smokes hot really hot! Nancy helped with my hair. It was surprising how fast she was with getting things done. I knew I would be traveling, so I went with a light breakfast. I'd snack if I need to. That should work. I must confess, not knowing the day's plans was quite strange for me. From what I've observed so far, this is a team of carefully handpicked people with highly developed skills and oddly none of them have egos. The entire group are pleasant people, warm. The children are well mannered, a unique family. I was beginning to feel very at ease with everyone. I had a little time before the meeting, so I strolled around the gift shop. I had been thinking of a nickname when I found Zack in the lobby reading a newspaper and sipping coffee.

"Can I join you?"

"Of course, my dear, park it here."

"Zack, can I ask a question about you?"

"Sure."

"I understand you have money. Is that right?"

"Well, yes, but if you'd like trying it, you're welcome to."

"What are you saying?"

"Mary, like I told Nancy, I can put three million in your hand in less than a minute with only one string attached. I have the right to see you day or night for one year just to see if you have the money or the money has you. Only takes a minute, what do you say, bodyguards, people to watch over your friends and family? Oh, the security system on your home and don't forget everyone you've ever been nice to will show up on your doorstep."

"You make it sound not all that wonderful."

"Mary, not even a year ago I sold an idea, my dream, and almost overnight I had money and power just like that. Trust me, in the beginning I didn't sleep. I was afraid to go out for anything. It was a job just to get the mail. I hope I haven't freaked you out."

"No, not at all. I guess I should apologize asking something so personal."

"No, it's OK."

"You have a meeting to attend shortly."

"Right."

Back to the room. Nancy is in the bathroom. I'm trying to get my bag packed to leave. I noticed Nancy's necklace on the dresser. My curiosity of her gold necklace drew me to it. I held it up to my neck.

"It's a one and a half ounces solid eighteen carat. I watched it being cast."

"It is beautiful, Nancy. Will I be able to buy one?"

"They're not sold. You earn a necklace. About everything else is given. It comes with a wicked price tag."

"How's that?"

"You do a shift six to twelve hours in the field on the job just like the men do before you get one. It may sound silly, but at a distance you don't see them moving. The day I earned that it was the hardest physical work I'd done in my life."

"Will I have a chance of earning one?"

"I think so."

"May I try it on?"

She helped putting it on. I looked in the mirror.

"It's so beautiful, it's worth any price, I have got to earn one. Take it off before it makes me crazy."

"Once you have one, you are naked without it."

As I watched her put it on, her words made sense. I could see a change in her that could not be put into mere words.

In the meeting room Zack handed me a booklet, I began looking over Allen Johnson's paperwork. This guy is superman or something. He has three degrees and was on the honor roll.

"Zack, I hear someone in the hall."

Zack walked to the door.

Zack: Come in, gentlemen.

The foursome came in and went to the opposite side of the table.

Zack: To start, you are here for a job interview, right? I'd hate to think I'd just pulled four people in here on their way to breakfast.

"Yes sir, the interview."

Zack: Very good, Mary would you sit here please. Jake here. Rodger there please. I'll do the introductions. The lady next to me is Mary Jo Door our onsite company doctor. To my right, is my righthand man second in charge, Jake Pauly. Next to Jake, Rodger Cook, the man who knows where and why when we can't. Myself, Zack Mulholland, for lack of a better word, boss. Rodger, would you hand out the notebooks please.

Rodger: Martin Cruz, one for you. Allen Johnson, yours. Terry Singer, yours. And Mr. Jack Porter, yours. Gentlemen, ink pens are here. Zack, start anytime.

Zack: Gentlemen, there is a subject I must bring up first before we go on. That is, how many of you know of Terry's letter sent to me?

Jack: All of us, sir.

Zack: Please first names. Gentlemen it was never written. You should never speak of it to anyone. I have my reasons and it's in your best interest believe me.

I saw another side of Zack, like someone just flipped a switch. He was answering questions left and right, like he had been doing this for years. He explained everything in detail, rules and what was expected. The last two pages, he slowed down. It was the non-disclosure form. He made sure it was understood by all. Then with the last page, he told them the second it's signed they were on the payroll. They have three days to get to Vegas. Jack asked, being married with children, if there might be a grace period. He was told to call on the third day to check in.

When the meeting ended, we had four more people. On the way out, the strangest thing happened. Allen asked me to lunch. Martin whispered to me in the years he's known Allen, it was the first time they ever saw him talk to a woman. It was odd. He was very nice, but painfully shy.

∞

December 17, 1984, 2:30 P.M. Zack

Jean found the fast lane to Norfolk, Va. This could be gold. From what Art told me, these guys have been together for a few years. I called ahead to make sure they would be available. Now, if the airport has a meeting room, this could turn into a great day. Six Krew welders in one day. Unheard of. The long shot of all times. My lady with wings was thinking ahead and had a meeting room lined up for us. Once we were on the ground, a shuttle was waiting to get us to the terminal.

Inside we found Bill Cox and Fred Miles were already there. The meeting room was ready, so we wasted no time. The introductions were made. I didn't have applications, so it was going to be a bit rough.

I took out an application to show them the last page and began asking a few questions.

"Are you gang welders?"

"Yes."

"How thick have you worked?"

"Twelve to sixteen inches."

"Ever work in a cool suit?"

"Yes."

"Gentlemen, the job is on a time frame, the sooner we are off the bigger the bonus is, and that is your base pay on the job site.

Bill: It looks good on paper where do we sign on?

Zack: That's where all I can say is a handshake and my word, as I'm not carrying extra paperwork.

Fred: Zack, look I'd take a chance on this job. Where is the office to get an app?

Zack: Vegas. That's where we base out of. Bill, Fred, I may have an answer to this wait here please.

I went to find Jean. She was in the coffee shop.

Zack: Jean, do you carry cash?

Jean: How much do you need?

Zack: 3,000 Dollars

Jean: It's in the plane. I'll bring it to the meeting room.

Zack: Thank you.

I returned to the meeting room.

Zack: Gentlemen, the answer will be here shortly. I hope relocating isn't a problem.

Bill: Vegas is a good three-day drive, in good weather.

Zack: The group will be doing three more interviews. Call this number four days from now to let me know where you are.

Fred: No problem.

Jean was knocking on the door.

Zack: Thank you, Jean. Alright gentlemen, this should help things along $3,000 cash for fuel, food and so on.

Bill: Zack, I think we could be on the road in the morning.

Zack: Thank you Bill, thank you Fred. I'll see you in a few days.

Our meeting came to an end as I walk to the door to the parking lot. Jean was standing with me as I watched them leave in a service truck.

"Jean, is the plane and paperwork all set for New Orleans?"

"I got the flight plan set all the way to Arlington, Texas. Are you ready to go?"

"Yes, ma'am."

We were on board and ready to go when Jean said we may have a delay before takeoff. It was only fifteen minutes; it wasn't so bad.

Once we got off the ground, Jean did her best to get us back on schedule. It was getting near supper time when we touched down in New Orleans. At the time, I knew two things. Food, and sleep, in that order. We had a reservation at a hotel not that far from the airport. Jean had told us the food here was the best. She wasn't kidding. My problem was that I was tired.

∞

December 18, 1984, 8:00 A.M. Nancy

We checked on Zack at ten last night. He was out cold. Mary is great company. It's nice having another woman on the Krew. The interview is at 10:00 this morning. I haven't heard a thing from Zack's room. We went down to the lobby. The hotel had a breakfast bar, emphasis on the bar side. There sat Zack having a coffee and reading the newspaper.

"Zack, when did you get up?"

"Oh, a little after six. You two were still in bed so I got ready for the day and here I am."

"When are you calling Mr. Perfect?"

"About nine. Where's Mary?"

I took a seat to have a light breakfast. Mary found us to have something to eat. We finished breakfast; Zack signed for everything as always. The hotel would handle all of our transportation needs. That was a concern of mine, as I hadn't seen a cab at all. Zack had made the call and we got a limo to Lloyd Sherry's apartment. The building looked old, but very well kept. Zack rang the doorbell at the front door. It took a while, but someone answered on the intercom.

"Hello, who is this?"

"Zack Mulholland to see Lloyd Sherry please or are we at the wrong place?"

"No, this is Lloyd's place. You're the job people? I'll buzz you in."

We walked in then went down the hallway to the last apartment on the left. Mary knocked on the door as a woman opened it.

"You're the people to see Lloyd? He's helping a friend. I'll get him. Please have a seat."

We had a seat; Zack was busy getting Lloyd's paperwork out. The door swung open.

Lloyd: I'm sorry. I was under the impression it would be at least an hour before you arrived. Welcome to my home. I'm Lloyd Sherry.

Lloyd and the lady friend were both standing in the doorway.

Zack: Lloyd, I am the person you spoke with a while ago. Now, please don't take this as being rude, but this is a private interview. I do thank your lady friend for being so helpful.

Lloyd: Thank you, Donna. I'll see you later.

She departed then Lloyd took a seat.

Zack: Maybe some introductions are in order. This is Nancy Bergman, our company nurse and Mary Jo Door, our company doctor. I'm Zack Mulholland, the boss on site. We studied a large number of applications and yours was one we found very suitable. Any questions?

Lloyd: What kind of job is it and how long will it run or last?

Zack: You will be doing in-field specialized welding. If all goes according to the plans, the job will end about this time next year.

Lloyd: Just a year.

Nancy: You will be welding in a cool suit. Outside temps can reach two-hundred degrees.

Lloyd: Now you're talking my language. When you say a thermo suit, that tells me it's big and the pay is good. How much can I make?

Zack handed him the notebook open to the pay and benefits page. Lloyd studied the page.

Lloyd: This can't be right. You are going to pay me the standby pay to wait and I'd be paid for every hour I'm at the job site? These numbers are the biggest I've ever seen!

Zack: Well, Lloyd, does this look like something you would want to be part of?

Lloyd: You bet!

Lloyd was a fast reader as Zack gave the high points for every page. Twenty minutes later all was signed.

Zack: Lloyd, you're on the payroll. Pack your bags and we'll see you in Vegas. Will you need travel money to get there? And here are the instructions for you and any van line you use in moving.

Lloyd: Well, a little money wouldn't be bad. My car does need a tune up.

Zack: Would five hundred be enough?

Lloyd: That should do it.

Nancy: Zack, could Mary and I have some time to talk with Lloyd?

Zack: Sure, take your time I'll be outside.

Mary and I had a talk with Lloyd about all the dress shops in the area. Somehow it didn't shock me. The shops were mainly for cross dressers. He was also a former cross dresser, but because of age he no longer goes out. He was a tailor and a dressmaker as a side job. He had no problems with nudity, as he was a card-carrying nudist himself.

Zack asked to use the phone to call the hotel for the car to take us to the airport. Lloyd saw us to the front as the car was pulling up. The trip to the airport was fast. Jean had the plane ready to go. In no time, we were on our way to Texas. Abilene was the next stop for one Miss Ann Stevenson, our cook.

∞

December 18, 1984, 3:30 P.M. Zack

I'd called her the second I got inside the terminal saying we would be at her home as soon as possible. She said she would be here, but her home was not the best place for an interview. She asked if somewhere else was possible. I told her the motel to come to and I would have a meeting room reserved. We had just got the meeting room arranged. We hadn't even set down our bags and she had arrived.

The usual round of introductions and all had been done. Nancy and Mary took over on the questions and answers. These ladies weren't fooling around. They hit the rules the life in camp. They hit everything. Ann was sitting there smiling.

"I can't find any part of this I don't like. You know, maybe the high heat, but I'm in. Now what?"

Twenty minutes later we had a cook. Ann Stevenson had signed on. I had given her all the relocation information. I could see she had a lot of pride, so I carefully pulled five hundred in cash from my billfold and handed it to her.

"Just get the receipts to me. It will save on paperwork."

"Thank you. I will be on the road by noon tomorrow."

One more to go and that would be tomorrow. As we weren't far, the motel shuttle gave us a ride back to the airport. We went through security and straight to the plane. Jean had finished all the preflight business. We boarded and were enroute to Arlington for the night.

Jean was filling us in on the flight plan. We needed to head south, turn north, and come in low and slow. If all goes according to plan thirty-five minutes tops. We just settled back and it was quiet. I could feel she was making a long, gentle banked turn. We looked out the window at maybe Two thousand feet as we glided into Arlington.

The limo was waiting, Jean said she had to stay on the ground sixteen hours so no one could question her about air hours. I decided we would leave between 3:30 to 6:30 tomorrow. Jean said the earlier the better. We got in the limo and headed for the hotel to catch up with the rest of the group. I was starting to feel the day. My ladies believed it would be a good idea to get me in the pool. I said okay to it. In my favor, I slipped in to the pool and was floating around before they knew I was even in the pool.

The next thing I felt was hands on my back as they walked around, guiding me around, it was okay. I was starting to get the feeling that I had two mother hens with me. I asked them to just let me float, which they did, but they never left the pool until I got out. I'd talked to Abby earlier and was ready for a long sleep. The hotel had a bed and pillows that were perfect for sleeping!

∞

December 19, 1984, 8:00 A.M. Jake

The kids and I got up and got ready for the day. Everyone was in the diner for breakfast. Zack stopped at our table to tell me Jean would be here soon with the flight plan for today. Janet was becoming a pintsize jet setter; she is definitely growing up. My son was ready to go home. I think the theme park got the best of him. I know he was on every ride at least twice. Good, Jean's in the lobby. We should know something soon. Jean tells us our flight to Tacoma; Washington will take a full three hours and the weather is good all the way. She said an overnight stay would be ideal as we would have the winds in our favor in the morning for heading back to Vegas.

I can do another night on the road. The kids were all thinking the same thing--a pool. They would sleep on rocks as long as there was a pool. All of us agreed on the overnight. Zack went to call Miss Patty Booker. He wasn't gone very, long but he had a big goofy grin on his face. My first thought was that it was all set for an interview.

∞

December 19, 1984, 2:30 P.M. Mary

The flight from Arlington to Tacoma was bumpy, but quick. Zack and Jean had worked together on lodging for the night and transportation for any sightseeing. The hotel was first class. The meeting room had been booked, so we would have to do the interview in a hotel room. Zack was a little upset and had a talk with the manager. I'm not too sure how he did it, but all of us were put in penthouse suites for the night. Zack had called Patty to see if a 4:00 P.M. interview would be doable for her.

∞

December 19, 1984, 4:00 P.M. Zack

I had left word at the desk for Miss Booker, asking to direct her to my room when she arrives. She was a little late. I figured road conditions or parking. There was a knock on the door Mary answered it. A very slender, attractive black woman with a small boy.

Zack: Miss Booker, please come in. The young man as well.

Patty: Thank you, sir.

Zack: Nancy, would you see if the Cooks could watch Patty's young man for a while. I'd like Jake in here please. And your name, sir?"

Patty: Well, answer him.

Jim: Jim, sir.

Zack: My name is Zack. I get Jack, Sack, and a bunch of other names. It's a pleasure to meet you. Now, Jim, your mother and us have a very important meeting we need to get to. I hope it's OK with you waiting with my friends the Cook family.

Jim: It's okay. Mom said this could be a game changer of jobs.

Zack: She may very well be right on that one.

Nancy had returned with the Cooks and Jake.

Zack: Jim, this is Lisa and Rodger Cook.

Jim: Hi.

Lisa: Jim, the girls are watching a girly movie and Jake Jr. is watching a western or there's a game room downstairs. Take your pick.

Jim: Games please!

Jim and the Cooks departed.

Zack: Let's get started folks. First this is Patty Booker. Over here is Nancy Bergman, our company nurse, next to her is Jake Pauly. He is, I hope, our night shift foreman/second in charge. He's easy to work with. Here we have Mary Jo Door, our company doctor who will be with us 24,7. Least, but last me, Zack Mulholland. Its rumored that I'm the boss. Patty, do you have any questions for one or all of us.

Patty: Yes, what will my job be?

Nancy: Your job, or I should say jobs, would be communication first, cook second and laundry. I don't know what shift you will be on, so that's the short list.

Patty: I would like to know where I will be working.

Zack: Patty, I'm going to bend the rules just a little bit for you. We work in the desert. The days can be over one hundred degrees, the nights in the thirties. We are in an isolated area that is in partly operated by the government, so it's guarded by the military. This you must know and understand. Once you're at the job site, you live there until the scheduled work is done, which is figured to be ninety days at work. Patty, I'm going to ask you a question. I would like an honest answer. How much did you make at work last week or on your last paycheck?

Patty: My take home was four hundred twenty-five dollars.

Nancy: Patty, I make three hundred sixty dollars a day just waiting. It's called stand by pay. I worked eighty-seven days the pay and benefits came to 100,000 dollars.

Zack: You are well qualified.

Patty: What about Jim?

Zack: I know a home, good people. I might be able to make arrangements for his care.

Patty: I need the money to take care of Jim. Where do I sign?

Zack: Mary, Nancy, would you take over.

The ladies went right to work. At thirty minutes all but two forms for guardianship and beneficiary life insurance were filled out. I needed Bob for those.

Zack: Patty, we will have to get you to Vegas to handle these two forms. But as far as I'm concerned, you are on the payroll as of this minute. As for the two-week notice at work, you may just go get what is yours and leave. Patty, there is a subject I must tell you about. We live in close quarters to one another. Because of the heat, you will see men and women in forms of undress. Now that said, my rule is no sex at all. Sex on the job site is only trouble that we don't need. The part on the pay sheet that is not all there is the bonus program. We came in three days under the scheduled time. That comes with your daily pay and ten thousand dollars per day. Do you understand this job is serious?

Patty: Yes, I need to get going. Thank you, thank all of you.

Zack: Are you driving to Vegas?

Patty: Patty: Yes, I have a truck. I can make the trip.

Zack: Jake, did you bring that crazy big sweatshirt? I may need it.

Jake: Yes, and its dry

Jake brought the heavy shirt from his room. We collected Jim from the game room then went out to her truck. I checked it over then wrote out a list of items she should have serviced. I then gave her six hundred dollars to cover the service work and travel expenses. Goodbyes were said and she was on her way to start packing.

The rest of the day was for just relaxing and not much more if I could help it. Christmas is almost here. If I play it right, I might make it back to Iowa. Jean tells me if we can get to the airport by 7:00 A.M. we should be home well before noon.

THE ASSEMBLY OF BODIES /
SECOND PHASE ON STANDBY

Entries by Individuals

December 26, 1984, 8:00 A.M. Jake

Zack just got back from spending Christmas Day with his folks. The phone is ringing night and day, of course that was some of my handy work. Just something to get the people here and settled. It sounds like he's in the shower. The red eye he came in on was packed He's one of those people who doesn't sleep much when he is flying.

"Coffee, old boy?"

"Hey, thanks. You don't know how bad I need this."

"Bad flight?"

"The worst--bumps and pockets the whole flight."

"Not to change the subject, but the phone has been going nuts. I need help man."

"No problem Let's get all the paperwork on the table. We need the van-line listings. The list of houses and apartments, the power and phone companies, and all the folks that are enroute."

"Got it."

"Hey, did I hear something about a party?"

"Lisa will be over around one to fill you in."

After arranging all the papers on the table, Zack studied the mess in front of him for a full hour.

"Jake, Jake you busy?"

"No, what is it?"

"OK, we can work this pretty smooth, but the timing has to be right on."

"OK, what's the plan?"

"First off, we got a bunch of houses, more than enough. All of them are fairly close. So, we put them in a house and forget about the apartments. Now, as the new folks show up, we put them in the family car and drive around to the houses. They pick one and the power is on. We hand them a phone they contact the van-line. Maybe a night or two at a hotel and done."

"Sounds doable."

"Who's first in. You know?"

"Well, here's the way it stands. Sit back man. I think I can get it all out without any mistakes. The 23rd Mary's stuff was packed loaded, car and all, and then was supposed to be enroute that night. The group in St. Louis is kind of a mess but Martin, Allen, and Terry got it set up so all three are loaded in one moving van. They left on the 23rd. They should be here today. Jack and family loaded, and they left on the 23rd. Their van left late on the 25th. Bill and Fred loaded their trucks and got a deal on a flatbed going to L.A. Bill said they would need a loading dock when they get here. Ann, geez, I forgot! She's got a small moving company handling her car and stuff. She's flying in this morning--something like 9:30. Patty and son packed their things and loaded her pickup and should be here today."

"Look, for now you try to hold down the fort and I'll beat it to the airport."

∞

December 26, 1984, 11:00 A.M. Ann

I'm really here. It's almost like a dream. I was playing a quarter slot machine when Zack found me, and I was winning. He said gambling could take all your money. I believe him. Riding to Jake's I thought it was strange two men, and two kids, live together I have to ask.

"Zack, can I ask you a personal question?"

"Sure, Ann I'll try to give a sound answer."

"Are you and Jake a couple?"

He looked at me with the funniest of looks and then laughed.

"No, but I think I see how you had that idea. I suppose if a person didn't know us, they might think the same way. I'll be glad to tell you the story."

"Sure thing, I didn't mean to say what I said. It just sounded, well you know, like you and Jake."

"Don't even think about it, Ann. Jake and I are old friends--all the way back to our days in college, and after that."

His face got long I could see tears in his eyes.

"We had a double wedding. After the wedding, Jake moved out here. My wife died and I wasn't myself for a while there. One day, I decided to look up my old friend. Not quite a year ago, I traveled here. Damn near the first thing I read in the paper when I got here was Janet's name in the obits, She had had a heart attack. Well, the two of us weren't in the best of shape, mentally that is, but there was the matter of his kids. I became an uncle overnight."

"Zack, I'm sorry. I had no idea what you guys had been through."

"Welcome to the family, Ann."

My boss is a nice guy I just do my job. This should be a snap.

"Oh, Ann, there is one other thing you will find out about me, so I just as well tell you now."

"I'm still feeling funny about my last question. Maybe if you made it short and simple."

"Hey, simple. OK, I'm a multimillionaire."

"What? You? What the hell are you doing in a pickup?"

He was laughing

"Yes, yes, I'm rich. I drive a pickup. It's mine. I built it. You think because a person has money, they have to act like they're rich? Not me."

"You're different. I can say that Well not to sound to forward, but Zack will you marry me?"

Now he had me laughing.

"Ann, I'm sorry, but a marriage proposal in the first hour? No, really, I have a special girl."

"You're engaged?"

"Yes."

"Any brothers?"

"Sorry. My turn."

"OK."

"The scars, windshield?"

"No, the dashboard. I was a kid, so all I know is what I've been told. It was a bad car wreck. My folks were killed, and I was in pretty bad shape. My grandmother paid the bill. Oh, they put a real dent in a social life, but I still have a good time."

"You're quite a lady, Ann."

"Where will I be staying?"

"We got a block of rooms set aside at the Showboat. It's a nice place with good food and it's clean."

"It sounds good to me. I understand there are more people coming in. If you need help, I'm here you know."

"Thank you, Ann. I may need a person to man the phone. For now the room is paid for. Have some lunch, get some rest, and the strawberry shortcake they have is the best."

"Alright, but if you need me."

Zack stopped at the hotel entrance. A bell boy took my bags and I was in a room in minutes. I was sitting in this very nice hotel room and ordered some lunch. Zack's right, the food was excellent, as well as the shortcake. That was better than I expected. I couldn't just sit here. I'm being paid. I should be helping. I had the address, so I called for a cab to Jake's.

∞

December 26, 1984, 1:00 P.M. Zack

Lisa and Jake had finished talking about some party things. Jake told me that I needed to call Mary first thing. Then he'd give me the update on the new people. The call to Nancy and Mary was quick and had a benefit to it. I asked if Mary could pick up a rental car for showing houses. At least that was taken care of.

Jake was in the kitchen next to the phone.

"Hey, you said you got an update."

"Well, you better have a seat, old boy."

"Hey man, you going to drop a bomb on me?"

"Sorry."

"Let me have it."

"Oh well, Patty and son are in town."

"And the other shoe."

"One van-line called from Boulder City."

"Great, she has directions here."

"Yes, that was an hour ago."

"The van-line, did they say who they had loaded on?"

"Nope."

"Great, just great. Old boy, we aren't going to have time to pee. I'd kill for a nap."

"You drop on the sofa. I'll man the phone."

∞

December 26, 1984, 3:00 P.M. Patty

It took three phone calls, but I made it. We made it to Zack's. I rang the doorbell.

"Patty, Jim, I was starting to get worried."

"Zack, thank you for the money for moving. It really helped. I mean I could have made it here, but I would've been cutting it close."

"You're here now, please come in."

∞

"I would like you to meet your workmate, Ann Stevenson."

She stuck out her hand.

"Patty Booker."

Her face! My God!

"Patty, they don't move."

"Oh crap, I'm staring, I'm sorry, Ann, I mean it."

"Patty, if I carried a camera, you would be amazed the expressions I've seen. Hey, in a week, you'll forget they're there."

"Well, we're going to be working together."

∞

December 26, 1984, 3:30 P.M. Zack

Mary had gotten the rental car. As she and Nancy were in the back yard, I got the car loaded with the folders of the houses. Patty was easy, just enough for her and Jim, plus she had everything in her truck. Ann was nearly as easy. The key difference, bigger kitchen area. Nancy and Mary had convinced me they needed a place together to keep up medically. The sticking point was the floor plan. Both places were nearly the same. A flip of a coin and the house was picked.

We got back to Jake's I needed a shower and a solid one-hour nap. The ladies said they could stay so Jake and I could get cleaned up and maybe take a nap. Ann took over in the kitchen. Patty asked if they could move in now. Jake handed her everything they would need. Jim and Patty left for their new home.

∞

December 26, 1984, 6:00 P.M. Zack

My head had barely touched the pillow and the phone was ringing.

"Hello?"

"Hello, Zack."

"What's going on, Marshal?"

"I just wanted to say great job on the interviews. It was a real life-saver for us in the front office."

"Wow, thank you, Marshal. Coming from you that means a lot to me."

"Well, give me an update here."

"Sure, I've got four people so far in three houses. That's because Nancy and Mary need time to study and will be sharing a house. More are arriving."

"Very good."

"Marshal, they're having a New Year's party and if it's possible, I'd like Abby to be here if the office could be closed. And you too, of course."

"Zack, Atlanta is getting a major remodel. This place is a mess. Call me at noon on the 29th. I won't say, but I have a schedule. I'll talk to you then. Goodbye."

"Bye."

It sounded like there's a chance the office might be closed for a little while. If I could just get a few hours of sleep, I would be fine.

∞

December 27, 1984, 7:30 A.M. Ann

Janet and Jake Jr. are up. I took it on my own to get in the kitchen to help out. Janet's been showing me where everything is. It's a nice kitchen to work in. The space is good. The counter space is super.

"Janet, does your dad have a special breakfast?"

"Oh yeah biscuits."

"Just biscuits?"

"You know, hot with butter, jam, sometimes an egg and coffee."

"And you?"

"Cereal. I let Dad have the biscuits."

"Jake something for you?"

"I'm going to have cereal and toast. I got a jug of juice at the stables. Thank you."

"You're being easy on me, but you got it."

The young ones finished and put their dishes in the sink.

Mary is showing signs of life.

"Good morning, Mary"

"Good morning. That sofa is so comfortable I don't think I moved once."

"Coffee?"

"Yes, please. Thank you Ann. Are the guys still down?"

"Yes, I got here at six and started in the kitchen."

"I need to get to Nancy's to help pack. I need a ride. What cab service did you use?"

"I got a card here."

"I should call Nancy first."

She wasn't on the phone very long.

"Well, I need to call for a cab. She is packing boxes."

∞

I could hear someone moving around down the hall.

"Good morning, Jake"

"Morning, what time is it?"

"7:50 Coffee?"

"Where did you sleep?"

"The Showboat."

Jake went back down the hall to Zack's room. He came back to the kitchen.

"Ann, one more coffee, a biscuit, butter, and jam."

The cab showed up for Mary and she was out the door.

∞

Jake: The truck in Boulder City, he's been parked there all this time with three of the guys from St. Louis. He's thinking that he's going to get demurrage billing. When I told him he was a half hour from his unload point, he knew he was talking to a trucker.

Zack: OK here's the plan, they have enough time here to use the john then into the four-door rental.

∞

December 27, 1984, 10:00 A.M. Jake

Alright, all the ladies are taken care of. Now, we got three of the guys in houses. Only four to go, plus Mary's load. Zack had pulled a house folder, saying that he would handle it himself. Lloyd's van line was calling from Henderson. Let me see, Zack said he was just dropping Ann off at her house and he'd be right back. He must be checking on the trio. Wait, good he's backing in the drive right on time.

"Hey brother, have I missed anything?"

"Why no, in fact you're right on schedule."

"Can I come back in say an hour?"

"No, because in about twenty-five minutes you, yes you, will be able to play Mr. Realtor."

"Can I call in sick?"

"Sorry, only if you're dead."

"Who?"

"Lloyd and his load."

"You are having way too much fun."

"Have a cup. You know more about Lloyd than I do. Go in towel off."

"Jake, where are they parked?"

"At the truck stop on Nellis. I've talked with Lloyd and the driver so they should still be there."

"Well, I guess I best get over there so I can get him set up in a place."

It took roughly half hour before Lloyd and his load was sitting out front. Lloyd was driving some old Cadillac that sounded bad. Zack had the folders for the houses in the rental car.

∞

December 27, 1984, 11:00 A.M. Lloyd

This is all new to me. A house the company pays for along with standby pay. Whatever the job is nobody is talking about it.

"Zack, I'd like to take a look at this one."

"Sure, it looks big, but you know what you need."

He drove right to the place, it looked perfect. Inside, I checked the whole place over. It was the house for me. I'm sure.

"Zack, I like it now, what's next?"

"Just sign these forms and you're home."

"That's all?"

"That's all."

It's hard to believe I haven't had a house since the sixties. Zack said its time to get my stuff inside. We were back in the car and at Jake's house in no time, as it was only three blocks away.

"Lloyd, I think I know why your car is running so bad. I can't do anything with it hot, but I should be able to take a better look at it in a few days."

At Jake's, I told the van-line driver to follow me. I was moving in! Boy, did it feel good to be in a house again!

∞

December 27, 1984, 3:00 P.M. Zack

Back at home, Jake was at the table going over notes.

"Man, did you lose something or just trying to put it in order?"

"I'm not sure. I had a note this morning and put it on the table."

"So, what was it?"

"Bill and Fred are pinned down in Vega, Texas, in an ice storm. The Porter family should be out front any minute."

"Do me a favor, check the weather channel on TV. From Vega to here is still a straight through hard eighteen hours nonstop."

"Someone's out front, old boy. You got the folders?"

"In the car already!"

Jack's wife, Betty, with his sons Jeff five years old and Tom four years old. I noticed Betty was, for the most part, in charge. Betty had picked out five places she had to see. After seeing all five, she chose number four. I was concerned about the non-disclosure part, so I got Jack off to the side for a talk. I was told she could be hard to deal with, but he could make it understood. I put the call out for anyone that could help get the Porter's moved in. It was all hands on, the only ones not hauling boxes were the children and Lisa, as she was doing the babysitting.

When Jake showed up, I had to ask him who was taking care of the phone.

"Janet, she's looking for money for sunsuits, so I gave her a pencil and a fresh notepad. I told her to write down who and what the call was about. She can handle it."

I caught Ann to ask if she could be a traveling chef for the kids, knowing Lisa that may be overwhelmed. She was on her way. The best part of that I found out later was that they were served gourmet grilled cheese. I was trying to figure out how she did that.

Everyone was working hard, hauling the last of the Porter's household goods in when I heard Jake.

"What are you doing here?"

It was Janet on her bike. She handed Jake some papers and hurried back home. Jake handed me the notes; the first one read Door's load in St. George be in by nine. The second was roads are clearing, should be in town early afternoon. By sunset, the Porters were moved in, with all the boxes in place as marked.

The group started to break up for the day. Everyone went home. Jake and I walked back home as the streetlights were coming on.

"You know old boy; I wouldn't want to do this for a living."

"What? Your back sore?"

"My legs."

At home Janet pointed to the refrigerator letting us know that Ann had made supper. Heat and eat! Great. We ate supper. Jake Jr. must have put in a long day himself, as he ate and went straight to bed. By 8:30, all of us had turned in for the night.

∞

December 28, 1984, 5:00 A.M. Mary

Nancy and I have worked out a plan for the library. If the plan works, one day is all it should take to put everything together. I've found living and working with Nancy is easier than I thought. It seems that in this collection of different people were bonded like old class-mates at a reunion. We've gone through the whole house, making sure there would be clear walkways to every part of the place. Now to sit and wait.

By 7:45, the garage was full of people. They were the people I would be taking care of. Ann showed up with a large pot of coffee and Patty brought a tray of sweet rolls. The only people that aren't here were the Porters and Jake, as he's staying by the phone. Jake called saying the trucks were parked at the shopping center on Charleston. Zack left to get them.

At 8:15, the two semis were parked out front. The first thing unloaded was my car. Between the van-line guys and everyone here, everything was in the house by noon. Janet came over with a note for Zack. Zack told me he needed to use the phone. He might have to leave sooner than he had figured.

∞

December 28, 1984, 1:30 P.M. Zack

Janet handed me this note. Call this number now. It had Jake's initials. Because of all the moving of people and boxes, Nancy said to use the phone in her room. I called the number.

"Hello?"

"Hello is this Zack?"

"Yes, who is this please?"

"This is Kay, Kay Bishop."

"Your voice is very familiar."

"You know me as Alice."

"Yes, Alice, OK so Kay, how can I help you?"

"Well, Zack, as soon as you get your last two fellows in, I need all their paperwork to be taken to the new office. Here is what I would like you to do for me. Get them into a house and then tell them they need to pack an overnight bag. With bags in hand get them to the Showboat. I will take over from there."

"Alright Kay. I'll get Bill and Fred to the Showboat soonest and the unpacking will have to wait. Correct?"

"That's it, sweetheart."

"Will you be Alice or Kay?"

"Kay, my dear."

"Kay, I should be seeing them about any time now. I'll do my best to get them there as quick as possible. Anything else?"

"Why yes, there is. Marshall said something about calling you. Oh yes, have me paged when you get here it's very important. So, bye-bye for now."

"Goodbye."

I didn't know there was a Mrs. Bishop. She sounds like a very nice person. Well, I'll meet her later on, I guess. I called Jake to check in. No word yet. It was almost 2:45 when Janet showed up to tell me her dad was going to get the two men. I said I had to leave and I wasn't sure when I'd be back.

I drove to the house I picked out for them and waited. The wait time was starting to get a little bit long, like, what's going on here? Jake's in the family car. It made the corner two blocks away with two really nice pro-service rigs right behind. I flagged Jake to the side. The trucks did the same.

Zack: Jake, what happened Did you guys do lunch?

Jake: Yeah, what's wrong bro?

Zack: The front office is on me about no apps on Bill and Fred.

Jake: Not that it matters, but who is making the fuss?

Zack: Bishop.

Jake: Marshal, damn the dude. That guy is scary.

Zack: No, Mrs. Bishop. I think she has more power than Marshal.

Bill and Fred were coming our way.

Fred: Zack, we made it. Texas was not much fun, but really the whole trip has been a pain in the ass.

Zack: Before someone starts reaching for a gun, knife, or club, I overstepped my bounds. That being said the front office is telling me that they want your applications. Look, here's what must be done before everything goes off the rails. I need you to park your trucks, pack an overnight bag for two nights and get in this camper A.S.A.P. Now, who has the longer truck?

Fred: Mine is thirty-two foot.

Zack: Here is the door opener and the keys. Pack a bag and get back out fast. Do you have something for an overnight bag?

Bill: Not me. The truck is twenty-six foot.

Fred: No extra bag.

Zack: OK, one second.

I had some new cloth shopping bags in the camper.

Zack: This is as good as I can do for the time being. Bill, your opener and keys. Please hurry.

The two of them wasted no time; trucks were parked, doors closed, and ten minutes later we were on our way.

Bill: Zack, this camper you got is really set up well. Did you do this?

Zack: Yes. It's old and when I was putting it together, I didn't have the money to make it like new. I had enough to make it tough.

We arrived at the Showboat and the valet parked the camper as we entered the hotel. At the desk, I asked to have Kay Bishop paged. The clerk lifted the phone, then pointed to my side. A very attractive woman was standing just behind me.

Zack: Kay Bishop.

Kay: Zack, my dear, we finally meet face to face. Abby wasn't kidding. I might throw Marshal away and give her some competition.

Zack: Kay, this is Bill Cox, and this is Fred Miles. Gentlemen, Kay Bishop, one of my many bosses.

Bill: Ma'am, we would have been here sooner, but we had to stop for lunch. My apologies.

Kay: Bill, sweetheart, please do not use ma'am again. It's one of those words that makes me uncomfortable. So, I see you have your bags. I have your room keys. Now, come along. I'll take you to your room.

Kay showed them how to use the key cards. Once on the elevator, it was nonstop. The door opened into the penthouse.

Kay: Gentlemen, this is your room. I will guide you through all the paperwork I require to get you on the payroll. I hope the accommodations are to your liking. Now, if you would like to freshen up, there are the bedrooms with a bath on the inside wall. So, if you will excuse us, I have business matters to go over with Zack.

Kay walked over to some light switches and instantly the drapes opened. We stepped out a sliding glass door.

Kay: Zack, there are things you need to know. First is the company is missing a rather large sum of money from petty cash. Next, my personal business account was broken into and well, a considerable amount from it has vanished.

Zack: Kay, I'm not familiar with much of the front office. Please forgive me, but you were the voice on the radio, so what's your job or position?

Kay: You really don't know?

Zack: What I've told you is fact.

Kay: My dear, I own seventy percent of Greater Southwest Steel Surplus and much more.

Zack: Well, it sounds like someone close to you is stealing. From the inside I would say. This may sound, you know silly, but has there been a department-to-department audit done?

Kay: Yes. The only one that didn't turn in their numbers was security.

Zack: I will let my people know not to give out their account numbers to anyone. You are very concerned about this. If I can help, just ask. That's all you need to do.

Kay: Thank you, Zack. Now, are you ready for the party? And before it slips my mind, you will need this tomorrow. Don't lose or give this to anyone. At noon tomorrow, I will close the office until the second.

Zack: Is this the key to the office?

Kay: Zack, my dear, that key is not listed on inventory. I have one and Art has the other locked away. Oh, if Abby turns down her ring, look me up, dear.

Zack: That's nice to know, but I think she will like it. We need to get inside, as you've got a pile of paperwork. I need to find a men's wear shop.

Kay: Go to this place dear. Here, I know they have the best.

Zack: Thank you. Before I get out of here, Kay, can you tell me anything about my crane people?

Kay: Yes, they are in New York and should be here for the party. They already have a house here and an apartment, I'm very sure they will be here.

I had all the paperwork for the guys on the table. Kay got the elevator for me and I departed.

I learned more I think than I needed to know, yet there had to be a reason for it. Regardless, Marshal was a person you chose your words carefully around. I got back home, and it was almost supper time before I knew it. Janet came in the front door with two bags of hot dogs.

"Jake, I can't believe you're that hungry."

"Look in the backyard."

Everyone is out there. It's a pool party in December. Jake must have turned on the heater earlier today. If anything, that evening was a blast. The kids played until they dropped while the grownups could have set a better example for the young folks. It was good clean fun. It was almost 9:00 P.M. as the party started breaking up. It was something to see to believe. They left like family. The single guys were carrying kids. Lloyd was there to trade off.

I didn't know how the Atlanta remodel was going. I made the choice to called it a day. By 10:00 I was in bed.

∞

December 29, 1984, 7:30 A.M. Jake

The coffee is on; it sounds like the washing machine is running. The house looked like it had been picked up. Zack was sitting in his room reading.

"Morning old boy. Thanks for getting a jump on the housework."

"No problem, man."

"The kids still in bed?"

"Yeah, Junior is up and moving slow. Janet is out cold. Right now, I'm waiting on a phone call from Marshal."

"What's going on with him at this time of day. He's always called at night or late in the day."

"Something's going on in the front office. I'm not sure of exactly what it is just yet, but something."

I went back to the kitchen for more coffee. At 8:00 A.M., I heard Zack's phone ring. It was a short call not even three minutes. He came to the kitchen for more coffee and took a seat at the table.

"Zack, you look like you're a thousand miles away."

"I'm calling Kay. Maybe she knows Marshal's whereabouts."

∞

December 29, 1984, 8:45 A.M. Kay

Well, I know Marshal is in town. And I know he is at home, so the only thing he's upset about is that he lost access to the Atlanta office. Art needs to know what's going on. I told my sweethearts here I needed a few minutes to take care of a little company business. I called from my suite.

"Hello, John darling, Art please."

"Of course, Kay, and a good day to you."

"Hello Kay, good morning. What, pray tell, would have you calling at this time of day?

"My dear man, we, that is the company, has a serious problem. It's Marshal. I checked petty cash, Art. It's been drained. Ten million gone. Then I checked my business accounts. One had a twenty million withdrawal."

"Kay, at present, I'm not happy with Marshal's use of company planes. Last month, he logged two hundred hours in travels with no report of any findings."

"I know what I want. The first is Marshal off the board of directors. Now. Second, a divorce from that thief."

"He did sign the prenuptial papers."

"He sure did. Get a vote on it as soon as possible. We don't need any more trouble."

"Kay, I will have an answer for you by noon; just stay safe please."

"I'll be by my phone at noon. Bye for now."

"Talk to you soon, bye."

If Marshal is in town and I'm sure he is, I need to call Abby now. Once she was on the phone, I told her not to let anyone in the office including Marshal. She said the place would be locked up. I returned to help get my gentlemen through their paperwork.

∞

December 29, 1984, 2:00 P.M. Zack

I had just talked to Abby on the phone, and it seems that Marshal was told he was no longer part of the company in any form. The police hauled him in for shooting up a power transformer station in the warehouse district. With the money he was carrying and the guns, what really put him behind bars was the fake F.B.I. badge. Kay served the divorce papers to him in jail. I was told he was to be held until he admitted where the money went. I heard he had gotten pretty vulgar.

Abby called when it was safe to come over. The drive across town gave me time to think about how it went so crazy. The security to get in Abby's place was nuts, but I could drive right in. It's huge. My truck parked, I began looking for Abby. It took a while, as she was floating around in her pool. The rest of the evening we spent holding one another.

∞

December 30, 1984, 6:00 A.M. Jake

I had a wonderful time with the girls and my kids yesterday. I slept straight through the night. The old boy must have stayed out late, as he's still in bed. I just can't believe he found a gal he can get close to. If the kids will let me, I may get some time to work on the truck today. I'd gone out to open the garage to find Lloyd at the end of the drive. He was on his morning walk. We talked for a while, then he continued his walk. Back in the kitchen I could hear Zack was up and moving. The coffee was ready for him.

"Morning. Late night?"

"Yeah, but we got a lot of shopping done."

"Say, Lloyd was by a while ago asking if you might have a look at his Caddie."

"Oh yeah, I forgot about it."

"What's going on with it?"

"Wrong parts. I'm pretty sure of it."

"Big job."

"An hour tops. Now the trick is finding the hour."

Zack had a full plate. He said he would be bringing Gabby by on the way to Lloyds. Kay called for Zack last night saying that Jill and Brent have made it here. They would be at the party. I asked Nancy if I could be her escort. She agreed.

∞

December 30, 1984, 9:00 A.M. Abby

Zack just pulled in. I had our shopping lists made out. The office was locked, and we were off on a shopping frenzy. Everything we got, we agreed on--the color as well as the size. About 11:00, he said he needed to get to a parts store to pick up some things for Lloyd's Caddie. On the way there, we stopped at his home, as I had to visit the little girl's room. Zack showed me his room. It was nothing like I thought. There were no pictures, and no art, just books, a bed, and nightstand. We only stayed at Jake's for a few minutes before going to Lloyd's. Zack had this weird smile.

"What's so funny?"

"It's a visual joke. You'll see."

We parked at Lloyds and rang the bell. A tall slim man answered. We were invited in. Every chair and stool in his place had a woman or girl standing on it.

"Lloyd, if you need me, I'll be in the garage."

All of them were wearing beautiful gowns. Mary introduced me to everyone. She told me Lloyd was a master dressmaker. I asked Lloyd where he would like me to sit.

"Wait right there!"

He dashed off to another room and we could hear him talking to himself. When he returned, he was carrying a cream-colored silk gown. It was incredible.

"Try this on, Gabby."

He didn't have to tell me twice. It fit like a glove. I walked back to the living room. Lloyd zipped me up and I stood on the coffee table.

Lloyd was smiling and laughing as he was running from place to place. I noticed that we were in and out of the dresses and we were standing around in our underwear. No one cared. He was so busy. I don't think he would have noticed. The gowns on us looked fantastic. It came to a point when I thought he was done. He then produced a pair of very large shears and began changing the hems with slits in the sides or back. He went from one to the next. Lloyd would help each of us slip out of our gown so he could do the last of the machine sewing on them. As he finished them, we would try them on one more time. These had to be the most beautiful gowns I have ever seen.

∞

Zack was at the door.

"Lloyd, the Caddie is ready for a test drive."

"Be out in a few minutes."

Lloyd was putting the dresses in bags to keep them nice for all of us as we started out the front door. Lloyd and Zack were talking then were laughing, but all I heard was green.

∞

December 30, 1984, 8:00 P.M. Zack

What a day! Being with Abby was like a dream. The stops, the phone calls, along with the stores. Everything is working.

THE PARTY,
THE PHASE TWO MEETING

As told by individuals

December 31, 1984, 9:30 P.M. Zack

The upper floor at the Dunes was rented for the party. The hotel was handling everything--food, drinks, even our valet parking. As I watched, I noticed two wallflowers. One rather tall and the other much shorter. Something told me it was Ann. Then I remembered Lloyd said Green. Abby and I walked over to say hi. I asked Ann who is her friend.

"Zack, Abby, I would like you to meet Sherry Lloyd."

I must say, even face to face, he made a pretty fair looking female.

A little while later, I let Abby in on Sherry's secret. She was surprised, but was a good sport and kept the secret. For a Monday night, the whole town was alive with a party going on around the next corner. Everyone was dancing and having a great time. Jake and Nancy made a nice-looking couple. At midnight I knew who I wanted in front of me. I'm fairly sure she had the same idea as well. Kay stopped by with us to talk shop for a minute.

It was coming onto two in the morning as the party started winding down. By three, the last of the guests had started for their hotel rooms. It was a job, but I got Abby to her place then made the trip across town to Jake's and bed. What I had heard was that almost everyone at the party was using the first day of the New Year to sleep.

∞

January 2, 1985, 8:00 A.M. Jake

Well, the phone is working just fine this morning. It was Kay giving me the time and location of our phase two business meeting for everyone. Well, that set my morning up for a good hour on the phone, except Jack would have to be face to face. Zack said Kay was going to take Betty for tea and a talk. I got Nancy on the phone and passed the word on about the meeting. I asked if she would tell Mary. She said no problem. I drove to Jack's place Betty had gone for groceries, so I filled him in fast, so he wouldn't have to deal with his wife.

∞

January 3, 1985, 8:00 A.M. Mary

Our meeting place was a conference room at the Showboat. There are only a few people here so I took a seat next to a Major Davis.

"Hello."

"Good morning. You must be Mary, the doctor for the KREW."

"Why yes, Major Davis, you have to be a member of this group. Well, may I ask a question?"

"Of course."

"What group or department are you attached to?"

"Doctor, I thought you were going to ask something much more in depth. My department using your words is transportation."

"I ask only because you're wearing pilots' wings. So, my guess is no bus to the job site."

"Correct."

"We fly to it."

"Yes, at night, Mary. It's the safest way."

"This is some very high-end company to have the military handling the transportation. They're starting."

8:30 A.M. Robert

Robert: First, I thank everyone for being early today. Now, for our new members I hope you have taken the time to study the Rules and other documents. Does anyone have any questions?

Jack: Robert, I may have a small problem and I feel I should bring it up now. I have studied all the paperwork for this job carefully, so I understand. It's my wife. She got a hold of the rules, and she just does not understand the security and secrecy or the need for it. I did not have my paperwork under lock and key.

Jake: I don't believe that's a big problem. Zack, do you have a copy of the abbreviated rules?

Zack: Yes, right here. May I make a suggestion.

Robert: Alright.

Zack: As Jack may be looking at an uncomfortable time at home, wouldn't it be wise to have our head of security have a chat with Mrs. Porter?

Robert: I like it, let's check. Kay, what do you say?

Kay: Jack, I understand your concerns. I also appreciate your honesty in this matter I will arrange a meeting with your wife, as I believe a woman to woman would be the best. And Jack, buy a lock box please.

Jack: Yes ma'am.

Robert: Anyone else? Very well. Next good news, bad news take it for what it is. There will be a two-week delay in starting phase two. Now I am turning it over to Collin.

Collin: Ladies and gentlemen, the reason for the delay is first, the government has permitted the site for our mining operation. That is raw Manganese, a very large deposit. This puts a good deal of money into the company bank accounts. Next, based on geological surveys as to the usage of nuclear, that has been dismissed. The tunnel left from the mining operation will be cut in such a way it will allow the vessel to slowly drop the two-and three-quarter miles, straight down.

Martin: Say Collin, you know like, where is this big hole from the job, man?

Collin: The hole on center is ten- and one half-miles.

Zack, Jake, Rodger: WHAT!!

Collin: Art, would you take over please.

Art: First, you should know, we, the company, is making money this minute. The manganese we found is the best find in over fifty years. That said, it is selling as fast as it comes out of the ground. Now, as for the distance, that has been mapped out already. John, the map please.

John: Yes, sir.

Art: On this map, looking down on the site, this grey line will be the path the vessel will travel to the mine. The full ten plus miles is a down grade. The first eight miles is one long sweeping turn on a mild down grade. The last part of its trip, the grade increases as the road is straight to its final stop.

Jake: Art, is that a second road to the site?

Art: Yes, a railroad to be exact. That is how all the plates will be arriving and other supplies. Smokey and Fats will still be making their daily runs. Rodo will be handling all the rail service. Major Davis, you said you have an announcement.

Major Davis: Yes, thank you. January fourth, tomorrow, all members of KREW will be at the southwest gate at the base for training at 6:00 A.M. sharp. Do I make myself clear? Good, I will see you then.

Robert: Is there any other business, very well this meeting is adjourned.

9:30 A.M. Art

Zack and I had a quick talk in the hall before I went to my suite, I found it intriguing in many ways. It was time to talk to Patty. John went to get Patty. She entered the suite.

"Patty, please have a seat. Now Zack spoke with me about having your son. Jim is that correct?"

"Yes, sir."

"He would board with me in L.A. while you're at the job site. So, what would you like that I might be able to teach or help him with?"

"Sir, well a roof and meals of course. But my son is not learning values in money or friends. His ability to have respect for anything or anyone it's just not there."

"Patty, I am a man who has never turned down a challenge. This is a challenge the likes of which has never been put in front of me. I will take guardianship of your son. Who knows, I may learn something from him?"

"Mr. Fellows, thank you. I know you can help him."

"I will give it my best effort. Now I must get ready for another meeting."

"Thank you."

"I'll see you later. John, escort Patty to her car. Thank you."

11:00 A.M. Lisa

It seemed simple enough just watch Jim. Easy if I would have had a tranquilizer dart for the monster.

12:15 P.M. Kay

I decided to take the Jaguar. It fits me better than the Bentley and it's sporty. A quick call to Betty.

"Hello?"

"Hello, Betty, Kay Bishop calling."

"Do you need Jack?"

"No, I was hoping you might have some free time this afternoon."

"I believe I can make some time. What do you have in mind?"

"Betty, I know a simply wonderful Tea-room in Northtown. Would you care to join me?"

"I'd love to. I'm going to need directions."

"Oh, no dear I'll pick you up. It's much easier."

"About what time, Kay?"

"Oh, 1:00, or 1:30 is OK."

"1:30 maybe OK for me. I should freshen up a little."

"That will work perfectly dear. I'll see you then. Bye."

"Bye-Bye."

1:00 P.M. Gabby

Patty should be teaching me the equipment. She showed me how to monitor two channels. She even pointed out my cooling fans were backwards. She said working with Zack should be a snap.

1:30 P.M. Kay

Betty was dressed nicely, and she seems to be a nice person. So, I think we will have a lovely time.

Betty: Kay, your car is gorgeous. What is it?

Kay: A Jaguar. Get in.

Betty: It's so close to the ground.

Kay: Well, you do sacrifice some lady like movements getting in and out, but it's fun.

Betty: All right.

I thought she was going to jump out of her seat when I started it up.

Kay: Dear V12's sound funny when they start.

A ten-minute trip and we had out-front parking; it couldn't be better.

Kay: Here we are. You are going to love this place.

Betty: Kay, I'm not well versed in tea.

Kay: Not a problem. I know one you will love. Trust me.

The tea and cakes were served, and Betty didn't waste any time.

Betty: Kay, are you part of the company?

Kay: To tell you the truth Betty, I am the founder of it. Why do you ask?

Betty: Honestly, I've always known where Jack is at work, what bar he stops at after work nearly from the time we met.

Kay: Oh, my dear please let me put your mind to rest. I toured your husband's workplace just the other day. Well, I can tell you, I have seen his room. It's called a cube. To get there you have to fly in, and no one is permitted to walk or drive there. Oh, that reminds me, anyone caught in the area of the site that is not permitted is shot dead. Isn't that wonderful? No one can sneak up and harm Jack.

Betty: Kay, did you just say people are killed, shot dead?

Kay: Why yes, I was under the impression you were concerned for his safety. He will be as safe as if he were in your arms.

Betty: Do you know if I will be able to at least talk to him?

Kay: Yes, that's a radio phone call. And the calls are short. I don't remember three or ten minutes also. Only so many per week.

Betty: I worry about him, Kay. He's never been away from home and there'll be women there.

Kay: I've seen the effects on the guys coming back from the site. They are beat. Also, Zack does have a rule more like law. No sex allowed.

Betty: They're fired!

Kay: Well yes and no, from what I understand he has the love birds sent to an island with a house for two for the rest of their lives. You may have heard of it. Guantanamo?

Betty: He has that much power?

Kay: On the job site, he is the law. Betty, please, I wish I could give you an exact amount that is at stake here, but it would be hundreds of millions. With that kind of money at stake and the number of businesses, jobs lost over someone talking about it, hell, I'd kill a person.

Betty: Seriously!

Kay: If you knew the good this one project is going to do for this country, you would be amazed.

Betty: Kay, so this is big, and my Jack is working on a key part of it?

Kay: Yes, for the moment, as this is top secret, he is making the heart of it. How is the tea?

Betty: Very good.

Kay: Oh, dear I need to get back to the office. Debbie put this on my tab, dear.

Debbie: Yes, Ma'am.

In no time Betty was home.

Kay: Betty, we need Jack well rested. This is the list of clothes and and goods he will need to have for his time at work. I must get going. Bye-Bye.

Betty: Bye.

I hope my visit takes some pressure off the poor henpecked bastard.

∞

January 4, 1984, 6:00 A.M. Zack

All of us are here and the security check went faster than I figured. The girls, well Nancy and Mary, were taken to medical study group training. Ann and Patty had a fairly serious class on food handling in high heat, as well as all the normal first aid classes. As for the guys, first, the new welding machines nice super high power, lightning-fast wire speed. All of us knew all the basic set up information from our time on the job.

The part that everyone was really working hard to get the hang of was the baskets that would be our work platforms. Terry and Martin were the first to figure out the combination. It was so weird. The baskets could be set for exact travel speed to match your weld. The simulators for the baskets were a blast. All of us it got to the point each of us could set the travel with the speed in seconds of one another. The classes were long, but never dull.

The next class was on the cool suits with all the systems. The part of the class that I was most interested with was fitting for best performance. I knew I would be needing to know that if Mary or one of the others may want a shot at a necklace. I pointed out to the instructor of the class that we had more than one model of suits on the site. He was quick to respond saying there could be three different models. And he gave the details of the differences. Before that class ended, I managed to get a copy of the fitting guidelines along with cleaning instructions.

The class on vehicles was fun. More than anything, the ladies were having a good old time on the golf carts all the way up to the water truck. The platform service truck was taken over by the girls on first sight. Each one of them climbed in or on it like, it was something they had worked with for years. To save time, the operator on the small crane on the truck didn't have to get back in the cab to move it. This thing had a control panel up with the crane. Controls for driving the truck the top speed on the remote was ten M.P.H. In the cab at the wheel forty M.P.H.

Jill and Brent had put most of their studies on all the lifting equipment, as well as doing the math to check the true load weights. It was four very long, very intense days of studies. We had notes and cheat sheets. Still, we had a lot to think about.

∞

January 9, 1985, 8:00 A.M. Nancy

I managed to get all the women together to go over the required items they would need to have ready to go. They all had the same look on their faces I probably had when I read the amount needed, based on time in the field. I had seen how much stuff we needed to carry. It was time to call for help.

I walked over to Jake's house for some ideas. Jake was always cool about things. He asked some questions and said the surplus store might have just what we were looking for. Jake finished his coffee and told Zack we were going to Northtown. Traffic was not bad getting there.

Inside the store, I asked the clerk where the bags for travel might be. Aisle three, half-way back, right-hand side. I was expecting everything to be olive drab. Not here. There was several colors. I unfolded one of the big ones. Yes, these would work. Jake got a cart. The shopping spree ended with twenty enormous bags and twenty large gym bags.

Jake had the idea of delivering all the bags today, so everyone had a way of knowing how much they could take. We made the rounds. All the stops went fairly fast until it was time to deliver Brent and Jill's.

The trip to Henderson was going to need a phone call first. Surprisingly, they had call forwarding. They were at their apartment only a half mile away. That was a piece of good luck. They lived in a real nice complex. Brent gave directions and we were there in minutes. We visited for a few minutes. It turns out the two of them had just got back from the site. They had built all of the new crane units. Jill made an off-color remark regarding the team finishing up the cranes.

"All idiots!"

∞

January 12, 1985, noon Zack

It seems the shopping frenzy is over for this go round. I'm splitting my time staying at Jake's, and Abby's. I've noticed Nancy stops in daily at Jake's. As she was helping him with just about anything he needed.

PHASE TWO

Start Date January 20, 1985
Told by Individuals

January 19, 1985, 8:00 A.M. Zack

I learned just a few days ago that Kay would be doing the house sitting. Gabby called earlier. The word is to be ready to go at 10:00 P.M. I called everyone and passed the information. Because of the number of us, a plain, unmarked bus will be picking us up. I finished my packing for the third time.

8:30 A.M. Jake

I made the call to Grandma and Grandpa to say I'm going to work. They said their bags were packed and they would be here by noon. My boy, I could see wasn't crazy about me going to work so I told him that I work and he's one step closer to being an animal doctor. He gave me a hug. Packing up the garage was a job by itself. It took two hours with Zack's help it was done. The house was in order for Mom and Dad.

9:30 A.M. Rodger

It's time for work. My wife and girls will do fine for money. We have plenty in the bank, no problem. Lisa has the emergency phone number so she can call. Being away is a pain, but the money's good. We will make it. I'm ready. The training classes were great. The van is in good shape, so no worries there. My bags are ready. I decided to pack extra writing paper mainly for the girls. Sometime today, I'll have to catch a nap.

10:00 A.M. Nancy

My bags are good and all. Mary is a little nervous. I made some additions for the kitchen stock. We're traveling at night. I wonder how weird it will be this time. I need to get busy cleaning. Mange has been to the vet and is in perfect health. The animal knows we're going. She's been dragging her towel all over the place and now has left it next to the bags. Kay called saying she would be stopping by to get a key for the house.

10:00 A.M. Bill

The two trucks fit in the garage like it was made for them. Locking up and picking up is the order of the day. Trash day is tomorrow, so I bummed space in Jake's trash can. It looks like others had the same idea. The training for the machines was real intense. Fred is the machine wizard. Set it and forget it. From the size and power, we're dealing with some heavy-duty stuff.

10:00 A.M. Fred

For the moment, about all I'm thinking about is what my bed in camp will be like. Bill is shaky about running high speed wire. Weather is cloud cover tonight so we can't plot by stars. I packed my whittling tools for down time. Jake said there was wood to be had--not great, but not too bad. The job itself doesn't sound too tough. I'm more interested in the people. Who knows how long we'll be out there?

10:30 A.M. Allen

It's finally time to go to work. I'm ready, but I still don't know the size of this thing. I guess I'll know soon enough. I figured I may need some tools, so I've got a travel bag put together.

10:30 A.M. Martin

Wow. Time to go, I don't know why at night. Time to burn wire, whatever this thing is, it's got to be a monster. All my stuff is ready I'm ready. Oh yeah, a tool bag. I almost forgot!

10:30 A.M. Terry

Time for work. Won't know much till we get there. I got everything gathered and my guitar. Kay got the key earlier. It's time to go.

11:00 A.M. Jack

I heard earlier it's time to go. Betty has all the information. The kids will be fine. It will be rough, but we'll make it. I promised the boys I would write them letters, as time allowed. Right now, I just want to be with my family. 10:00 tonight will be here soon enough.

11:00 A.M. Lloyd

It's time to go The house is ready. Kay got the key and was thrilled when she saw the sewing room. We had a nice chat. She remarked that she would like to stop back after work. The bags are by the door. I believe I should call Ann to see if she needs help.

11:30 A.M. Patty

A half hour ago, Jim left with Art and John for L.A. I hope he stays out of trouble. It's been like pulling teeth trying to get packed. I'm calling Nancy. She has to help me.

11:30 A.M. Ann

Lloyd called to see if I needed help. Am I glad he called! The housework was my main concern. He showed up ready to work. By 3:30, we were done. We went over my list for packing, the only things left were my knives. I'm ready. Everything is ready, and I need a bath so bad.

4:00 P.M. Mary

Six hours to go then 24/7. Nancy got back from Patty's and went down my list with me. It's a good thing she did. I forgot my med bag. I must admit, I am nervous about this job, but it may open other doors later on. All is done that needs doing.

10:00 P.M. Zack

The bus was out front on time. Jake gave everyone a hug. The second we were in our seats, we were moving around the block. Next on Mary, Nancy, Mange, Allen, Lloyd, Martin, Terry, and Ann. Then down two blocks for Bill, and Fred. The next stop was Patty, Jack, and Rodger. The driver handed me a note saying Jill and Brent were already at the base.

As each one of us got on the bus, Jake would hand out stick on name tags. When the last butt was in the seat, our driver wasted no time getting us to the air base. At the gate, we picked up Jill and Brent. It was different this time when we rolled through the gate. The driver radioed someone. Next we traveled to a hangar at the far end. The back side of the hanger was open.

When we stopped at least four guys came out of thin air to get our bags. Inside the hanger, Major Davis was directing the loading.

"Major, what's the movie on this flight?"

"Sorry Gentle, no movie, no stewardess, no snacks. Just me."

"What's the arrival time?"

"If all goes well, a little after midnight."

"That's not bad."

All the bags were in and tied in place. We were seated. The hanger doors were moving. Next, the tow hooked onto us. The ladies, less Ratchet, were about to freak out. The tow pulled the Chinook helicopter out. The Major came through the cabin checking seat belts and when he was up front the engines fired up. I was watching everyone, Buzz and Dog in particular. Yeah Navy Seals. Take off was quick and very smooth. The first leg was figured to last around twenty minutes. The Major put us on the ground a minute before a training squad of fighters came through. Well, our time here wasn't a total loss, as the flight line kitchen smelled good. We had a break not like the first trip out.

∞

INDEX OF NICKNAMES OR CODENAMES

[Zack.......Gentle]   [Bill........Buzz]   [Jack.......Pooch]

[Jake........Pink]   [Fred......Dog]   [Mary.....Nasty]

[Rodger...Cable]   [Allen......Wire]   [Ann........Salt]

[Nancy.....Ratchet]   [Lloyd.....Boomer]   [Patty...Pen]

[Mange....Mange]   [Martin...Slim]   [Jill.......JJ]

[Terry.......Cutter]   [Brent......Bud]

We shared some finger food. It was alright. The drinks were not bad at all. The hour layover was quick. We did enjoy the stop, but we had to keep moving. In minutes, we were airborne and moving. I could feel that we had some speed. I checked the time. We should be slowing. In a very short time, we were hovering as the Major set us down.

The blades slowed to a stop; the door was unlatched. The Major was taking the straps off the bags. The door opened and there was Smokey with a flatbed pulled right up to the door. The bags and us were quickly moved onto the truck. Along with our stuff, there were four very large coolers and two large flight bags. Smokey said the extra stuff was food and drink as getting settled may take three days.

We had landed a good four miles away from the site. As the big top came in sight, the entrance had moved. Inside, we could hear a small engine running a generator. Smokey turned on the lights. It was a good thing he did. None of the camp trailers were near the deck. The bags were left on the deck. Everyone found a bed and the day ended.

∞

January 20, 1985, 6:00 A.M. Gentle

I got up about 6:00. Salt had found the gas grill and breakfast was being made. Cable was going for coffee. I got some coffee. It wasn't quite daylight yet.

Cable: Gentle, it looks like a lot of work.

Gentle: I hope Smokey has a trick up his sleeve or the plans.

Smokey: I sure do.

Cable: Well good morning, Smokey. Coffee is on the deck.

Gentle: The camp needs to be first.

Smokey was back with a mug in hand.

Smokey: We can have the whole camp set up by 9:00 this morning.

Gentle: Who do you need?

Smokey: To make the job faster, JJ and me will run the small cranes to set the trailers in place. Pink and Dog can set the corner locks. The leveling should go just as fast with everything tied together.

Gentle: Smokey, the rest of it?

Smokey was sipping on his mug.

Smokey: I would say Pen and Pooch on the LP line. Then I'd put Wire and Bud on the power lines. The water line, that would be best for Nasty and Buzz. The wastewater should go fast. Not much digging Ratchet, Slim and Cable can handle it. And you have plans and prints to start going over.

By 3:00 P.M., all the systems for the camp were being tested. As for myself, if the showers and kitchen are running, its fine by me. By 4:30, it was good to go. I made the cube assignments by day and night shifts. The Krew filed off to their cubes, bags in hand, to make a temporary home. I went to my cube unpacked, grabbed my shower goods, and started to the showers. Oddly, all the old timers had the same idea. It was obvious we wanted to get cleaned up. The new folks slowly fell in line. Once I was dressed, I finished my unpacking and then straightened up my cube.

∞

Nasty was at the door with a glass of wine in hand.

"Gentle, here, you look like you need a mild sedative."

"You're the doctor, have a seat."

She took a seat on the edge of the bed.

"How are you fairing up, this being your first day?"

"OK. I just keep telling myself it will smooth out."

"That's the plan. How's your office doing?"

"It looks good. I need to go over the stock."

"That reminds me, I didn't see the second day work schedule or plans for areas set up."

"That sounds important."

We walked to the radio room; Pen was still working.

"Pen, have you seen any more plans?"

"There's some big rolls in the cabinet."

I found the starting plan, but not the one we needed. Smokey must have them at the supply yard.

5:00 P.M. Pink

Everyone did a great job today. Gentle has been looking for the camp plans. If we can hold this pace, we should be working in six days.

9:00 P.M. Cutter

Busy day and I can't believe the food is the best. Better than home cooking. I think this job is going to be one to remember.

9:00 P.M. Gentle

I was wondering how Gabby is doing. I need eight hours of shut eye! I finished my wine and went to bed.

∞

January 21, 1985, 5:00 A.M. Salt

This place is incredible. The air is cool and clean. If it wasn't for the generator, I think you could hear a pin drop a mile away. Breakfast. I should get moving.

5:30 A.M. Slim

The food and coffee. I'm hitting the showers. This is great man.

6:00 A.M. Gentle

Slim was in line for breakfast. The second day of real food may put him in shock. Coffee in hand, I had time to see where Smokey and Fats were. Well, the telescope says an hour or so. The sky looks a bit over-cast. We don't need a delay. Salt is a wizard in the kitchen.

6:30 A.M. Pooch

Something's going on, as Gentle and Pink have been in the radio room for a good twenty minutes. Sounds like they're calling for a meeting.

6:45 A.M. Pink

Pen had found the weather channel as I was taking notes.

"Is everyone here? Gentle is watching for Fats and Smokey, what's happening? We got a dust storm heading our way and it's a big one. We can't say how long it will last but we know it is going to be a mess around here."

Gentle: "Smokey has water, Fats has LP."

7:10 A.M. Smokey

"Gentle, I'm topping off all your water today. Go easy on it as I can't say how long to the next run. Fats is doin the LP, diesel fuel should be fine. Anything in the field been opened?"

"That I don't know, I'll check. You need help?"

"I'm good, just send Salt my way."

7:30 A.M. Gentle

Smokey and Fats weren't messing around. We well full. Nothing was opened in the field. Smokey said they were taking the interstate back. It was the railroad tracks. The trucks had dolly wheels for the rails. In minutes, they were heading straight into the storm. I had the golf cart floored back to camp. The cart was put away in a container. The next order of business, a head count sixteen and a dog. We stood out front watching the wall of sand and dirt coming our way. Mother Nature gave us two days off with two long days of clean up.

∞

January 25, 1985, 5:00 A.M. Salt

The storm business is over. If anything, everyone is caught up on sleep. I know I am. The oven has to be warmed up by now. This is going to be a great day.

6:00 A.M. Bud

I have been going over the electrical side of the tower crane and something is not matching up. It has no functions, no matter what. All it does is pop the circuit breakers. Something is seriously wrong. JJ and I started going through the check list and spec sheets. We went over the entire control system piece by piece. Every system in and on.

The tower is right. All the connections are in place and right. We had decided to get Cutter and Wire involved. The two of them may have an idea why it's not powering up.

6:30 A.M. JJ

As I was working with Bud, I noticed the primary beam was bowed. I put on my safety harness. I got on top of the main boom catwalk. As I walked out, I was nearly sick. Those idiot bastards! Every bolt is backwards! Walking back, the news didn't improve any. Where the hell are the counterweights? As Bud was finishing in the cab, I started pointing out all the problems.

7:30 A.M. Pink

Gentle was out at the generators as Cutter was explaining what was going on with the tower. The generator that was connected to the tower was the generator for the welders. The other generator wouldn't work with anything we had. It looked like the old boy's head was about to explode.

8:00A.M. Gentle

I knew I was going to have to move fast on all these crane troubles. Smokey was called first. I knew he was working on opening the road here. So, I got him on the radio.

"Hey Smokey, you there?"

"Sure am. What's for lunch?"

"Quick question, are the rail cars still in the yard the ones that carried the giant crane frame parts?"

"There sure are and there's a bunch of crates that have never been touched."

"I know you can't do it now, but we need those parts. Are there any extra generators out there?"

"As soon as we get there we're starting on the interstate, and the generators, nope."

"Lunch is grill steak sandwiches and tater salad."

"We'll be there by noon. See you then."

Alright the crane parts are in the works now. Not my department. Someone must know something about the generator problem. I called Gabby. She said she would start looking. I called the Major to see if anything may have been left at the base. No, we had everything. Art was called, and I explained what we were dealing with. I was told he would call me back. That was one really long hour to wait. So, while I waited, we had a thrown together meeting, which worked out pretty good. These people are seeing the way of working together. They were coming up with great ideas. As it moved along there, were drawings to support the ideas.

Art called back in about an hour. Our power plant was in a warehouse in Richmond, Virginia. The one odd ball we had should have gone to a hospital in Mississippi. Art said something I didn't really expect. The power plant would be here first thing in the morning. All we had to do was have the one for the hospital ready to be picked up. It had been determined the generator now connected to the tower was for the welders and needed to be moved.

Nasty got with me asking if she and some others could look over the area layout. I agreed to it for the moment, as we would be waiting. The rest of the day they continued studying the camp and field. I wonder what Nasty was working on.

7:00 P.M. Buzz

I haven't done anything yet in the way of welding. I don't understand the codename business--just as long as I see one fat bank book.

8:30 P.M. Boomer

Ratchet, Pen, and Nasty are in the radio room working on the area's layout plan. Cable and Salt are in the kitchen setting up tomorrow's feed. Dog, Gentle, Pink, and Pooch have a card game going. Wire and Buzz are out front walking around. Cutter is sitting at the table playing his guitar and I'm just sitting with a glass of wine.

9:00 P.M. Nasty

This day is done, a fast shower and bed. It looks like some of the others have the same idea. Oh well, the line should be short.

∞

January 26, 1985, 4:45 A.M. Salt

It's a cool morning, feels like forty degrees. The kitchen is warming up. There are lights in the valley.

6:00 A.M. Cutter

Salt said it looked like Smokey would be here soon. I went to get Cable, as I didn't know the first thing about end loaders--even with the classes.

6:00 A.M. Cable

Coffee to go. Cutter had a cart waiting and ready to go. We headed across the field to warm up the end-loader and wait. From out in the field, it looked like he pulled in and made a pitstop and was coming out to us. By 7:15, our generator was in place. The odd ball was on the truck. He said on his way out that he would be back around noon.

They would be getting the switch engine to help clean up the tracks. Nasty talked to me about some changes in the field. Maybe now she should say something.

8:00 A.M. Gentle

The ladies and I are having a get together. The ideas Nasty has have been quite valid. First, the lift lines are only used to remove the plates from the rail cars, having them in a central location by the track. The cables used for loading, as well as the cables used for fixtures, needed to be on the field side. Nasty had a place picked out by the southeast corner near the diesel tank. I knew she was trying to make a safer working space. Moving the containers needed to be centered at the south end of the field made sense.

The one idea that I wanted to hear more about was the idea Ratchet had for reloading the baskets. She received help from Boomer and Slim for drawings with a detailed layout of the east side. I told them to make it happen! I want it ready to be put in place as soon as the mat is down. Work started on the spool rack in minutes.

It was time to check with the team working on the tower. JJ said they needed a bucket truck to fix all the bolts that were put in wrong. A quick call to Smokey and a bucket truck would be here in an hour. Bud was running system tests and said it was looking good. By noon, everyone was in camp for lunch. Smokey had pictures of some of the missing parts still in the rail cars. JJ pointed out the crates that would make up the missing counterweights. The problem was moving the weights from the rail cars to the field. Rodo remembered the mine had a surplus of end-loaders. At 5:00 that afternoon, all crane parts and then some were in camp.

∞

January 27, 1985, 5:00 A.M. Boomer

Salt brought me a coffee. I liked Nasty's ideas. I had a few ideas, so I decided to try some on Nasty just to see her reaction. She joined me for breakfast. We talked about our ideas and we did share, one which was lights in the reload area. Bud and JJ no more than got breakfast down and got Cutter to start up the tower power plant. I really wanted to see how they were going to get the weights over thirty feet up and fastened in place.

9:00 A.M. Ratchet

I had the telescope at the railroad door watching the staging area. I couldn't guess the number of rail cars already sitting there. It wasn't long when Gentle found me.

"It's going to be a monster."

"Do you really think we can build this in 110 days?"

"Ratchet, I'm not sure this rotten start hasn't helped. Hey, come on. The guys are starting the tower crane."

10:00 A.M. Bud

Programming this beast isn't bad at all. JJ did a great job laying out the controls. Now to put this through some basic moves then and park it.

Noon Gentle

When lunch was finished, it was back into the field. The spool rack looked plenty strong. I can't tell how many it holds. I knew it was time to make the shift selection. This is one of those things from the classes with the Major. It was my best guess! I found Pink, only to tell him I was making out the shift list for personnel.

"Just put me on nights, old boy. Please."

"Thanks for making it easier."

First, I need to pick out the night shift that will fit together. Ladies first Ratchet and Pen, the nurse, and a cook. Pink and Slim should match up Boomer and Dog or Wire. That's all four baskets for welders and Bud in the crane. Next, I figured it would be best to have a talk with Nasty and Salt. JJ was in the crane making test runs and system checks. My conversation with Salt was quick. She said the kitchen and laundry, along with the radio room, gave her a full plate. I understood her completely. I was looking out from the deck as the rubber matting was being put down in the field. It was to protect the edges of the plates from damage.

Nasty was in her office doing paperwork.

"Nasty, you and I need to have a chat."

"Sure, when?"

"Now. Let's go for a ride. You'll need your binoculars."

We took a cart, as I was working on the best way to approach the subject.

"Gentle, what's on your mind?"

"Well, I believe I painted myself into a corner. It's like this, I'm still short-handed."

"Look I can't sit in the office like some damn princess. If you have got work that I can do, I'll do it."

"Thank you. OK, let's get you set up."

We gathered all the tools she would need.

3:45 P.M. Nasty

I have a section. Now I need to refine it. Make it fast, simple, and safe. I asked Slim, Boomer, and Ratchet for help getting everything set up. By 6:00 I had a working model complete with lights.

7:30 P.M. Pen

I heard the guys out on the deck. I had just gotten a call from Smokey saying he and Fats would be here at sunrise with four trailers of supplies. Sounds like plenty to do tomorrow.

10:45 P.M. Pink

The camp is quiet now, with only the one generator running. Going on nine days and the welding towers are all that's left.

∞

January 28, 1985, 5:00 A.M. Smokey

Those folks on the hill are going to jump for joy. They're getting mail. Now, the rest of the stuff I got, who knows? There is one thing and that's Salt's breakfast. I should be pulling in about twenty minutes.

6:00 A.M. Cutter

Slim and I are fueling everything here, diesel and gas. Thought it would take hours, but we were done in less than an hour.

6:30 A.M. Ratchet

Cable and Gentle are in a basket on the tower crane looking at the top of the welding towers. I went to get the binoculars. Too late. They were coming back to park the crane.

7:00 A.M. Pink

The old boy is mad. Something on the towers has him really upset. He was in the radio room the second he was back in camp. The moment he came out, he and Smokey were heading to the supply yard. Pen stuck her head out the door saying Art would be here this morning. Well, if Art's involved, its big!

9:30 A.M. Gentle

We found a lot of the missing parts based on what JJ and Bud had shown me in rough drawings. Now it was a matter of hauling it back to camp. Rodo was in the yard. Smokey got him lined up with all the goods that needed to be moved. Rodo was on it. Hopefully it would be the last of the missing parts that should have been in place.

Smokey gave me a quick tour of their home in the supply yard. All I could say was wow! It didn't look like much on the outside, but the inside was huge. It had all the comforts of home from end to end. Then it was back to camp with a load of water in tow.

12:30 P.M. Buzz

Nasty and I were looking down the valley on the telescope. Maybe fifteen minutes out it looks like Smokey.

"Nasty, I would say we should be ready for whatever is thrown at us."

"I think you're right."

We passed the word and waited.

1:00 P.M. Gentle

When we pulled into camp, the bulk of the Krew was on the deck. Pen came out of the radio room and was heading my way.

"Gentle, Art and Bob are flying in. They said they should be here in fifteen minutes."

"Thanks, Pen. Anything else?"

"I left your mail on the bed."

"All good news I hope."

"I think it is."

Smokey was on the radio trying to get a time Rodo would be starting this way. I got with JJ and Bud to see how much it was going to take to get the basket cranes in working order. The two of them said they would go over every inch of the cranes and have an answer by sundown.

Cable and Pooch got some carts to go out to pick up Art and Bob. I noticed as our guests arrived with bags, not briefcases. Strange, nothing was said about an overnight. After a round of greetings Art made his way over to me.

"Art, welcome to camp. WILL IT EVER WORK?"

"Gentle, give me a tour please."

"No problem."

We left the camp in a cart heading for the railroad side.

"Gentle, a penny for your thoughts. American money."

"Keep the penny, just tell me how this got so screwed up."

"That was my mistake."

"You? Really Art, you know this is about speed out here. Everything from the time we got here has been screwed up or wrong."

"I was told by someone I trusted about the construction group to prep the place for phase two. I made a bad move in hiring, so I'll take the blame."

"Bishop?"

"Yeah."

"Well, you have eyes and ears on us?"

"Yes, but only to know how it's going."

"It's Smokey. You two are old buddies?"

"It's a little more than that. He is my half-brother."

We talk business for a while then, Art asked something that caught me off guard.

"Can you show me where Spin died?"

"Sure. It's best to see it from above. Bud can give us a lift."

Bud was rounded up; Art was in a harness, and it was an open-air elevator ride to five hundred feet. Bud swung the boom over then he set us down next to the spot. Art was very quiet.

"Thank you."

Bud lifted us up then set us in the parking place.

"So, what's your itinerary?"

"First, get a ballpark estimate on how much time it will take to be operational. Then I need some time with Pen about her son."

"Not bad news?"

"No, no, quite the opposite. That young man is brilliant."

"Maybe that will help her with their separation."

"I will be staying to talk to everyone and have supper here just to see if what I've heard is true."

"So, you're going to be looking for a reason or an excuse to come out this way for Groundhog's Day."

"I can say this. Yes, no, maybe."

I could tell Art was as concerned with the project as I am.

4:30 P.M. JJ

I'm not sure Gentle will like what I found wrong. All I can do is tell him. He was sitting at the table studying blueprints.

"Excuse me, I have the list of areas and items requiring attention."

"Is this for the main tower or the basket towers?"

"The main tower only has the locating system to be installed and Bud can put that in at any time."

"The basket towers. What about them?"

"They are totally screwed up. We have to have the main hooked to each one just to do the connection on top. This is the one that tells me all four were broken into and damaged. We had locked the panels on the hydraulic systems. All of them have been messed with. As far as the time to make repairs, I'm guessing a day each at best."

"Thank you, it's enough for today. Close up shop out there and hit the showers. OK."

"OK."

Holy cow, I thought he would go nuts.

5:15 P.M. Dog

Oh man, Gentle is coming out here and Bud is some kind of crazy in the containers.

"Gentle, the dude, he's crazy. Like snapped, you know?"

We heard him carrying on inside one.

"Not crazy, pissed off. No problem."

5:20 P.M. Bud

I can't believe it! Those idiots unpacked everything and dropped it in a pile. This is not good.

"Bud, what the hell are you carrying on about?"

"Oh, Gentle, I didn't hear you come in. It's like this everything you see here was boxed up and labeled. I don't know how long it's going to take just to sort this out."

"Bud, let's close up. Tomorrow you are going to have help. For now, hit the showers. You don't want to be late for supper."

"OK."

6:00 P.M. Art

I gave a little speech to the Krew. Then I settled down to a meal suitable enough to be considered fine dining, less the linens. My talk with Pen came as quite a shock to her. She couldn't believe the grades he was getting in school. I can say this, having him around is a true challenge. Dog and Buzz are very interesting gentlemen. The surprising thing about them was having master's degrees in rather odd subjects.

8:30 P.M. Bob

Art just left with Smokey for the storage lot. Nearly all the paperwork is done for everyone in camp. It still makes me wonder how all of this is put together. This day has been long enough for me. Time for some sleep.

∞

January 29, 1985, 4:30 A.M. Salt

It's cold this morning. The temp must be forty degrees. The showers will be fast this morning. Best get the coffee going. They'll be up soon.

5:30 A.M. Nasty

The shower was an eye opener. The guys are studying the camp layout plans. Bob was the last out of bed, which worked out well for Salt. Not much in the way of leftovers.

8:00 A.M. Gentle

Bob said his flight out was about 8:30. We talked right up to the time his ride showed up. For the next four days, from sun-up to sundown, it was all hands working on the cranes. On the morning of the fifth day, the loading of the field with the two hundred twenty-ton plates began.

∞

February 6, 1985, Noon Ratchet

I started the hotel radio link key switch.

"Atlanta A. K."

"Atlanta A. K."

"Hotel A.K."

We are running.

PHASE TWO RUNNING

Told by individuals

February 10, 1985, 6:00 A.M. Nasty

Getting the first row of panels up was something to see. I've been watching everyone's health closely. The timing of all the work is to the minute. The funniest thing to me is at 5:30 in the morning, its breakfast for the day shift. At 5:30 in the afternoon its breakfast for the night shift. The guys are starting the second row of panels. Pink said once the first two rows of panels are up, it should take only a day and a half to lock it in then start the next row.

∞

February 12, 1985, Noon JJ

Row three is in progress. When everything is going smooth, I can almost do five panels an hour. I was afraid this job would be boring, but it's great. I love it! Bud has it rough at night with limited light.

∞

February 14, 1985, Midnight Pink

Slow and steady on the crane. As far as this welding goes, it's hot and fast. I figured three spools of wire in three hours and the gas figured out to four tanks for twelve hours. Slim is the fastest guy with a welding gun out here, next to Gentle.

∞

February 20, 1985, 9:00 A.M. Gentle

We're not far from two hundred feet. Bud and JJ were telling me about a wireless locating system for the crane. Bud had seen one in use on a container crane. I felt, why not. I called Art to run this stuff down and get it to us A.S.A.P. The scheduling of days off wasn't as simple as I had thought, but it got worked out. The thing I noticed is everyone has settled into their shift fairly well.

∞

February 28, 1985, 6:00 A.M. Ratchet

At three weeks, everyone was doing very well medically. Sleep for the guys was a good eight to nine hours. Art and the Major flew in with some crates and a fast meeting. Art handed Gentle a briefcase, then Pink took it after Gentle got papers from it. Nasty has been exercising to get a chance at a necklace.

∞

March 2, 1985, 6:00 A.M. Gentle

Art had found the locating system for the cranes and a whole lot more. Bud, Wire and JJ did all the installation work. The generators were being serviced along with everything else. The night shift turned in at 9:00 A.M. Smokey and Fats rolled in around 8:00 with water. We were thirty thousand gallons down. We would be getting more water, mail, food, fuel. Everything was to be at the max; the goods received were parked, stacked, and stored in record time.

6:00 P.M. Pink

All that's left is moving spools of wire into staging or storage. Barely two hours of work and the time was ours. It was funny in a way--time off, free time. We just plain stopped. Everyone relaxed in their own way.

∞

March 3, 1985, 6:00 P.M. Nasty

All have had full exams. Salt and Pen have provided the diets of all in camp and in the field. Stress is centered on safety for themselves and others. To this point, all that I have had to treat for is cuts and scrapes. Buzz and Gentle have given me a list of exercises and goals for welding.

∞

March 6, 1985, Noon Buzz

It looks like another two or three days and we'll be at the halfway point going up. Gentle and Pink both said seven to eight days to finish weld the bottom half.

∞

March 8, 1985, 11:30 P.M. Bud

That's it, the last plate to the halfway mark! The locators have cut the time to set a plate to near nothing. I know the guys burning wire are going to go nuts with the cruise controls JJ and I installed.

∞

March 9, 1985, 6:00 A.M. Gentle

Bud explained the cruise control to everyone. All four baskets on the same weld, Slim drew up a set of weld patterns then said we could run the machines five percent under the high limit no problem. It took a while for us to get in position. With the controls set, we were running.

6:00 P.M. Pink

Gentle filled us in on how they run. The old boy wasn't kidding, you're moving. That figured out to just over eighty-six tons of wire per shift.

∞

March 16, 1985, 6:00 A.M. Cable

Smokey and Fats just left for another load. All the usual service work is under way. I would like to know what are we doing with the giant pile of cables in the bottom of that?

11:30 A.M. JJ

The tower is in excellent shape. The field is empty, so there's more than enough room for the cables. The baskets are parked at the camp end. If I play this right, it should take two hours to put all of it in the field.

1:00 P.M. Gentle

All of the day shift were in the field putting away the cables. By 6:00P.M. we had made a sizable dent in the pile.

6:00 P.M. Slim

Wow, what a mess! This could be an all-nighter. It was like real work. By 3:30, we had all that crap put back in the containers.

∞

March 17, 1985, 7:00 A.M. Nasty

Checkups for all, then reports to do. Maybe lay out in the sun for a while. I got my necklace for a full 12-hour shift. It was different. Even with the welding gun resting on the rail of the basket, the concentration needed to stay focused was incredible. Pink has sized me for my necklace. Ratchet wasn't joking. I hurt for two days after just one shift. I tried talking to Gentle about how they built up the stamina for this kind of work. His and the others all gave the same answer. TIME. For now, it's our day off and I'm taking advantage of every minute.

∞

March 18, 1985, 6:00 A.M. Gentle

We only have maybe three more days of straight welding to do. We got the word. The new lift and suspension cables were in the storage yard. The method of assembly is something like the lower half. The welding was more detailed on the blueprints.

Salt tells me that someone is on the road, moving fast this way. One call to Smokey and he said the Major was enroute. Nasty was in the railroad door watching as I was in the driveway doing the same. This was weird. Someone got passed Smokey. We were wearing our headsets for talking to one another in the field.

"Gentle, it looks like a school bus."

"Yeah, school is about to start. Look down the valley."

"What are those?"

"Attack helicopters. Gunships I'd say."

"Do you think there'll be killing?"

"This place is supposed to be a super top-secret Area 71."

"So, you weren't kidding when you said no talking about this place."

"That's right."

It didn't take long before the bus stopped. The blast from the machine guns may have had something to do with that. The bus turned around and was leaving the valley. My guess would be whoever was on the bus was going to have an unpleasant greeting at Smokey's. The balance of the day was our usual rhythm.

∞

March 24, 1985, Midnight Pink

The plates are nearly falling in place. I was studying the order of welding and found it just too strange to be workable. Boomer and Slim looked it over. I asked Gentle to call the engineer on this; he agreed it was weird.

The Major stopped in yesterday at shift change, along with the storage yard trio. Mainly for breakfast, but we got updates, mail, and the shipment timetable. The bus from a few days ago was full of officers that had slipped in behind a semi. In short, they were sightseeing. Pooch has had problems calling home, as it seems his wife has gotten a job. He asked me if my folks could check on the boys. No problem.

∞

March 26, 1985, 2:00 P.M. Buzz

Something is going on. First, Gentle is called to the radio room, so he's on the ground. Then an hour later, Pooch is on the ground. Gentle gets me on the headset asking me to train Nasty on tack up. I said OK. Nasty, I can say this, as a person who knows nothing about welding, she is easy to teach.

6:00 P.M. Nasty

I did four more hours in the field. Buzz gives really good and direct instructions. Art, Bob, and a stranger were dropped off a while ago. The Major stayed with the helicopter. Pooch and Art flew out immediately.

∞

March 27, 1985, 6:00 A.M. Gentle

Bob was reviewing the inventory and usage sheets. Art had brought the engineer out to explain the odd assembly process. At breakfast, our guest was introduced Mr. Earl Jones. He was familiar. Slim recognized him immediately.

"Gentle, that's Earl Jones. The dude that wrote the book."

"That Earl Jones?"

"I took one of his classes. The dude knows his stuff, man."

Mr. Jones gave a detailed explanation of the welding process. He suited up and at 9:00 A.M. Cable, Buzz, Cutter, and Earl were going up for a shift.

Bob got with me about Pooch. It seems his wife Betty picked up a rather bad drug habit. She overdosed and had wiped out the family bank account. His boys had been living at Cable's place for almost a week. Her body was found in Henderson, but the police say her death was questionable, as her fingerprints were not on the syringe. Art had all the information but said we could talk about it at camp. Kay hired a live-in nanny.

From all this bad news came a ray of hope and help. Earl said he would be glad to fill in for Pooch if it was OK with the management. As he was part of the office team, all he needed was work clothes and a toothbrush.

∞

April 1, 1985, Noon Salt

Word spread that Pooch would be back in a few days. Earl works a noon to midnight shift that takes the pressure off both shifts.

∞

April 5, 1985, 6:00 A.M. Gentle

Pooch is back. He appears to be in good shape. Earl asked to stay on a few more days. I couldn't say no to his offer. If anything, we have three lady welders now. Earl got all three trained in a week. I must say, they're good. Like really good. One thing I noticed, was that it took a while. Earl was not a wine drinker. His choice of drink was sherry. The rumor in camp is that the first week of May phase two will be done. From my point of view, the second week sounds doable. The usual routine was back in rhythm.

∞

April 7, 1985, 4:30 P.M. Cutter

We just set the last plate for three quarters up on the job. Tomorrow morning is service work. Someone said Art would be here on our down day.

∞

April 8, 1985, 6:00 A.M. Pink

Day shift was on the job. I checked the list with Gentle and the night shift would still have plenty to do. The list was not our normal list. The first thing that caught my eye was the amount of food and water.

10:00 A.M. Gentle

Service day madness! Pooch, Cutter, and Cable on generators, then they move to the cranes. JJ and Buzz were doing the tower. Nasty and I will be topping off everything needing fuel. Then we move to gas tanks and spools. Pen had a message for me earlier from Art. It was about Pooch's boys saying they were doing exceptionally well. He was planning on being here on our next day off.

∞

April 9, 1985, 4:30 A.M. Pen

The kitchen is loaded. It's going to be a warm one today I can feel it already. We finished all the jobs at 4:00 A.M. All that's left is water for the camp tanks and diesel in the main storage tank.

7:00 A.M. Bud

Well, all the girls hit the showers and were on their way out front for some tanning. I've got some letters to write, but for now I'm going to clean up and get some sleep.

2:30 P.M. Gentle

I had concerns about Pooch. I'm hopeful Art might have a counselor he can talk to. I do believe the ladies are trying to set a record for bronzing themselves. I just spent twenty minutes on the phone with Gabby. This visit with Art on our next break has me wondering. We haven't got shut down orders yet.

∞

April 10, 1985, 6:00 A.M. Cable

JJ was up early and the generators were running! She was checking the systems in the tower. I got her on the headset to ask why so early. She said Rodo and Smokey would be here at 6:30. A fast breakfast happened, then all of us were ready to unload railcars. Gentle has been watching Mange, as she's been acting funny. Smokey was about to pull into the field when Mange went nuts barking. The dog ran off the deck barking. Smokey stopped his big rig to see what was up with Mange. He walked to the front of the truck.

"Gentle, get out here."

Gentle left the deck. Mange was still freaking out. Smokey was getting something from the cab. It was a snake stick and a bag. They walked over to the crane hook, where a fairly large rattlesnake was resting. It took a minute or two, but they got it in the bag.

8:00 A.M. Gentle

The train was here shortly after Smokey arrived. The snake didn't help start the day. Salt brought me my headset; it was Fats on the line. He gave me the news that rain was heading straight for us. Great, all the wire and baskets had to be covered. It took an hour to get everything covered. Nasty was in the driveway with the telescope.

"Smokey and Rodo were moving fast and from the looks of the sky, so is the rain."

Well, it's down time, the nightshift was waiting to see what it would be like. Everyone grabbed a cart and went to join Nasty. Pink and the night Krew joined in. Cable had a big goofy grin. So did Pink. We watched as it was heading right to us. It was a heavy down pour. The question was is it a warm rain? We could hear it coming then. It's warm. In seconds, we strip down and were having a shower courtesy of Mother Nature. All of us just stood for a warm water thirty-minute soaking before starting back to camp. It ended in an hour.

∞

April 11, 1985, 6:00 A.M. Nasty

The vacation time is over. It was time to work. As it was still quite humid, everyone was dressed lightly. This is a very slow start. The guys were checking everything. These guys were ready to sew this phase up.

∞

April 21, 1985, 10:00 A.M. Buzz

It's taking three days per row. The travel time on the tower crane has slowed down. Regardless, safety comes first, because if someone gets stupid around here, someone could die.

∞

April 29, 1985, Noon Gentle

The last plate has been put in place for phase two. My best guess now is six days of burning wire and it would be shut down. Then Phase Three. By the end of our shift, the tacking should be done. The nightshift will start on the service work. So, it's a little head start. The usual list was handled in the usual way. Everyone pushed themselves to get as much done as possible. The day shift called it a day at 9:00 P.M. Pink and the nightshift should have no problem finishing up.

11:00 P.M. Pink

My guess, two and a half hours to finish. We went in for midnight chow to find Ratchet and Pen were standing on the tables.

"Snakes."

"Yeah."

"How many?"

"Six, I think."

We got the stun sticks and proceeded to zap rattlers, ten in all. Someone forgot to turn on the electric fence. Lunch was late. It was 3:00 A.M. when we finished.

∞

April 30, 1985, 5:30 A.M. Pen

I just received a call from Atlanta saying Art would be here at 8:30 A.M. Knowing that I made up a few dozen muffins for Major Davis to take back with him, as everyone flies here.

6:00 A.M. Gentle

I was having breakfast when Pen reminded me that Art was coming out. Nasty and Ratchet sat down with me. The two of them said I needed exercise.

"OK, like what?"

"A jog."

"Sure, I can do that."

Little did I know, they were going on a morning snake kill. I got some shoes on, my low tops, I had the kill stick, while the ladies had both sticks a kill and stun sticks. The two plus mile jog and kill took an hour. Seventy plus snakes had a bad day. We were heading for the showers.

"Gentle, the Major said he's fifteen minutes out."

The three of us made a mad dash for the showers then the run to our cubes to get dressed. I could hear the helicopter coming in. Guests is all I remembered. For the most part, who or why, no clue.

Nasty was on a cart to deliver muffins and pick-up guests. I had a weird feeling that something was not right. Nasty parked the cart, Art and two other big guys hopped out. Once they were on the dec Art started the introductions.

8:40 A.M. Art

"Good morning everyone, the gentlemen that are with me today are your Krew into phase three. At this point in, the program is one month ahead of schedule. Thank you. Now this is Dwight Lee, codename Deuce, This gentleman is Maurice Smith, codename Morry. Gentle would you take over?"

"Sure, Art. Would you round up the others? Two are on the road and two out front please."

"No problem."

8:50 A.M. Gentle

"Deuce, Morry, welcome to camp hell or codename Hotel. I am Gentle. Not boss or anything like that please. I came up with the original design for this monster. On dayshift, I'm the lead person in the field. This ridiculously handsome gentleman is Pink, nightshift lead man and second in charge. Next is the support team. First and foremost member, Mange, our camp dog. She earns her keep by warning us of snakes nearby. Now our medical team is Ratchet, registered nurse and our doctor, Nasty. The two of them are working on a paper on high heat workers. At this point, I believe mingle would be best."

Salt and Boomer were nearly dressed heading for the showers. Wire and Pooch had been out picking up dead snakes. I was trying to help Nasty with her suit when I heard Morry.

"Sherry? Sherry is that you?"

"Smith, what the hell did you do to land here?"

"Lloyd Sherry, you crazy bastard."

"Lee, you too? Both of you clowns. So where is the rest of the circus?"

Nasty was stuck in her suit.

"Boomer, help me I'm stuck. It won't unzip."

"OK guys it's past my bedtime. I'll see you around six. Nasty, you, and I will fit this suit later, please."

Art and I got in a cart. Then I got the rest of the story.

"Gentle, this crew that's coming in are the people that will assemble the inside of the Hotel. I'm trying to make this seamless."

"Makes sense to me."

"I got a small problem, however."

"OK let's hear it."

"I don't have cooks or medical people."

"Now, that is a problem Art, but there may be an answer. It's fairly simple. Money. Double time plus bonus for work on site seven to ten days. Ask and wait."

"That's so crazy it might work."

"I heard the rest of the folks will be coming here this afternoon."

"Correct, that is so they are set up as you finish their housing."

We went back to camp. Art had the plans in the office. I took a good deal of time studying them. These guys have got a lot on their plate. There's a hundred plus miles of cable to be put in.

10:30 P.M. Nasty

Smokey is in the valley and Rodo is moving our way. The guys were sitting around the deck waiting. JJ has gone out front for some sun with Buzz. All the exams are up to date. Art is all over the place. It's looking like we were going to lose some down time.

11:00 A.M. Cable

Gentle, Art, Deuce, and Morry have been in the office a half hour. No one has a clue of what's going on. Smokey was starting to get a bit upset. There were some words said by Smokey. It didn't take long after he put his two cents in that we were working. Their housing was set in by Noon. By 1:00 P.M., move in ready. By 2:00 P.M., the field had been rearranged for them to begin work.

3:30 P.M. Gentle

Looking out the railroad side, I could see Rodo loading our staging area. Looking towards the supply yard on the horizon there was a Chinook helicopter coming this way. Bad enough working in this heat. Now I'm a zookeeper. I just know something is going to go sideways. I drove back to camp wondering if Art had made a mistake.

"Nasty, we need the service truck. Where're Deuce and Morry?"

"I can have the truck ready in a few minutes, Deuce was in the radio room. Morry and Art are on a joy ride."

"Get Deuce and head for the truck."

I made it to the truck and started unloading the racks for the baskets. Nasty and Deuce pulled up and we were on the road. The Chinook looked about five miles out as we were on the hill. Major Davis had a spot where he lands. Nasty was at the wheel; she drove just passed it and turned around to pull in alongside. He set it down and we waited for the signal to pull up, The Major said we needed more deck space. We unfolded the back end and loaded bags, kitchen goods, medical items, and ten people.

The trip back to camp was slower, as I wanted some time in the sun. Of course, the new people needed to know the meaning of overdressed. The short fifteen-minute drive back would help their acclimation. In camp. the unloading of all the goods went fast.

"Morry, Deuce you'll have to figure who is on what shift. So, we can get your folks moved in."

"You got it, Gentle. Everyone over here. Now please."

Mange started barking. We got up to check, Pooch and Cable, grabbed zap sticks and went hunting.

5:15 P.M. Boomer

JJ and Bud were going to get me up to date on the tower crane. It's going to be great working with Deuce and his people again. I guess that in one week most of us will be home. Deuce and I had a long talk about the place and Gentle. He was surprised when he heard Gentle had big money from selling the plans for this. I explained the bonus plan on this job, I thought he was about to pass out. It was breakfast time for me.

6:00 P.M. Ratchet

The new people aren't going to make it. The two gals with them are about to drop.

6:30 P.M. Art

"Great meal Salt. Now the short list we have some of the best craftsmen and women here. I asked Gentle if some help might be provided by the Krew from tower operators, kitchen, medical, and ground Krew as support."

Deuce: "Art would you tell everyone here the pay and bonus ratio."

Art: "Certainly, everyone here is paid one-hundred dollars for every hour you are in camp. Your scheduled for seventy-seven days you will make let's say $185,000. That said should you complete the job say fourteen days early you will still be paid the $185,000 plus a half million per week. I will be back here in the morning so if you have any other questions please make a note. Where is Pen?"

"Here."

"Office please."

8:30 P.M. Gentle

Morry had his nightshift team picked out. Pink would be doing ground training to start the first four hours. Ratchet would be doing the next four hours on diet for the nightshift personnel. Boomer and Bud would be doing the training on the baskets. Deuce and I had a long talk about what might make the job faster for his team. He was paying attention, only saying that he wanted to study the layout and plans more.

∞

May 1, 1985, 5:00 P.M. Salt

More people here, isn't a problem for me. The new folks eat like they were starving. It's tricky making sure all of them get a balanced diet. It's going to be another hot one today. My guess is one-hundred-fifteen degrees.

5:50 A.M. Deuce

Everything on the prints is straight forward. What I see is a time and distance problem. Finding Gentle was easy, he was in the showers. Slim was running for the shower. Gentle was still dripping wet with Slim, right behind him.

"Deuce, one of your people is in the field cutting banding you get out there and stop them, NOW!"

It was Moose, my troublemaker.

"Moose, stop it!"

"Stop what? I'm just doing my job."

"Where did you get that necklace?"

"I found it."

"You stole it. Hand it over."

"No"

"You're out of here pack your bag."

The idiot stealing from these people. I gave this guy too many breaks already he's off the team.

6:00 A.M. Gentle

It was Cable's necklace that was missing. Deuce was back from the field with one of his people. Slim showed up with more bad news. The cable tightening systems were damaged. This big dude struts across the deck.

" I'm leaving."

"You're leaving the necklace on the table."

"Screw you."

As he went to his cube for his things, Buzz slipped onto the roof with a zap stick.

"I'll take you out to the helicopter myself. Just leave the necklace and all your travels will be handled."

"You must not hear too good. I said SCREW YOU."

The fool was coming out the screen door. Buzz nailed him in the back of the neck.

"Buzz, nice job."

"Now what?"

"Strip him and tie him up please or I will kill him."

Smokey and Art were pulling in. Buzz, Nasty, and Salt had the bull line and was neatly binding him up. Ratchet came back from the field with more news. The generators were opened. The diesel tank was dripping, and the welding wire was cut on the spools.

"JJ, Bud, get on that tower and check it, end to end. Cable, Pooch, the diesel tank. Salt, Pen, check the camp inside and out. Cutter, Wire, the generators. Boomer, Slim the baskets. Nasty, Ratchet, check the water supply. Deuce, Morry, you pick three from your team to strip and sanitize that cube. You two do a fine-tooth comb inspection on all your goods in the field. Morry, run out there and bring back a one-foot sample of the banding. Thank you. Art, one slipped through the cracks. As it stands, at the moment, there's got to be over a half million in damage. Time wise, unknown."

"Why is he still alive?"

"Oh, I want to kill him, but having him locked away, far away. I believe he will like island life."

"Guantanamo?"

"That's right."

Smokey was on the radio to Fats and Rodo for what to bring here for repairs.

"GENTLE!" It was Salt carrying Mange. "She's dead."

That was the last straw. Ratchet's dog killed by this sick animal. Guantanamo for the rest of his life, naked. The water in one the twenty-five thousand-gallon trailers contaminated. The damage reports just kept coming in. The unwanted former employee was moved outside. Smokey had a load of damaged tooling. Pink brought me my Speedos and vest. Art was on the phone to the manufacturer of the cable tools. All he had to do was get them to Sweden, as they had replacements.

The list of damage and destroyed items and areas was all in by 9:30A.M. The misfit was on his way to Guantanamo, but Ratchet got to him before he was hauled away. For the life of me I could not figure out where she got a six-foot length of barb wire. By 1:00 P.M. the supply problems were under control. When I say we suffered a time loss, I'm being kind. At 9:00P.M., I ordered sleep for all!

∞

May 2, 1985, 5:00 A.M. Salt

The guys are fighting to get back on track. Gentle is as mad as a wet hen. My hopes are that low life that killed Mange lives in hell.

5:30 A.M. Deuce

I got all my team up and moving. There is a lot to get done. Morry and I are put in a real screwed up way. We are supposed to band or reband our stock. Thanks to Slim giving us some pointers, we got it done. Gentle and I had a talk about making the job faster. My idea was putting lift eyes on the field toilets and have lunch delivered.

"Sounds good, make it happen."

8:00 A.M. Nasty

Ratchet and I are in the reload area. We've got no gas tanks for running. Ratchet is doing OK She was really attached to that little dog. The last word I got was if all gear is in working order, all the touch up welds were to be done on the nightshift. Gentle and Buzz are at the supply yard with Smokey cleaning the water tanks. Pink and Boomer stopped to say the gas tanks would be here about 10:00 this morning.

11:00 A.M. Pink

Tests on the welders checks out. I asked Morry to round up his night team and to get some sleep. Boomer was in a meeting with Gentle and Deuce about a guy in Florida to be hired on Deuce's team. Art had called saying they were refueling in New York and would be here soon.

4:00 P.M. Buzz

Cleaning the water tanks was some brutal work. All that super-heated steam. Art showed up with the new tools. I was looking for more to do.

4:30 P.M. Gentle

Salt was cooking up a storm. The camp smells wonderful. Deuce was talking to Art about the guy in Florida that Boomer knew. I knew Art wanted to help.

"Gentle, we will get this man tomorrow. I want you, Boomer, and Deuce ready to go at 6:30 in the morning. For now, one of Salt's fine suppers is in order. I will be staying at Smokey's for the night."

The balance of my day was on the deck writing a letter to Mom and Dad. As night set in, I just listened to the hum of the generators.

I was nursing a glass of wine when I was approached by Ratchet and Nasty.

Ratchet: "You want me to fill in for Boomer?"

Nasty: "And me."

Gentle: "Where's Pink?"

Nasty: "In the shower."

Gentle: "Get Pen for me, please."

The four of us marched into the showers.

Gentle: "Say old man, you busy?"

Pink: "No just changing my stink. Are you broke? Did you sell tickets to the ladies or what."

Gentle: "Look, the girls want time on the finish welds."

Pink: "OK, it's not the same as joints, you know."

Gentle: "Right, so like you and Ratchet, Nasty and Wire, Pen and Slim. What do you think?"

Pink: "I like it, no problem."

The ladies couldn't be happier as they left the showers.

Gentle: "Hey old man, how're the necklaces coming along?"

Pink: "They're done, I even got one for Salt."

Gentle: "Thanks"

The A.M. would be here soon enough I called it a day.

∞

May 3, 1985, 5:00 A.M. Boomer

Ratchet was in a basket at midnight and she did fine. Now her and Pen are working with some of the rigging crew quick changing the baskets. I would say I got four hours of good sleep. I asked Salt for something on the light side, as I was traveling today.

6:30 A.M. Deuce

When Art said 6:30, he meant it. The helicopter landed right on time. The one thing I can say for sure is these people do not waste time. The lady doctor, Nasty, was in a suit and welding. Unbelievable. The trip in the helicopter was short, maybe fifteen minutes. We landed at a military base. In minutes, we were in a jet and airborne. The Major said it would be a two-and-a-half-hour flight.

10:30 A.M. our time Art

We landed at MacDill air base. A van was provided. Both Deuce and Boomer were familiar with the area so in a very short time we stopped. This is the place? A music store. Whitman's music. We went in.

Art: Sir, we are looking for an Al Whitman.

Clerk: Well there are two. I'm Albert and my brother is Alfred.

Lloyd: Is your brother here?

Albert: Yes, he's giving a music lessen. He should be done in about ten minutes.

Art: Thank you.

The ten minutes passed quickly. A young lady came from the back of the store followed by a giant.

Alfred: Lloyd Sherry, is that you?

Lloyd: It's me.

Alfred: I heard you moved out west.

Lloyd: Maybe I should do some introductions here. This is Art Fellows. He's the guy in the corner office. This here is Zack Mulholland, the boss on the job site. His handle is Gentle. Here we have Dwight Lee, foreman of the cable team. He's called Deuce.

Alfred: Are you offering me a job?

Art: Mr. Whitman, we flew out here because I need the best working this job.

Alfred: Just tell me about the job.

Deuce: Al, have you worked with Timmons connectors?

Alfred: Yes, by hand.

Deuce: We have machines for setting them.

Alfred: Well, now you've got my attention. The pay?

Art: You will receive not less than 185,000 dollars for the planned seventy-seven days estimated, as well as a bonus ending or finishing early. That can all be explained later.

Alfred: When do I start?

Lloyd: Here is the list and here's your bag. Fill the bag with what you have and when that door closes behind you, you're on the clock.

11:25 A.M. our time Gentle

Al was short on a few items on the list. I told him not to be concerned. We have a concierge.

Gentle: Art, I need your phone.

Art: What for?

Gentle: To call Gabby, Al needs a bed. Al, what's the length on your bed?

Al: Seven-foot, six inch.

Gentle: Firm?

Al: Yes, please.

Gentle: Pillow?

Al: Fiber fill, firm.

Art handed me his phone.

Gentle: Hi Gabby, is Kay in town?

Gabby: She's right here.

Gentle: I need to talk to her.

Gabby: Sure, Kay, it's Gentle.

Kay: Hello, sweetheart.

Gentle: Kay, my dear, we are in need of your special skills.

Kay: Which one, dear.

Gentle: Shopping.

Kay: My favorite. What is it? I have a pencil and paper.

Gentle: One single wide mattress, length seven foot six inches, firm, Pillow king size fiber fill, firm, two sets of sheets with cases, and king size blankets to fit. This is for your magic. All at the Hotel by 3:30 P.M. today. You will have a small list of personal items to do shopping for, but I would prefer you and Al, our new person to go over it.

Kay: 3:30 at the Hotel. I think it can be done. Anything else dear?

Gentle: Yes, Gabby please. Deuce who's your handyman?

Deuce: Lew.

Gabby: Is this Deuce?

Deuce: Yes, I need to get a message to Lew.

Gabby: OK, let me record it so she knows it's you.

Deuce gave all the information of what was needed for Al's cube. Then he said good-bye to Gabby as we entered the air base.

Once on the base we got food at the flight line kitchen. The Major had the plane ready to go. Al was looking like he'd just won the lottery. By noon, we were enroute back to Vegas. I was sure of one thing. There had to be a reason for all the problems with personnel. I needed to ask Art if he had noticed this as well. The flight back was smooth all the way.

4:00 P.M. Boomer

If I do a shift tonight, I'm going to hurt. Pink said all the welding was done. Al was settling into his cube.

5:00 P.M. Al

It was so strange. I'm at home this morning and not even six hours later, I'm on a job that is going to pay me when I sleep. I was at a table filling out the last of the application when this very attractive woman sat down across from me. I knew her from a magazine some time back.

"You must be Al."

"You must be Katharine Mayfield."

"Thank you, my dear."

"Would you be the person that took care of my sleeping area?"

"Yes."

"The bed is very nice. Thank you for your fine shopping skills."

"Please call me Kay. Let's just say, Miss Mayfield retired some time ago. When you finish, I'll take it with me to the main office. Let's go over your list."

"I still have more to fill in. It shouldn't take long."

I can't believe this place; everything here is massive. I finished the paperwork and went looking for Kay. This place is shaded and it's still hot. A golf cart was coming this way.

"Hi, you're Al, right? I'm your doctor out here. The name is Nasty. This is Pen, radio room and cook. Look, you may not know it, but out here you're losing a lot of water. Hop on. We'll get you back to camp."

"This is a first."

"What's that Al? A first?"

"The first time I've been picked up by two naked women."

At that, the two of them were laughing.

"Al, you'll get used to it. Everyone here is naked at some time, we were out sunbathing."

"As your doctor, you should learn out here, less is better."

That's food for thought.

"Good, Kay is on the deck. Thank you for the lift."

We had supper together as she went over my list. She said she would dig out a photo from her days modeling.

7:00 P.M. Gentle

Smokey, Art, Kay, and I were having a chat outside the truck entrance. Smokey asked Art who was doing the hiring for the between phase folks. Kay said it was Marshal doing the hiring. I asked Kay about background checks. She said the only checks that were done was on my Krew. Art said they had found twenty-two-million dollars he had stolen. For now, he was living in Cuba. Kay was clearly unhappy with him running around on her.

It was a little past 8:00. Kay and I were sipping wine when she said something I felt a bit off guard by. Since she had all the service work done on my camper, she was using it as her bedroom at the office with Abby. I couldn't help myself but asked anyway.

"How do you sleep?"

"In the nude. Your bed is just so nice, I promise it will be spotless when you get back."

Kay was staying the night in the hospital bed. It was time for me to turn in.

May 5, 1985, 3:30 P.M. Nasty

We still have work to do, but Gentle got the list. It doesn't matter. We're here ten more days as supply staff. I wish I knew when the camp would break up. The nightshift is already up and reworking two baskets. Pink said if the cutters for the cable anchors work right, we'd be done in a day or less.

∞

May 6, 1985, 6:00 A.M. Gentle

Pink tells me we could be done by noon. I went over our phase two shut down list. It's only half a day of work maybe. Deuce's team pitched in to help. By 2:00 P.M. all of the list was complete. Only one thing left to do.

It was time to bury Mange. We drove out to the far corner of the big top on the west side of the railroad tracks where Smokey had dug a grave. Mange's remains were in a finely made coffin that Slim crafted. Pink had done some carving on the lid to dress it up. Once we finished that, we took our last look at the spot where Spin had died. Some of Deuce's team hadn't heard about Spin.

Back at camp it was time to make the call, I made my way to the radio room.

"Atlanta Goodnight."

"Atlanta Goodnight."

"Hotel 1, 2"

I switch channels.

"Gentle, how many are coming back?"

"Eleven of the Krew will be going home."

"And you?"

"I'll be back in ten days."

"Good enough, see you soon."

"Bye."

"Bye, bye."

Then came the announcement.

"If you're hauling something home, get packed now. Sunset, you are out of here."

There was a mad dash for the laundry, as everyone wanted to wash their things and store as much as possible at camp. Salt had cooked up a masterpiece in the way of food.

After supper, I made a call to get the pick-up time. I was told by the Major 7:30 P.M. on the flats. At 6:45, everyone heading home was on the service truck with bags in hand. We moved out to the flats as the sun was setting. We were in the shade of the hills as the temp started coming down. The wait for the Chinook was only twenty minutes. The Major set down ahead of us, so we didn't get covered in sand. My Krew on board. It wasn't long and they were gone. Nasty and I made our way back to camp. I set the cruise control at thirty M.P.H. and just glided back. In camp, we drove over to look at their baskets. To me they just looked weird. JJ and Boomer were going over crane operation and techniques for loading the long bundles of cable.

∞

May 8, 1985, 6:00 A.M. Boomer

These folks doing the rigging don't mess around. It's one speed and that's fast. JJ told me they're doing five levels a day. If they can hold that pace, that will be a nice bonus check.

∞

May 16, 1985, 6:00 A.M. Pink

We got an early flight to the flats. Ratchet and Bud came out, Boomer and Salt are working straight through. Ratchet and I keep the generators filled, spotting for the tower crane, stacking the wood shipping slats. Plenty to do around here.

∞

May 16, 1985, Noon Gentle

I did my best to be with Abby as much as possible. She is everything to me. I do owe Kay a huge thank you for having the cleaning done on my camper. She had it parked inside with Abby. Kay is sitting in for Abby, so we were able to go have some fun.

∞

May 26, 1985, 10:00 A.M. Gentle

Nasty, Cable, JJ, and myself arrived in camp just after six this morning as Pink, Ratchet, and Bud were heading home. Deuce's team put in the last deck panel. All of them went to work on clean up. As members of the grounds Krew, their tear down and packing went fast. At 3:00 P.M., everyone was in camp; Art had come out for the occasion. At the 6:00 P.M. meal, Art announced for anyone interested, loaders would be needed in four months, if not sooner. Everyone was on the list for the loading work. Art then told everyone to check their savings accounts at the bank.

I talked to Deuce about lodging in Vegas or to make sure Alice Krew had his phone number. I let him know that if he or any in his group were staying in Vegas. Kay might be of help with housing.

Art had took me aside. Kay's divorce was final. She was selling off the homes they had, along with a lot of other items. He said she had been living at the office with Abby while she was having a new place built. Art then told me the one-hundred dollars an hour was for everyone that started on phase two and adjustments were made because of the work we had to do just to start. What he then told me did come as a surprise. The site was going to be locked up. The only people to be here are the supply yard guys for two plus weeks. The reason was to move all the empty rail cars out as the storage yard. They would need every inch of track for phase three. Then to load the Hotel.

∞

May 27, 1985, 6:30 A.M. Nasty

Smokey had the bus next to the camp. As all of us loaded ourselves and bags on board for the ride to the flats. I knew we would have a payday to remember. All of us Krew were home by 8:30 A.M.

∞

May 28, 1985, 8:00 A.M. Art

I have spent a great deal of time on the phone with Smokey and our rail service providers. It appears to be two train loads are delayed in Ohio and one in the Denver area. Smokey has loaded the Hotel camp with all their needs, less food. This reminds me that I need to talk to Kay about gathering everyone for supper or something. Deuce and the bulk of his people have found places to stay in Vegas.

Noon Kay

Abby and Zack have been just wonderful to me. Now I can start over. Maybe meet someone with real values. Art had called about a get together supper. I begged him to just let me handle the parties. Sometimes Art gets an idea and it's almost impossible to have him rethink it.

WAITING TO START

Told by Individuals

June 1, 1985, Zack aka Gentle

I've been helping Jake with his old truck rebuild which was becoming a monster of a project. Abby would help when she could. The one thing she is good at is painting with a spray gun. Nancy would stop by at lunchtime, almost daily. Patty and Jim are living at Art's place in L.A. because of Jim's schooling. Mary is busy writing her medical study, which Nancy said is highly detailed. Rodger and family are on the go, doing everything as a family. Martin stopped by on the weekend. I asked what he was doing these days. I was surprised when he said that he was studying some books on welding. Jack is with his kids. The company found a counselor to help him and his kids with their loss. Ann and Lloyd from what I hear, are nearly living together. Bill and Fred are into cooking out. If it can be grilled, that's how it's cooked. Jill and Brent are living out in North Vegas, so we don't see them as much. Nearly all the cable crew is in Henderson. According to Nancy, Mary and Allen are dating. Terry is a home body and plays his guitar. Time it seems to be moving faster than ever.

∞

June 2, 1985, Jake aka Pink

Janet and Jr. are on summer break now. Zack likes spending time
with them. Janet has finally learned to shut the refrigerator door. I
can thank the grandparents for that miracle. My son is working almost
full time at the stables these days. The two of them are growing like
weeds.

∞

June 3, 1985, Rodger aka Cable

I decided with the girls out of school, we would rent an R.V. and
drive around the Grand Canyon. We're going to have a great time
being tourists. Jake said he would watch the house while we were gone.
By noon, we were on the road.

∞

June 4, 1985, Nancy aka Ratchet

Between helping Mary with her study papers and my feelings for
Jake, I keep a full day. I've dropped hints of how I feel about him. Just
wait is all I can do. Janet and I get along great. We do things together. I
took a two-night stay at my folk's home. It was fun. Dad has become
quite a gardener and Mom was learning how to can and freeze everything he grows. I'm sure that the most of us are ready to finish this job.
The hours arc brutal. But when it ends, who knows what will happen.

∞

June 5, 1985, Abigail aka Gabby

I'm spending as much time with Zack as I can. Phase three has to
end by November first. It's not going to be easy on anyone, as the

summer heat can be deadly. I'm trying to keep Kay from having a melt down over Marshal ripping her off. The one thing I found out is she's as crazy for Zack as I am. She'll sleep in the camper every chance she gets. Financially, the company is making money. Millions daily. If the ore sales stay like this, bonuses will be huge.

∞

June 6, 1985, Arthur aka Art

Today, finally everything is enroute to the storage yard. The ore is some of the purest ever found. It sells as fast as it's made into ingots.

∞

June 7, 1985, Bill aka Buzz

I would say when we got back in town, I slept for two days. I checked in at the bank and nearly fell over. Three quarters of a million bucks. Damn, if we can finish this thing ahead of time, who knows how much it could be. If I keep eating like I've been doing, I'm going to need to adjust my cool suit.

∞

June 8, 1985, Fred aka Dog

Bill told me about his trip to the bank. Well, he wasn't pulling my leg. That's a lot of money there. For right now, Mary gave me a list of foods to avoid. She knows her stuff. I'm pretty much ready to go back to work.

∞

June 9, 1985, Allen aka Wire

Mary really likes me. She's great to me. I'm thinking of asking if she might want a more personal relationship. All in all, she is fun to be with. Martin and Terry are super friends, but maybe it's a change I'm needing. I did stop at the bank to check my account. That's unbelievable!

∞

June 10, 1985, Lloyd aka Boomer

The word from Jake is this phase three is going to be free welding. No support cables for a lot of it. In my time, it means slow going and dangerous. This is something I can't talk to Ann about; she is very special to me. I can't cause stress for her or others.

∞

June 11, 1985, Martin aka Slim

I've been going over the Earl Jones book on welding and Bowman and Lenge's book on bonding steel. Both have a section on making arches. The trick, or key, is the method of size and placement of tacking for the job. There was a math equation that was way over my head.

I asked Nancy if she knew like a math teacher. She said she knew a professor in the math department at the university that might help. Nancy set it up for me to meet this professor. When I got there, it was this really cool lady professor. She spent like hours with me making sure I understood this math problem from front to back. This is like important. I've got to show this to Zack. This is a time saver!

∞

June 12, 1985, Terry aka Cutter

This time off is turning me into a cream puff. Eat, sleep, and write music. I'm wondering what life will be like when I own my own studio. Everyone seems so busy running around doing things. We'll be on the go before they know it.

∞

June 13, 1985, Jack aka Pooch

The company has been real helpful. They found a grief counselor as well as a nanny. I'm trying to keep it together for the sake of my kids. I don't know what happened that caused this change with her. I may never know. The boys are doing better than me for the moment. The nanny, Jan, and her daughter Anna are live-in people. They are very nice. I feel my boys will be taken care of with her.

∞

June 14, 1985, Mary aka Nasty

The report for the study in phase two is complete. Allen has been a great help to me. He took care of everything so I could work. He doesn't know how I feel about him. He should know I'm more than just fond of him. I'll tell him at the right time. As for going back to work, I'm ready.

∞

June 15, 1985, Ann aka Salt

Work will be starting soon; I can feel it in my bones. I'm being careful of what's in the fridge. Lloyd and I have been doing a lot of carry out. He is wonderful just to be with.

∞

June 16, 1985, Patty aka Pen

I don't know how in the world Art did it. My son has transformed into a perfect young gentleman. Art surprised us with a trip to his getaway home on Santa Catalina Island for a whole week to be tourists. John stayed with us, as Art had business in the cities. He only stayed two days. Being with Jim is so much better now that he's not a little hellion. Art said he is welcome to stay with him until the end of the job. I asked Jim if it was OK with him. He said OK!

∞

June 17, 1985, Jill aka JJ

Rumor is the twentieth is phase three start up. Brent and I are already packed, so we're good. I'm still surprised no one has said anything about us being married. It's OK. I still love him.

∞

June 17, 1985, Brent aka Bud

Jill has got us all set to go. I would be a basket case without her. Work is going to be hot, so we are going to make some adjustments on the cab AC first thing.

∞

June 18, 1985, Dwight aka Deuce

Everyone signed on for phase three. The company moved us and has put us in a very upscale apartment unit. It has a pool, an exercise room, and much more. We are used to being together, so it's cool.

Al was the only one that went back home. At the bank, each of us made just short of three million with bonus and pay.

PHASE THREE

Told by Individuals

June 20, 1985, Noon Gentle

Gabby was calling me at Pink's home.

"It's time to go, 6:00 P.M. at the base, have all your things ready. Be safe, love you."

"I will, love you too."

The call ended. It's less time off than I had hoped to have, but we're in the home stretch. We have our work cut out for us. I should get busy and finish packing. The phone hadn't stopped ringing after that. My answer was:

"That it was real."

I had my packing done by 1:30. I decided to make a fast trip across town to see Gabby one more time. When I arrived, Gabby and Kay were in the pool. My future bride was happy to see me before it was time to go. I asked if I could leave the camper with her. She said it would be fine. The time with her went by so fast. Kay came over to remind me of the time. I kissed Gabby goodbye and got in Kay's Jaguar for the trip to Pink's.

On the way there, Kay told me a little more about herself and why she decided to sell off the houses Marshal and she had bought. I asked

S. P. BENNETT

where she was living. She was at her studio, but for now she would be staying with Gabby. It was coming on to 3:30 when Kay pulled in Pink's driveway. She kissed me on the cheek.

"Be safe."

∞

6:00 P.M. Pink

Mom and Dad are here for the kids. Mom asked how long we would be at work.

"I don't know."

Gentle and I got on the bus, waving goodbye as it pulled away. By 6:30 everyone was in a seat. JJ and Bud drove to Boomer's place and parked in his garage. My guess was we would be in camp by 8:00 P.M. It turned out the bus stopped right behind the Chinook. We went straight from the bus to a seat on board with bags in hand. In minutes we were moving to the runway. The doors were left open for air. The inside of the Chinook it was ninety degrees or so. The Major said we're taking the scenic route. It took forty-five minutes to reach the flats.

The welcoming committee of Smokey, Fats and Rodo were there with one flatbed trailer for us and two refrigerated trailers of food. When the last person was on the flat bed, we moved out at a good speed.

∞

8:00 P.M. Nasty

There are times out here when nothing is said. If it needs to be done, you just do it.

We put our bags in our cubes and started loading the kitchen. Pen and Salt directed the traffic. Smokey told Salt the canned and dry goods were in the back of the kitchen. Slim had the snake sticks charging. By 9:00 P.M., our corner of hell had started looking like home sweet home. All three guys from the supply camp brought supper, fried chicken and all the sides with a cooler packed with wine. Afterwards, we cleaned up then took care of our unpacking, putting our cubes in order. The storage yard trio would be staying the night. By 10:30 the only person still busy was Pen in the kitchen. I would be doing exams one hour after breakfast Time to turn in.

∞

June 21, 1985, 4:45 A.M. Salt

Its morning and breakfast was in the works. It's a steady stream to the showers and all. In some weird way, I love this place, It challenges me to create the healthiest meals possible. Best get back to work.

6:00 A.M. Gentle

Nasty is doing exams soon. Fats and Rodo are heading back to the yard. Only six snakes were caught on Slim's electric snake fence. JJ and Bud said the tower needed some fine tuning. I told them to go over the whole thing. It has to be one hundred percent plus. Boomer and Ratchet started on refilling the racks for the baskets. Pooch, Pink, Buzz, and Dog were checking the baskets. Cable and Slim went to see how the rail cars were set for order of unloading.

Smokey and I were looking over the blueprints, as we had some things that didn't match up at all. The key problem was the starting point. Smokey explained by his prints was how the rail cars were arranged. If anything, Smokeys prints made more sense. By noon, the place was looking like it was time to fill the field.

Noon Bud

We just completed testing the auto locater system. Now we get plates fast and safe. Lunch and we can fill the field.

2:00 P.M. Cutter

The panels are coming off the train like lightening. Bud is putting the tower to work. Gentle has called a stop to all work at 6:00 P.M. for a meeting.

4:00 P.M. Ratchet

Not even 24 hours and it looks like the guys can start burning wire tomorrow. The meeting at 6:00 has everyone guessing. What's it all about?

6:00 P.M. Gentle

The train pulled in, so the supply yard trio is here for supper. I figured food first then the pep talk. Salt had made a very special supper for all.

"Well folks here we are and here is the game plan. I or we got the wrong plans, but fortunately Smokey got the right ones. Why we got the dog and pony show plans, I don't know for sure. From this, I can see once we get our Mojo back in full swing, I would say fifty-five days. You may start a pool and that is with five breaks. Slim, you have the floor."

Slim got up came to the front then gave a dissertation on tacking requirements for the arches. He then gave the math equation, including how it works. Dead silence for the whole speech. Our crazy genius hippy had blown them away.

"Would the nightshift Krew please become night owls? I am asking if you will stay up and turn in at about 8:00 A.M."

Pink was looking at me smiling.

"Thank you, does anyone have anything to add?"

Nasty: Everyone be careful around the panels the edges are very sharp. Boomer was the first to find this out.

Gentle: What's that?

Boomer: I was turning around to get out of the way and barely bumped an edge, nine stitches.

Gentle: Nasty when did this happen?

Nasty: A little before 6:00.

Gentle: Well thank you for the update. It might be a good idea for those in the field to wear their snake boots.

It was the only thing I could come up with at the moment. By 9:00 P.M. the day shift was in bed.

∞

June 22, 1985, 2:30 A.M. Pink

I have got wild people to work with. Bud, Dog, and Wire were cart racing on the main road around the big top. Pen and Ratchet are in the kitchen making bread or something. Only thing strange about that is they're nude. Boomer and Slim have been in a discussion over Earl's equation. Boomer got the parts breakdown and tooling spec list. Slim reran the equation and found the tacks he first believed to be big enough were undersized. The two of them added and refigured all the tacking sequences.

The old boy was up at 4:30 heading for the showers. I knew his every move from the time his feet hit the floor. I had his coffee at the table to ease him into the day.

"Good morning, old boy."

"Morning. Coffee, thanks"

"Sleep OK?"

"Yeah, how did the nightshift do?"

"Well Dog won the cart racing. The girls spent their night in the kitchen naked, Cable and myself have solved the world's problems. Boomer and Slim refined the tacking sequence on the arches."

"Really?"

"It looks good on paper."

Gentle was studying Slims numbers and patterns.

6:30 A.M. Nasty

The guys are almost done loading the field. Pink and Gentle have been at the table for nearly an hour. It seems Gentle wants Slim on days and Pink is asking for Gentle's speed man. I was called to the table.

Pink: Nasty, a person being changed from days to nights. Is that a high danger stress condition?

Nasty: It could be if an insufficient amount of time was not given for rest from one to the next.

Gentle: Would you monitor and supervise getting Slim on days and Buzz on nights?

Nasty: Sure, I can start now if you like.

Pink: Alright, they're yours.

I got on a cart with Gentle to get Buzz. Slim was in the showers, so I asked him to wait up for me. I knew this shifting of personnel was key to the project yet wasn't sure why or how.

10:00 A.M. Slim

Me on days! Gentle told me the arches are critical to the safety and speed of the project. Buzz was totally cool with going on nights. Him and Dog are a team. Nasty said I had to stay up until 5:00 this afternoon. She will be watching me. Only seven hours. I can do it.

2:00 P.M. Gentle

The field was at maximum capacity--cables attached and all. Slim was still up running the numbers again. By 3:00, I brought the Krew back to camp. Pink was up at 4:30 and at the table by 5:00.

"Well, old man, do you think you can stand one more night off?"

"Sure, Oh I'm taking a ride to the top. According to the plans of Smokey's, the top is supposed to be all marked and laid out with part numbers as well as locator spots."

"Enjoy the time, old man. If Slim's numbers are in fact right, JJ and Bud will be working their butts off."

At 6:00 P.M., Nasty went to get Buzz out of bed to start adjusting him to nights. He had breakfast to start his first easy shift. Nasty said Slim was out like a light. The day shift was starting for their cubes at 8:30. I was in line at the showers when Nasty and Salt came in. They were talking shop as food goes. Before long, I was heading for bed.

∞

June 23, 1985, 5:00 A.M. JJ

Gentle caught me just out of bed.

"Hope you got a good night's rest. You're going to need it."

It was already eighty-five degrees. A quick trip to the bath. I stopped Nasty for advice on heat stress. She told me to keep the A.C. where I feel comfortable and alert. It's just that simple. I made up my mind that less is better.

6:00 A.M. Slim

Man, I'm on the day shift. Cool suit, a bag of notes. This is the big leagues. All there is, is my A game. Nothing else.

6:15 A.M. Gentle

Slim was not his usual self. He was quiet, focused. Something inside me knew he was going to make it happen. Slim took over the day shift. Panel by panel, Slim directed the size and placement of every weld with flawless accuracy. By the end of his first day, Slim had gotten four arches up, for a total working distance of two-hundred-eight feet. I watched as he gave Pink the tack up information for the nightshift. Pink and his Krew were heading out for their shift. I called Slim over.

"Slim, you old hippy, how's it feel being on days?"

"Not bad. Not bad at all. I see why you wanted the arches done on days."

"You did pretty damn good out there. The million-dollar question is how many days to center?"

"In a perfect world, five."

"Hit the showers. Salt will be bringing out supper soon."

Salt had made another masterpiece in food. I was timing the crane trips--twenty minutes. Pink and Boomer are sharp and those two will get it down to fifteen minutes by morning. I did an hour in the whirlpool, then some time on the radio talking to Gabby. I turned in about 9:00.

∞

June 28, 1985, 5:00 A.M. Pink

The baskets are parked and have a full load of gas and wire. The center arch is going in today. The day Krew was up for the day. I knew Gentle's team was good, but the center arch panels are monsters fifteen feet wide, forty feet long, and eighteen inches thick at a weight of three hundred plus tons each. No room for mistakes.

6:00 A.M. Gentle

Everyone was checked by Nasty before we went out. JJ was in the tower doing a locator test. Everyone was on headsets even ground Krew. The size alone said slow going was the rule. Once we were on top, it was a short trip to center. Slim was ready as the first panel was enroute. For the rest of the day, it was all serious business. We moved as a team. By 5:30 P.M., the keystone last panel was set in place. The last of the tacking was done at 6:05. I looked at Slim as I had a little smile on my face.

"That's how it's done brother."

We parked the baskets on the change-out spots. Climbing from the baskets, we made our way to the carts then back to camp. All of us made a bee line for the showers. When we had cooled off some we got into dry clothes and had supper. Everyone was in camp.

"Pink, old man, I've been thinking."

"Yeah, on what?"

"How about a maintenance, clean up, and reload day? Then a day or two off."

"Sounds good to me. When do we start and where do you want us to start?"

"Clean up. I need the tower in perfect running order."

"You got it."

"I've got to talk to JJ and Bud. Then I'll call Smokey. I'll see you after a while."

I caught JJ in the shower.

"JJ I've got a question."

"Sure."

"How much time do you and Bud need to do an end to end, total check up on the tower?"

"A total check four to six hours or so."

"First thing in the morning that's where you start, please."

"OK. We on break?"

"Yes."

Pink had a list of jobs to get done. I took a seat by the railing, staring at the work we had done. I turned in around 8:30.

∞

June 29, 1985, 6:00 A.M. Nasty

Thank goodness its break time. Both the guys and machines have been nonstop. JJ and Gentle have been talking for a long time. Cutter and Wire are working on the generators. Cable and Slim are topping off everything from fuel to water. The nightshift took care of all the trash.

Looking down the valley, Smokey and Fats are heading this way. They were traveling slower than usual. By 9:30, JJ started running tests on the tower. Fats was backing in his refrigerated trailer to the deck. A food delivery plus. Smokey was carrying L.P., Gas, and diesel.

Noon Gentle

JJ was out of the tower. I asked how the tower was doing. She explained that Bud needed to do a recalibration on the electronics, as the field locators were not accurate. I said OK. Bud would be out of bed in five hours. Besides, we were ten and a half days ahead of schedule. Salt was cooking out on the grill, did it smell good, burgers and potato salad. Everyone was finished with all the maintenance and odd jobs.

About 5:00P.M., Bud was up. I stopped him on the way to the showers.

"Bud, you and I can talk at breakfast."

I got a cart and made a trip to the train door. Looking out to the holding area for us, I counted nine cars of panels, maybe six hours of work. Tomorrow morning, we load the field. Bud and JJ were at the table going over the service records.

"Well, have you figured it out, Bud?"

"I believe so. It's on me, I missed a step on the last service."

"Fixable?"

"Oh sure. I missed a battery change."

"Is it a major job?"

"About an hour, I'll get my tool bag."

Both of them were in their harnesses and on headsets. I listened on my headset as Bud gave JJ detailed instructions on all the controls. In fifteen minutes they started changing out batteries in the whole system. Bud calibrated the system then field tested it. The locator system is now accurate to one eighth of an inch.

I talked to Pink to see if he could have two of his Krew stay over in the morning. He said someone would be up for it. I made a call to the supply yard to ask about having the last of the arch panels brought into camp in the morning. Smokey told me they need forty-five minutes to get moving. It was too late in the day to unload so the announcement was made.

"6:00 A.M. We unload the rail cars, have the panels ready to go and two days off."

11:00 P.M. Pink

The old boy is beat. All of us are. Two days off should give us time to get rested up for the next push. One thing is for sure. The whirlpool is going to be standing room only. I took a good long look at the field plans for the last of the panels. Lots of space for the carts. I think we will get all the equipment fueled and checked by 5:00 A.M. or so.

∞

June 30, 1985, 6:00 A.M. J J

Bud is taking the first two hours of my shift to make sure the locators are perfect. At noon, I parked the tower then powered it down. It's break time.

∞

July 3, 1985, 6:00 A.M. Nasty

The guys are in the field. The tower is running. I had the speaker on to hear the cross talk. Slim is in charge on the arches. The field is loaded and ready. Ratchet and I have been working on the refill station seventy-two spools of wire per shift. Well, the upside is when the last of the fill panels go in, JJ and Bud will be on the ground.

9:00 A.M. Gentle

Slim has his A-game in place. If we can hold the pace as before, we should be near sixteen days ahead of schedule. Seven and a half days to the next break. I checked with JJ on the outside temperature, one-hundred-twenty-two degrees. The cool suits were doing their job. By the end of our shift, five arches were up with the sixth started.

10:00 P.M. Pink

Just like the north end, the panels are fitting perfectly. Bud is in motion for the whole shift. I think Gentle nailed the seven-day guess.

∞

July 11, 1985, 6:00 P.M. Boomer

Gentle and the gang are coming down. The last arch panel is in. Some service work and break time.

6:00 P.M. Gentle

Nasty tells me Art is coming out to the camp. Kay maybe with him. The nightshift refilled the baskets. JJ and Bud were checking the lifts for the baskets. Wire and Cutter checked power boxes. The rest of us loaded the refill area. Wire and gas was ready to go. By 8:00 P.M. we stopped. The rest of the list could be done in the morning.

∞

July 14, 1985, 5:00 A.M. Salt

Pink and Gentle are working on getting me some time away from the kitchen. I wouldn't know what to do.

6:00 A.M. Pink

Gentle is telling me we haven't received the half time list. I know we're going to be packing at some point. Pen said Art and Kay would be here by 9:00 this morning. JJ and Bud are doing some serious inspection on the welding towers.

9:30 A.M. Gentle

The work is nearly done for the moment. Kay and Art arrived a little while ago in, of all things, a really fancy motor home. Art was talking with Pen on the deck as the nightshift was heading for their cubes to sleep. Kay was on a cart driving around the place. Smokey had done the driving to get the motor home here. He said Fats was bringing groceries this morning. I joined up with Art on the deck.

"Art, what brings you out to the camp?"

"I'm holding paperwork you may need."

"The setup papers for the time between halves on phase three?"

"Yes, here you go."

Art handed me a briefcase. It was packed. All the paperwork and photos right up to the day we say good-bye to this place. Pink is going to freak out when he sees this list. Art was staying with me as I flipped through these heavily detailed instructions. First, we were going on a two-day break. Art and I talked at length about the amount of work in the between time of the halves. I did get a bit more information from Art as to equipment and the amount of packing we would be doing. The fork trucks to be used are electric.

Noon Cable

Slim and I were looking over the things to do list for the start of the second half. We agreed we would be busy, real busy. Slim was studying many of the clean-up jobs to be done. We continued leafing through the plans and papers.

2:00 P.M. Kay

I got my swimsuit on to go sunbathing with the girls. Only I forgot they sun in the buff. Well when in Rome. The itinerary was simple. Sun, shower, whirlpool, and then dress lightly for supper and wine into the night. Now this is some girl time I believe I will enjoy.

6:00 P.M. Pink

Art was talking with Salt over by the kitchen when out of the blue Salt gave Art a big hug and kiss on the cheek. All I heard was, "Thank you." It's still early I haven't called home for a week. I know the night-shift will keep the noise level at a low roar.

∞

July 17, 1985, 6:00 A.M. Gentle

The day shift would start the last of the major welding. JJ will be helping in camp but is ready to get in the tower. Cable, Slim, Pooch, and Cutter manned the baskets. Ratchet and Nasty assured me the baskets would be refilled in record time. Art and I had business to talk over.

"How long?"

"I'll know more at the end of the first twelve hours. But if an estimate would be sufficient?"

"Yes."

"Fifteen days welding then one or two days taking down the anchor cables and a full day cutting off the anchors. Then pack up and set up, which is unknown."

"I feel it would be in everyone's best interest to have the cable team brought in."

"I agree one-hundred percent."

"Very well. I'll have them in fork truck training first thing tomorrow morning."

"Remember Al went back home to Tampa, in Florida. Kay and the Major could have him back here tonight."

"Where is Kay anyway?"

"Her and Ratchet went out front for some morning sunning."

Within an hour, Deuce was notified that training classes were starting. He should have his team ready for a 6:00 A.M. bus trip. Art called the Major to arrange a flight to MacDill air base. In ten-minutes, the Major had called back saying he would need a company plane if it needed to be today.

Art told him to use his plane at the North Vegas Airport. Kay was readying herself for the trip as the Major would be here in thirty minutes. Well, as the helicopter made its way into the far end of the valley Kay was ready to go, looking gorgeous. She was on her way to Florida.

∞

July 22, 1985, 6:00 A.M. Ratchet

Pen had just got off the radio. She told Pink and Gentle that the cable team would be here this afternoon. Smokey hauled the camper of Art's back to the supply yard. Gentle has been going over the half-time list and all the jobs. He said we need a day off.

Noon Nasty

No one in this camp was needing one more shift of work. I told Gentle everyone in camp is exhausted. He agreed with me.

"I was thinking of two days off maybe, three would be more appropriate."

The nightshift had gone to bed by 8:30 this morning. At 3:00 P.M. I was in the whirlpool when Salt said someone is on the road heading our way. It was Deuce and his folks coming by way of motor home. It seems the Major dropped them at the supply yard. Which makes sense at one-hundred-twenty degrees on the flats the fifteen-minute ride here could have cooked them.

5:00 P.M. Deuce

When we got in camp it was a ghost town.

Al: "Look here."

We walked over to see what he was pointing at. Looking over the deck rail, there was Pink and what looked like all the nightshift in the whirlpool.

Pink: "Deuce welcome back, did you miss the place?"

Deuce: "Only a little."

Pink and his team started out of the tub. It was strange seeing these people so incredibly buff. They looked like they lived in a gym.

Gentle showed up with Slim and Cable. The 6:00 P.M. meal was smelling good.

8:00 P.M. Gentle

Deuce's people had settled in. Al and Cutter had teamed up with their instruments. Cutter was on guitar, Al with his bass flute. They went out in the field to play. It sounded eerie at first but that passed. I was showing Morry and Deuce our things to do list. Morry said that he saw the machine for rolling the rubber mats at the supply yard. I gave the reason for us being on a break as a fifteen-day push to get the welding done was rough on all of us. I asked if they could start by getting their day and night shift people re-acclimated.

"Deuce, you got a day shifter wanting on nights?"

"Yeah, why do you ask?"

"Well, I would like it if Al was on days."

"Done."

My day was coming to an end.

∞

July 25, 1985, 6:00 A.M. Cable

The day shift is ready to go. According to the jobs list, we start on rolling the mats in the field. Simple. The machine rolls the mat up once the mat is unzipped. Then the tower takes the banded rolls to the rail cars. By 4:00 P.M., the field mats were on rail cars. JJ was bringing the rollover mat back to the field side. We got the mat rolled up to find a snake hotel. Gentle said it was time to call in the cavalry. He called Smokey. It wasn't long and all three of them showed up. They took care of the snake problem in short order. We lost count of how many they got. The nightshift would be breaking down and packaging the tires.

∞

July 29, 1985, Noon Nasty

I'm keeping a close watch on everyone because of the heat. The field is stripped bare. Smokey and Fats have been busy getting us filled up with fuel and water. The reload area for the baskets was holding enough for the last two panels and not much more. Smokey has been bringing some huge equipment in for flattening the road. The road work was done by 6:00 P.M.

∞

July, 30, 1985, 6:00 A.M. Pooch

The nightshift must have been flying. I couldn't tell for sure, but it looked like a conveyer system and more.

7:00 A.M. Gentle

Pink had left the assembly sheets. Well, if anything the plans were a start to finish set. It's not all that bad. The road is level, so it should go fairly quick. The west side was just over a quarter mile in length. The south side was nearly a half mile long.

I really missed my guess on the assembly time once the platform was in place for loading into the monstrosity. The conveyer system nearly put itself together. Very little adjusting for level was needed. By lunch, the conveyer only needed power. Odd there were no instructions on the power hook up. I called Smokey to see if he had something on the power supply. I was told our next load would have everything. He wasn't kidding. Rodo pushing in loads filling both tracks. The paperwork was coming with Smokey.

At 3:00 P.M., Smokey and Fats came rolling in pulling three sixty-foot trailers each. Smokey handed me the layout plans. All the hardware was here. It's just a matter of getting it in place. The first thing on this list was the A.C. for the Hotel. The inside was the same as a slow cooker.

Pink was out of bed at 5:00 P.M. With coffee in hand, we studied the list and layout. Power plants, A.C., elevator, small crane, charging station and more.

"Well, old boy, where do you want me to start?"

"For the moment, I would say try to get as much in place as you can."

Pink was downing his coffee while studying the list and field layout.

"Old boy, this is a serious twelve hours of work."

∞

August 1, 1985, 5:00 A.M. Al

Slim and I had been looking at the designs for the packing of the Hotel. It was sloppy. We showed Gentle our design and space gain. It was no time before Gentle had Art on the phone checking on any surplus or late shipments. We learned that the balance of what should be here was sitting in a warehouse in Washington, waiting for rail cars. I was seeing Slim more as a genius than a crazy hippy, even though he used the hook on the tower crane as his personal swing set.

We were trying to figure out a way to move large numbers of containers in a timely manner. Gentle was watching from the radio room. He walked over and asked if he could help. We said sure. In minutes. he had it figured out the tools for the job, then had them drawn out.

7:00 A.M. Boomer

The word in camp is forty-eight hours off. Art and Kay showed up at sunrise in camp. JJ is training Nasty and Rosa, a gal from Deuce's team, on the little tower. It seems for the loading there is a lot of talking going on.

8:00 A.M. Art

I just cannot understand the need for all of this time off. The train from Washington should be here in three days. There is something most peculiar here. Even though they are taking time off they are still busy with odd jobs.

∞

August 3, 1985, 5:00 A.M. Gentle

Everyone is rested and had a good breakfast. I gave the layout of how the containers had to be set in. Al, Boomer, and Slim had drawn up diagrams for each level to put the maximum amount inside. All of us knew there was no room for accidents or mistakes, as this stuff was deadly toxic. With the conveyer loaded, the process of loading was under way.

Inside the Hotel, it was very different, the fork trucks made very little noise. The headsets didn't work, but because it was so quiet, you could talk to someone fifty yards away. The A.C. in a word was as cold as people could stand. They would carry heavier clothes and get dressed inside. Nearly from the start, slowly everyone got in rhythm. As one shift would figure out how to save time, it was shared. At shift change, ideas were exchanged.

7:00 P.M. Kay

Art, Nasty and myself were in the whirlpool drinking wine and having a grand time. I do believe my tan lines are almost gone. I had notice that Art had been spending a considerable amount of time with Pen talking about her son would be my guess. I told Gentle we would be going home in the morning. It was late, so I told Gentle he should go to bed. Tomorrow night, I would be going to bed in his bed. He laughed. I gave him a kiss and said good night.

∞

August 4, 1985, A.M. Pink

Gentle is going to freak out. They will be starting on level four. The batteries were being changed out; nightshift is handling that. Bud and Boomer are the only ones that didn't get inside.

7:00 A.M. Gentle

Pink has been sharing tricks on shaving minutes on all the trickier operations. The rotation of people helps to keep them from burning out on the job. The push is on. It's going as fast as possible and as safe as possible around the clock.

∞

August 14, 1985, 6:00 A.M. Salt

The way it looks, my people are going to finish this job early. I'm keeping them on a diet for working folks. They will be healthy and well fed. We have a break starting today. I think it will be comfort food for all.

∞

August 30, 1985, 9:30 A.M. Nasty

The Hotel was loaded. All of them were exhausted. I was a little upset with Gentle for working fifteen days straight. I asked Gentle point blank if we were going home or what? He just smiled, saying that he didn't know. He did have a concerned look on his face. No one was sure what would be next.

As Gentle closed the door of the radio room, he was on the phone for fifteen minutes. None of the nightshift had gone to bed. When Gentle came out, he was all smiles saying.

"We are going home for two weeks. Be ready to come back to work on September 15th to finish up the job and pack up the camp. Put on your traveling clothes, folks."

We were going back home. Salt quickly closed up the kitchen. The guys covered the whirlpool as Wire put it on a timer. In less than a half hour, Smokey parked an old school bus next to the camp. With everyone seated, we left camp for the supply yard. Arriving at the supply yard, I had no idea of how massive in area it was. Roads, railroad tracks and buildings--I couldn't guess in square miles, its size. The Major was waiting for us with the Chinook helicopter. By noon everybody was home.

11:30 A.M. Kay

I had picked up Zack, Jake, and Al at the Air Base. I made sure there would be limos for everyone. The first of the fine men to be delivered home was Jake I had called ahead so there would be a wel-coming committee for him. I asked Zack where he was going. His answer came as no surprise.

"The office please."

"Thank you, Zack. Splendid! I can change cars. Oh that's right your truck is at the office. Silly me."

I put some soft background music on the sound system for the trip across town. Both of them looked completely worn out. I pulled up to the garage door at the office and punched in the combination. The door opened I pulled in, and then called to get the second door opened. Abby must have had her finger on the button. The inner door opened immediately. Pulling in, I turned for the parking area. I really do not like the Bentley.

"Zack, my dear this is your stop. Al, would you be a sweetheart and wait here while I change cars?"

"Of course, Kay"

I went to get the Jaguar. Abby was hiding as a stranger was in the office. I pulled up to Al and Zack.

"She must be in the ladies room. Get in, Al."

"Thank you, very nice."

The inner door opened and closed behind us then the outer door did the same.

"Would you like a small tour, Al?"

"Yes, I've never been in this part of Las Vegas before."

"Where have you been before?"

"The University, mainly giving lessons."

"You're a professor?"

"No, music lessons for the orchestra."

"You teach music to an orchestra?"

"Well yes, but I had found an odd blend at camp, Terry is quite a guitar player. I'm sorry, your tour?"

"Oh, I need to make a left up here. Well, you're in for a surprise. From here to the end of these buildings, what do you think?"

"Well, it looks like commercial and warehouses."

"That's absolutely correct. I own all of them."

"Really! Kay, I had a feeling you were a person of means. How many buildings are there?"

"There will be twenty-six in total at the first of the year."

"Forgive me for changing the subject, Kay, but where will I be staying during my time off?"

"Well, how would you like sharing a place? Let me explain, my dear. Presently, my house/home is for sale and being shown. My studio is being rented for a video production. I've been living at the office with Abby. Well, Zack will be staying there so I have arranged temporary housing for two. If you're OK with my idea."

"Well, I would like to see it. I hope I'm not sounding unappreciative."

"Not at all. I believe you will love it."

We started back across town to the Showboat. Al is going to love the penthouse. Arriving there I handed my key to the valet and showed him my room key.

"Al, this way."

We stopped at the desk to make sure the room was ready. The clerk, an old friend, assured me the room was perfect.

3:00 P.M. Al

Kay is a treat to be with.

"Kay, the elevator has no buttons."

"Al, watch, my dear."

I have used key cards for rooms, but never on an elevator. She slipped the card in a slot. The doors open. Inside the elevator, the card goes in another slot and we're moving. She had a big smile as the doors opened.

"Kay, are we in the right place?"

"Yes."

"This is magnificent."

"So, you're saying you like it."

"Kay, I love it."

"Good, now I'll show you the place. Here we have our full kitchen area. This of course is the common area. Over here is my boudoir."

We walked back across the very spacious main room.

"Al, this is your bedroom. Would you care to try the bed?"

"It looks to be the right size."

I sat down on the edge then stretched out.

"The bed is perfect. The curtains are there, windows all the way around?"

"You could say that."

She walked to the doorway and pressed a button. No windows, the wall was glass with sliding doors, screens, and all. I opened a door and we stepped outside the view was unbelievable.

"Kay, I will do my very best to be the finest roommate ever."

"I believe you."

She called the valet to bring our bags up. From that point, on it was relaxation as we settled in for the day.

5:00 P.M. Allen

I asked Mary if she would like to go out for supper. She said yes. We drove to a place in North Vegas for spaghetti. I wish I could find a way of telling her how I feel about her. Maybe if I ask to help on her report, it might help.

6:00 P.M. Jack

The nanny is a part of the family. I'll be able to retire and be a fulltime dad. I'm thinking about moving back east. I need to do some shopping. This weekend, I believe we will take a road trip somewhere.

6:00 P.M. Patty

I got to the house to find John and a limo in the driveway. I had just enough time to grab a few nice things to wear. Then it was straight to the airport. I thought it was funny. All I wanted to do was be with Jim. It took two limos, one jet, one helicopter, and one more limo to get to Art's home. My boy was thrilled to see me. Both Art and John said my boy was amazing to be with. Art had arranged for Jim and me to see as many places we cared to. Jim was very understanding when I said I needed a few days to adjust. From there, the next two weeks I was living in a dream.

6:00 P.M. Rodger

Lisa made a pot roast for supper. It was great. My family was surprised when I said it was bedtime at nine o'clock. It went over with them. Just being with my family felt good.

6:00 P.M. Bill

If anything, my truck started right up. So, me and Fred made a trip to the store for food. We stopped at a burger joint on the way. The shopping trip went pretty good it wasn't to stock up, but enough to have on hand at the house.

6:00 P.M. Ann

Lloyd invited me over for supper. He does do some real creative cooking. His lemon pepper chicken is delicious. I enjoy being with him. I need to find a salon and get something done with my hair. I'll ask Kay. She must have someone.

6:00 P.M. Jake

The instant change today is worth it. All the grandparents were here when I got home. I called Nancy to see if she had dinner plans and invited her over. The kids love her. I've been thinking of asking her out for a date.

6:00 P.M. Brent

Jill got in the house and fell asleep on the sofa in seconds. I didn't make a sound. I just went to bed. If I'm lucky, getting twelve hours of sleep will be fine.

6:00 P.M. Terry

Allen went out to supper with Mary. Martin was on the phone the minute he got here. He left at 2:00. I ordered a pizza and watched TV until 10:00.

6:00 P.M. Mary

Allen is great to be with. He's a true gentleman and terribly shy. I know he likes me, but he can't express his feelings. He asked if he could help with my report. I said yes. Maybe he only needs to be around me more to become more comfortable.

6:00 P.M. Abigail

My arms have been around Zack since Kay left. I only let go so we could eat supper. He looks so tired. I put him in bed.

∞

August 31, 1985, 7:00 A.M. Gentle

I kind of remember getting in bed, but I don't remember getting undressed. Abby may have been playing games while I was out. I headed for the shower. If someone saw this place, they wouldn't believe it. It was a fully functioning home with no walls. You could take a shower and see the whole place.

Abby was in the camper for the night. She must have heard me in the shower. She walked over to give me a good morning kiss. only saying.

"Good morning, I need a shower."

"Need help?"

"OK."

I washed her back so she could finish up.

"Zack, call Art."

"OK."

I sat down at the desk.

"Speed dial two."

"Thank you."

I punched it in, and John answered.

"John, Zack here. I understand Art was trying to reach me."

"Yes Zack, I will get him to the phone directly."

"Hello Zack, and good morning."

"Art, I didn't know you were so jovial in the morning."

"It's the mine, Zack, the mine, eighty percent of what's coming out of that hole is near pure manganese. The foundry we are working with is running three shifts and we can barely keep up with the orders."

"Art, you might have just enough money to start looking at some of my nice American money that is some of the cream."

"Zack, based on the bonus program in place you and your Krew will live very comfortably. Now, in regards your pocket change, I'd be interested to see your so-called cream."

"Very well. Come out to the camp after we have been there a week and Art, I'm serious."

"Zack, where the hell is Kay?"

"Just a second, Abby, where is Kay staying?"

"The Showboat."

"Did you get that?"

"No."

"The Showboat."

"Thank you. I should talk to Kay. For now, the office is closed."

"Thank you, Art we are going out for breakfast. Bye."

"Bye."

The call ended. Abby made a few quick calls and we got dressed to leave. She drove to a diner on Tropicana for breakfast.

After our meal we drove over to Jake's, the garage door was open, and Nancy was working alongside of Jake on the old truck. We talked a while then headed to Lloyd's place. Him and Ann were pulling in the driveway, so we parked out front and helped carrying the groceries in. Abby was talking to Lloyd about a wedding dress. He said he would take care of her.

It wasn't long before we were on our way back to the office. We made a fast stop to pick up some goods for the kitchen. We enjoyed every minute we had together. After a week Abby said she wanted to show me her hiding place at night. Because of the lighting, a week had gone by and I never saw the catwalk up in the roof's peak. We went up and after a few small doors were opened, we were on the roof. It was a helipad. We put together a late picnic and dined under the stars with the lights of Vegas to see by. Before I knew it work, would be starting again. Abby was helping me pack to go back. She had a funny smile as we shoved things in the bag.

"What's so funny my dear?"

"I was thinking how much bonus money we will have if you're done by October the fifth"

"Roughly how much?"

"If Art is honest with the pay scale, about fifteen million each."

"That's a fair amount of change."

"We would be set for life."

∞

September 15, 1985, 6:00 A.M. Abby

I kissed Zack goodbye. Kay had rented limos to collect everyone. He hasn't been gone an hour and I miss him.

7:00 A.M. Kay

Al is someone I would like to hang onto. He has a great mind for business. I'll see to that man's care and feeding when he gets back.

7:00 A.M. Major Davis

Hard to believe everyone is early.

"Everyone, your attention please. This will be a fast trip as the Chinook is scheduled for a mission this morning. Smokey is enroute to the flats. So, you do not overheat, the doors will be open and water provided. Also place your bag under your seat and use the strap to secure it between your legs. Handheld cases are just that. You hang on to them. We board in five minutes please move quickly, thank you."

7:10 A.M. Gentle

"Major, we're still on the ground. What's going on?"

"Low battery."

"What's the flight time Major?"

"Twenty minutes give or take."

In five minutes, we were up and on our way. I wasn't paying attention to the time, but it wasn't long and we were landing out on the flats. Smokey pulled up alongside the Chinook. In no time, the bus had all of us on board. The trip to camp was fast. Once we arrived and our personal things were put away, we got together on the deck. I was working at getting a plan put together on finishing the Hotel and packing up the area. The way it looks to me, is the elevator tubes were the first on the list. That would take a full day. By day three, we would be putting the last two panels in place. Nasty and Ratchet were busy mothballing the medical trailers. Pen and Salt were giving the kitchen and coolers the same treatment.

∞

September 25, 1985, 5:00 A.M. Pink

Some expanding foam stuff was pumped into the Hotel. Now that was weird. Once all the stuff was inside, a really wild chemical reaction happened. In seconds the vent pipes shot these three-hundred-foot giant noodles out. Then the Hotel was sealed up. The plan was to have the camp loaded on the rail cars by noon. The running joke was, has anyone called for a cab? At 2:00 P.M., Ratchet said it looked like three trucks coming into the valley. JJ and Bud were staying here to do the tear down on the crane, as they had made arrangements with Art.

By 2:30 P.M. Fats, Smokey, and Rodo rolled into camp. The caravan consisted of a large motor home, a large van, and the old school bus pulling a small box trailer. The bags went into the trailer. We got on the bus. Gentle was just standing there looking at the Hotel. No one called for him to get on the bus. This was his idea in the first place.

5:00 P.M. Gentle

The only thing left to see out there was just watching it disappear and Abby was by my side. Kay and Al dropped me off at the office. I only had some clothes and a few personal things left at Jake's home. Abby and I didn't have much to say that evening. It was mainly eat and sleep. Over the next few days, I helped Abby pack up the office.

Art showed up as the office was being loaded into shipping containers. We sat at the kitchen table and talked about the company's plans for a while. I knew why Art was here. My coins. I went to the camper and asked Abby to hand me my vest. Abby and I walked back to the table. I looked at Art.

"I guess you're hoping to see some cream."

He had a smile on his face. I took a six-coin cachet from the vest pocket and slid it to him. Art was staring at it.

"Is this the only one?"

"Nope I've got six more but only have one more with me right now."

"OK, I'll make an offer for both."

Art wrote down a number and handed it to me. I showed it to Abby.

"Ten million, I'm OK with your offer."

He got a draft from the bank. Art was now the new owner of twelve cents American money, six steel and six copper 1943 pennies.

Kay had a house on Sunrise that she was letting us use until we found a house we liked. We moved in on the first of October.

EPILOGUE

Told by Zack

November 2, 1985, 6:00 A.M.

Abby and I got up real early so we could be at the Air Base on time. Today the monstrosity known as Hotel would be tucked away never to be seen again. At the Base, we were directed to the hanger for our ride out. The Chinook was full, plus one. Abby was riding out sitting on my lap. Because of so many changes at the camp, we were able to fly in under the big top. There were at least a hundred people already there. I asked the Major if he had a head count. The guest list was for one-hundred-twenty-five people and thirty-five Air Force personnel.

I put my necklace outside my shirt then put on my bandana. One by one all who worked out here did the same. The announcement was made to put on ear and eye protection. The blast blankets were in place. Then the countdown--three, two, one, Art pushed the button. There were dozens of explosions and then it started moving. The wheels were making a high pitch grinding noise. The ground had a buzzing sensation like, traffic on a bridge. I hadn't expected that they would have food here. We both got a plate and continued watching. Even at the seven-mile mark, it still looked big. It was nearing the tunnel when someone announced that it was doing twenty-five miles per hour.

The KREW watched as nearly a year's work disappeared into the tunnel. A puff of dust turned into a jet stream. We heard a thump as the stream of dust was getting stronger. The gigantic vessel was now traveling straight down. Oddly there was no noise. Next, the ground shook three times. The job was done. Art was smiling. The hole would be filled in as soon as the railroad tracks were gone.

Abby and I walked over to the tower. She asked where I slept. I pointed towards the corner. Patty and Art joined us. Art invited us to their home in L.A.. Abby had never been there, so I accepted. The gathering started breaking up around 10:00 A.M. We were ready to go home and caught the first Chinook leaving. We were back home by 11:00 A.M.

That evening's newspaper had a small article about testing on the Mercury Range. The article stated that the test of a new generation of bunker buster bombs was a complete success. It went on to say the device was conventional not nuclear.

We decided to get married on the fifth of November. We made some calls. Kay made the arrangements for a large meeting room at the Showboat for us. On our wedding day, it was a full house. Kay gave away the bride. Jake didn't make any embarrassing toasts. Mom and Dad flew out for the wedding. It was a great day.

In time Jake and Nancy got married. Rodger and family moved southern Iowa and he became a sod farmer. Bill and Fred built a pair of welding shop semitrailers. They were going to be gypsies. Mary and Allen are living together, I think they got married. Well, Mary got a job offer in Oregon, so they moved away. Ann and Lloyd got married then left for Minnesota for plastic surgery on Ann's face. I hope it goes well for her. Jack and the nanny moved to the west side of Vegas and have a beautiful home. Martin and the lady professor are living together and have a home in Blue Diamond. I hear they travel a lot. Terry and Al opened a music store. Terry bought the house Jill and Brent were renting. Kay and Al now there's a pair! She's five foot maybe ninety pounds, aging model, white. Al is six foot six inches, two-hundred-sixty-pounds not an ounce of fat, white hair, Afro American. They make a great team. Patty and Art are living together with her son in L.A.. We may take Art's invitation into consideration. Jill and Brent moved to Ohio and opened a crane repair business. They been married and together eight plus years. Dwight and his crew headed back to the east coast. Robert is living in L.A., not far from Art. As for Smokey, Fats, and Rodo, no clue what or where they are. Me and my wife have been looking at some pictures of a piece of land just outside of Bonaparte. One good sales point, you could say it comes with free babysitting.

THE END

ACKNOWLEGMENTS

My greatest thanks goes to my wife Margaret for her help and patience in the time we spent putting this together.

Joanne Wiklund my coach and go to person who never stopped her encouragement. An author herself in eBook and print. She gave nothing but the best in advise.

Heidi Iffland the person that took time in doing a line for line proof-read and soft edit.

I want to thank an old friend of mine. Dennis Seaman, for reading the first draft. He called to memory the personal experience of welding: the shrinking of leather gloves, the little balls of hot metal under my shirt, the pain of flash burn, and the immense self-satisfaction of a beautiful bead.

Kast Laser Creations, Kelvin & Sara Tenboer, Kayla, and Sophie. The people that took care of template cutting for my books cover. Thank you.

Cover art was done by a father and son team, Chris, and Eric Murphy. Both of them proficient in art.

My beta readers were Barb, Beckie, Todd, and Dot. I thank all of you.

A big thank you to the Cordova and Port Byron libraries for a lot of help.

BIOGRAPHY

Greetings, a little bit about me. Born and raised in Illinois. My schooling was public schools then a trade school. My working career began at twelve years old, which continued to age sixty-five. About the only interruption in my time working was four years in the Air Force. I have had a variety of jobs mainly in welding and fabrication. At the end of my days working I managed a warehouse as well as being their mechanic. My home has always been in towns along the Mississippi River of north west Illinois. My writing started near thirty years ago. When I was between jobs. After attending a writers meeting, I put my writing away, I didn't fit in. My dad and mom moved to Arizona. I would vacation there in the winter. Dad passed away so I would travel to their home to help Mom. It was on their patio I started writing again, mainly short stories. Finding a local writers group at home worked out for the best. With some help and encouragement I finished this book and have started on others.

Thank you

Stephen P. Bennett